THAT PROMISE

THAT PROMISE

JILLIAN DODD

Editor: Jovana Shirley, Unforeseen Editing
Photo: © Regina Wamba
Cover Design: Mae I Design

Jillian Dodd Inc.
Madeira Beach, FL

ISBN: 978-1-953071-25-5

Books by Jillian Dodd

London Prep
The Exchange
The Boys' Club
The Kiss
The Key

The Keatyn Chronicles®
Stalk Me
Kiss Me
Date Me
Love Me
Adore Me
Hate Me
Get Me
Fame
Power
Money
Sex
Love
Keatyn Unscripted
Aiden

That Boy
That Boy
That Wedding
That Baby
That Love
That Ring
That Summer
That Promise

SATURDAY, AUGUST 17TH

The boy I used to love.

Devaney

DAMON AND I roll into the house, arms filled with bags. Our mom insisted on taking us back-to-school shopping. Now, we both have wardrobes full of hip designer clothing. My brother is totally into it. The flashier it is and more logos on it, the better as far as he is concerned. I like nice things, but I guess I fall somewhere in between him and my mom.

Damon sets most of the bags on the dining room table and then goes into the family room, where our stepmother, the actress Jennifer Edwards, is sitting on the floor, playing with our two half-sisters and our dog, Angel.

I follow him.

"Looks like you managed to find a few new things," Jennifer teases. She knows what our mom is like. How much she cares about appearances.

"We did," Damon says as two-and-a-half-year-old Weston jumps into his lap, calling out Day-Day, her nickname for him.

"We brought you a present," he says, causing her eyes to get big. He pulls a bag out from behind his back and hands it to her. The bag is pink and has pastel ribbons streaming from it.

"My birfday! My birfday!"

"It's not your birthday, sweetie," Jennifer says. "It's just a fun surprise."

"Surprise!" She pushes her hand under the glitter tissue and then pulls out the cutest stuffed unicorn. Its fur is a soft white plush, and it has bright green eyes, pink hooves, a silver lamé horn, and a sparkly rainbow mane and tail.

"It's bea-u-tee-ful!" she screams, hugging it against her chest tightly and running in circles, the dog hot on her tail.

"She looks like Damon after he scores a touchdown." A deep voice chuckles from behind me.

It's the voice of the boy I used to love—will probably always love—my neighbor and former lifelong best friend, Chase Mackenzie.

I turn around.

And holy hell.

Speaking of clothes, Chase is wearing very few of them. Just a pair of swim trunks with what appears to be a new shell necklace.

"Oh, hey, Chase," I manage to say, trying not to visibly drool over his naked chest.

Since we stopped being best friends, every time I talk to him, I feel like my voice is stuck in my throat, my heart ready to beat out of my chest. A few summers ago, on one amazing three-week family trip to the Ozarks, we went from being BFFs to something much more—before it got all screwed up.

Why did it get all screwed up? Because I'm an idiot. Mostly.

And I wish I knew how to fix it. Fix us. Fix, at a minimum, our friendship.

I still see him all the time. He still lives next door. He and my brother are still best friends. We are together often because our families are close and we went to the same school. We are cordial with each other, like he is being now. But since that day on the football field, when an older guy surprised me with a homecoming proposal and Chase thought I'd said yes, we haven't been best friends. We haven't been close. And it's really hard. It's one thing to miss someone you don't see. It's another to miss them incredibly and have to see them all the time. It's like a daily reminder of how badly you screwed things up.

Chase and my brother couldn't be more different. He wears nice clothing, but there's nothing flashy about him. While Damon chases the spotlight, Chase seems to prefer avoiding it.

But I get it. Damon is almost a full year younger than Chase despite their being in the same grade, and he's had to work extra hard to keep up. To excel. He's always been fast and always loved to run races—well, *win* races—and in football, he likes the glory of scoring. My dad—now-retired three-time-champion quarterback, Danny Diamond—always tells the same story about why his son didn't follow in his footsteps. Basically, it's that when they were little, Damon always wanted to run and would get Chase to throw him the ball. Usually, instead of throwing it back, he'd run it back, hand it to Chase, and tell him to throw it again. And it's sort of how it worked out. Chase became the quarterback and Damon his best receiver.

"What's with the necklace?" Damon asks Chase while Weston continues to run in circles, although now, she's prancing like a pony—or a unicorn, I suppose.

When she bops her baby sister, Easton—who was happily playing with an educational toy—in the head, Easton starts screaming bloody murder, causing Jennifer to pick her up and take her into the other room to calm down.

While Weston has been an adorable terror since the day she was born and is now a precocious toddler, Easton, who is a year younger, is much more easygoing. She entertains herself, gives the sweetest hugs, and does just about anything we ask.

To a point.

And once she reaches said point, you'd better watch out. A full-on meltdown is coming. I'm assuming since Jennifer removed her from the room, it means this isn't the first time Weston has been messing with her.

"Oh," Chase says, touching the necklace and rolling his eyes.

I squint mine, wondering what he means, but my brother goes, "Ah, Lacey's back from Hawaii. Gift?"

"Yeah," Chase replies and then quickly changes the subject. "How was shopping?"

Chase isn't one of those guys who will rub your face in his relationship and try to make you jealous. If anything, he downplays whatever it is he has with Lacey. They've been dating for almost a year now, although I know he won't commit to a relationship.

I overheard Lacey talking about it at cheer practice last spring. The girls on the squad told her she needed to lock that boy down. But she told them she didn't care what their status was as long as he was always on her arm and in her bed. Which made me want to throw up.

Adding to the nausea, I had to pass the torch to her as the next cheer captain.

"Sweet, dude," Damon says. "I'll be styling at school this year. *For sure.*"

"What about you, Chase?" I ask him. "You ready for school to start?"

He holds my gaze and then shakes his head. At least, I think he does. It's more what his eyes say than his body. And I know, even though we aren't friends, he's not excited about my leaving for college.

And when he looks at me like this, neither am I.

Because somewhere deep in those eyes, it seems like he still might care about me.

I've done everything to move on. Dated other people. Avoided him. But I'm still hung up on him. Some almost-magnetic force always seems to pull me toward him.

Chase's phone buzzes, and he says to my brother, "Go get your suit on. Everyone is waiting for us at the dock."

Damon smirks. "Of course they are. The party doesn't start until we walk in."

"It's outside," I tease.

"Whatever," he says, running toward the stairs. "I'll be right back."

Which means, now, I'm awkwardly standing alone with Chase.

Thankfully, baby sis breaks the ice. "Pony!" she says.

Chase gives her a big grin, puts her on his back, and gallops around the room with her.

"I wish I could still ride you," I blurt out, referring to how we used to give each other piggyback rides when we were kids.

Chase sucks in his breath so hard that he starts coughing.

"*Oh*. I mean ... I meant, like, when we were kids, you know? I don't ... I didn't. Um, I wasn't referring to *riding the pony*. I mean, I would but—"

Chase stops galloping and looks at me again. "You would?"

"Yeah, I mean—"

"Oh no, you *don't mean*," Damon says, shaking a finger in my direction as he strides across the room, takes Weston off Chase's back, and sets her on the couch while speaking to me. "No more pony rides for you. At least, not with Chase. We still haven't recovered from the last one." He turns to Chase. "Come on, dude. Let's roll."

And they are out the door.

Weston brings me the unicorn and dances it across my lap, babbling about its pretty mane and soft fur, but I'm stuck back in the moment.

You would?

"Earth to Dani," my dad says.

When he came into the room, I literally have no idea.

"How was shopping with your mother?"

"Oh, great," I say. "I'm, uh, gonna go put everything away. Do some more packing."

"When you're done, stop by the Mackenzie house. Jadyn said you still had some questions about rush."

"Yeah. I'm freaking out a little, honestly."

My dad sits down next to me and pulls me into a hug. "You have nothing to freak out about. You're smart and a good conversationalist, and everyone will think you are amazing. You'd get my vote."

I can't help but smile. "Thanks, Dad."

"Did that help?"

"Maybe a little."

"Good."

Jennifer and Easton rejoin us, and my dad picks up Easton, giving her a kiss on the cheek and then tossing her up in the air and catching her, to her delight. She definitely loves her daddy.

I decide to go talk to Jadyn now instead of dealing with the new purchases. Mom is sending me a list of what I'm supposed to wear for each day of rush, and I'll tackle putting that together tonight. I'm told that I won't have much time to unpack or get settled before rush starts, so having everything all together and ready to go will supposedly help me be less frantic during the week.

Plus, I know Chase isn't home right now, which makes it less awkward. I can't believe I basically said I wanted to have sex with him again. I mean, I do. *I would.* But it's complicated. Way, way too complicated to even consider.

THE MACKENZIE HOUSE is surprisingly quiet when I get there.

"Where is everyone?" I ask Jadyn. I call her Auntie Jay, although technically, she's not my aunt; we just call her that because she and my dad are best friends.

"Phillip and all the kids are out in the boat. Well, except for Chase. He and Damon were meeting some friends at the public dock to swim. That means, we can actually talk and not be interrupted."

She leads me through the kitchen. "You hungry? I made some chocolate avocado mousse."

I grin. "I would love some."

Once she gets us each a bowl, we take a seat at the kitchen table.

"Are you nervous about rush?"

"Yes. I'm not sure if I will pledge or even enjoy it, but I'm going to give it a shot."

"If nothing else, you'll meet a lot of new people. Do you have specific questions about anything?"

"I think I've read every article online regarding the process," I say. And I have. "Do you think I made the right decision, going to Nebraska?"

"I don't know," she fires back. "Why did you choose it? Because *you* wanted to go or because you wanted to piss off your mom?"

"Out of all the colleges I got into, she seemed most excited about Georgetown. It just didn't feel right to me when we visited."

"At some point in your life, you have to stop pleasing your parents and worrying about what everyone else wants and decide what you want. What's *your* dream, Devaney?"

I look up at her. "You called me Devaney."

"This is a serious conversation," she says with a grin.

"Or I'm in trouble," I reply with a laugh.

"Definitely not," she says. "So, what is your big dream?"

The cupcake I made Chase that summer at the lake immediately pops into my mind. When our individual dreams became a combined dream.

"I suppose since I decided to major in broadcasting—you

probably already figured out that's what I'd like to do—I specifically want to be a football sideline reporter. College or pro, either one."

"I think that's wonderful. You certainly know the game well."

"I do. Not sure my mom will approve of that career choice either. She's always wanted me to model or go the debutante route to try to marry me off."

"You might be surprised what your mom would say," Jadyn says, which shocks me.

She and my mom were close in college. Jadyn even set my parents up. They get along, but they aren't BFFs anymore.

"If she supported me fully, that *would* be a surprise. Although maybe there's hope. She seemed a little different today when we were shopping. Happier maybe. Van seems to make her happy."

"He does," she says. "And I hope that if you choose to pledge a sorority, you'll choose it because it feels right. You've always had a good head on your shoulders, Dani, and you're more intuitive than you give yourself credit for. Follow your heart, always."

I glance down at the table, my hand immediately sliding across where Chase and I wrote our names on it when we were old enough to do so.

She narrows her eyes slightly, sees where I'm looking, and says, "Are you two ever going to make up? I've never really understood why you haven't. You were best friends your whole life."

"I'm sure you saw the video of the fight, the one they showed their coach."

"Yes, I did."

"Remember when you told me about the time when my dad and Uncle Phillip got into a fight with your cheating boyfriend? You said you were mad at Phillip for dragging you away. Why were you mad?"

She frowns. "Lots of reasons, I suppose. In all honesty, it was mostly because I wanted to be able to handle it. I know that I should have gone up to Jake myself, told him we were through, and walked away. When Danny and Phillip got involved, it was almost like they were taking away my power. In the moment though, when your dad was pity flirting with me, it felt good to have them on my team. But Phillip making me leave the party—it sort of made me feel like a little kid who was in trouble and got sent home."

"And when I told Chase to go home that day on the football field, I wanted him to go home because I didn't want him to get in a fight or get hurt because of me. I didn't tell Hunter yes to Homecoming. Instead, I ran after Chase. Tried to explain what happened. But he wouldn't listen. Kept twisting my words."

"He didn't tell me that part," she says, looking thoughtful. "And you certainly don't have to."

"Maybe I need to," I tell her. "He accused me of lying to him about my feelings for him. Said he protected me from that jerk. Risked his place on the team and probably just effed up his entire career. And that the bitch of it all was that after what he did for me, I wouldn't even walk away with him. That I wouldn't stand up for him. *For us.* Which made *me* mad. I told him that I never asked him to punch Hunter. That I was going to handle it myself."

"Were you?" Jadyn asks.

"Yes, but I never got the chance. Doesn't matter now though. Chase doesn't believe me."

"Do you want to know what he told me?"

Do I want to know? Can I handle it? "Uh, maybe?"

"He said that, to you, what other people think of you is more important than what you think of yourself."

"There's truth in that statement. My mom has been telling me most of my life that I should care what others think. To worry about my appearance. Make good first impressions. How to speak.

And I don't see what's wrong with that."

"There's nothing wrong with caring about what people think, Devaney, unless it overshadows what *you* think. And that will be really important to remember when you go through rush. Because during it all, you will feel judged. What's really happening is that you are being assessed to see if you are a good fit. It's like the draft. Every year, there's a top-ranked quarterback coming out of college, but if the team who has the first pick already has a good QB, they will pass on him and take a different player. Someone who fits what their team needs. Rush is a little different though in the fact that the players tend to go where they are told. In rush, while they are assessing, so are you, and you are matched instead of chosen."

"You just talked football to me," I say with a laugh. "Actually, now, it all makes perfect sense. So, I'll be judging them and narrowing the field while they do the same. Kind of like at the combine."

"Exactly like that, *if* the player got to analyze each team in the process."

She gets up suddenly, going into her study and coming back out with a marker. "You need to sign the table again."

"Really?"

"Yeah, I think your signature has changed a little since you turned five. And it's a momentous occasion, leaving for college." She rolls the marker across the table at me.

I'm sitting in Chase's usual spot. Our names are signed halfway between here and the next seat. The spot I used to sit at. I consider signing it right above my original signature but don't. I will be at college but don't want to be forgotten, so I press the marker down in the spot right above where his place mat sits.

The front door bursts open suddenly, and Chase, Lacey, Damon, and a bunch of their friends come barreling in.

"Hey, Mom," Chase calls out.

"In the kitchen," she yells back.

I instantly panic, pushing the place mat on top of my signature. Which is good because next thing I know, Chase is standing in front of us along with Lacey in a skimpy bikini, holding his hand.

He drops her hand, which must piss her off because she looks at me and then speaks in a tone so sweet that it might as well have been dipped in sugar, "Dani, it's so good to see you. What are you doing here?"

"I live next door." I try to keep the *duh* out of my voice but don't really succeed.

"What did you need, Chase?" his mom says to him.

"The dock at the park was too crowded, so we're going to swim here. Any idea when Dad will be back with the boat?"

She glances at her watch. "Probably won't be too long. Why don't you send your friends outside?"

Chase opens up the door to the deck and motions everyone through it. Then he shuts it and goes, "Am I in trouble or something? You are usually fine with everyone hanging out here."

His mom gets up, points at her chair, and says, "Sit here."

She walks out of the room.

Leaving Chase and me alone.

Can't manipulate the truth.

Chase

I CAN'T HELP but wonder why Dani is here, talking to my mom. I also don't know why I instantly dropped Lacey's hand the second I saw her. Or why my mother told all my friends to go outside.

Or why I can't think of a single thing to say to Dani when

there are a million things I wish I could.

I go with the super original, "What's up?"

Dani looks a little shell-shocked. "Um, not sure exactly. Your mom and I were discussing rush. And then we got on the subject of that day. At school."

"The day you ditched me for Hunter?" I reply, trying to pretend I don't care when, in reality, just thinking about it still makes my blood boil.

"Yes," she says, nodding.

"And what lies did you tell her?" I fire back.

"I've never lied to you, Chase. Ever," she says, standing up. "And the fact that you would suggest that really hurts. That's it. I'm done. I give up."

"Giving up is nothing new for you, Dani," I practically growl, my voice getting louder. "You *gave up* on us that day."

"You're wrong. So wrong, Chase," she says softly. "But it doesn't matter what I think. You saw it a certain way in your mind, and nothing I say will ever be able to change it."

"You can't manipulate the truth, Dani. I was there!" I'm full-on yelling now. "I *know* what happened. I had to watch the video of you humiliating me *over and over* with our coaches just so I wouldn't get kicked off the team. So, don't act like *I'm making it up!*"

Tears fill Dani's eyes. She sadly shakes her head and walks out on me.

Again.

The moment the front door slams behind her, my mom comes flying back into the room.

"Chase," she says, shaking her head at me the same way Dani just did.

"What?" I sass back loudly. If I don't, I'm afraid I'll start crying. Better to stay mad.

"I don't think I've ever uttered these words to you in your life, but I'm disappointed in you. Disappointed in the way you just treated Dani. It's not okay to go off like that on someone you care about. It's fine to disagree. It's fine to be mad, but you acting so completely disrespectful toward her is only going to make things worse. Because it's *very obvious* to all of us that you still care for her. Even to Lacey, who you won't commit to. You think she didn't notice when you stopped holding her hand the second you saw Dani? Anger won't kill your feelings, Chase. It will only make you look ugly trying to hide them."

I want to justify my actions, but I can't exactly tell Mom that, earlier today, Dani said she'd *ride my pony* again, and it got me all revved up.

Because what the hell was that even about?

I've had sex since we ended things. But it hasn't been the same. What we had was special. It was love. The kind of stupid true love everyone dreams about.

And the kind of love I'll probably never feel again.

I was going to yell at Dani earlier at her house, but Damon interrupted us. And it's been simmering inside me all afternoon. The rage. The sadness. I'm not sure if there's even a difference anymore.

I don't reply to my mom. Just stare blankly at her, hoping she can't read all that's going through my mind.

She must not be able to because she keeps the lecture going, finally saying, "And I'd like you to tell your friends to leave. I think you need to spend some time alone today, contemplating the kind of man you want to be. Because the son I raised wouldn't treat anyone, especially not a friend, the way you just treated Dani. She wanted to explain why she did what she did, and you just yelled at her." When I don't reply, she gives me the mom glare. "Better yet," she says. "*I'll* tell your friends to head out. You can just go straight up to your room."

Which only makes things worse.

Because now, I find myself lying on my bed, staring at Dani's window, knowing my mom was right.

Not about what happened.

But about how I yelled at her.

And how I wish I hadn't.

SUNDAY, AUGUST 18TH

she lost it.

Chase

DAMON COMES BARRELING into my room, unannounced. He was kind of pissed at me yesterday after Mom told everyone to go home, and I maybe fibbed to him about why I was in trouble, mentioning some chores I hadn't done. As my best friend who happens to live next door, it's certainly not unusual for him to just come over, but today, he seems stressed. And Damon is the least stressed person I know.

"I had to get out of the house," he says, plopping down on a chair in the corner of the room. "My sister is freaking out."

And I can't help it. My eyes immediately glance out my window to his sister's bedroom window.

My mom was right. I'm not at all over her. I just feel stuck. I also know that, like many of my other friends, she'll be leaving for college next weekend. Which means I don't have much time left to fix things.

Or apologize for yelling at her yesterday.

"What's she freaking out about?" I ask.

"She's leaving for college today, and she's still not packed."

"Wait, what?! Why is she leaving so soon? School doesn't start for another week," I say in a panic.

Damon rolls his eyes at me as he picks a football up from the floor and starts tossing it in the air and catching it.

"Rush week starts tomorrow. Apparently, Mom made a list of what Dani should wear each day, and she couldn't find one of her pairs of shoes. She lost it. Started crying. I told her she needed to get her shit together. That she couldn't go to college, acting like a big baby. To which Jennifer gave me a dirty look, gave Dani a big hug, and took her into *her* closet to find a similar shoe. So, fine, I'm thinking, *Okay, that's settled. We're all good.* But Dani's still babbling about how she's worried she can't take enough regular clothes and blah, blah, and I was like, *You're a few hours away. It's not like you can't just drive home. Or call for the plane.* Both she and Jennifer looked at me—the voice of reason—like I'd just told them to go eff off, so I figured it'd be safer over here."

My eyes go back to the window. Even though Dani and I haven't been close, at least I still get to see her. She sits on her window seat and reads or talks on her phone, and she goes to my and Damon's games and to most of the family events. She's here. I see her every day. And it makes me sad to think that I won't anymore.

"I'm hungry," Damon says. "Let's go raid the fridge."

"You go on down."

"What's wrong with you?" he asks me.

"Nothing. Just sick of chores. I've gotta put these clothes away quick, so Mom doesn't get mad about it." Fortunately, there's a laundry basket full of clean clothes on my desk.

"Cool," he says, wandering out, yesterday apparently forgiven.

He goes down the hall, and I hear him stop and talk to my sister, Haley, who is probably in her room, doing the same. Our family's weekend chores.

I know what I'm about to do makes no sense. But nothing since the day we stopped being friends ever does.

I grab a piece of paper and start writing.

I look at it.

Laugh at myself.

Wad it up and throw it in the trash.

I grab another sheet and start over.

There are six rejects in the bin before I finally settle on a winner. Or at least, the best of the stupid things I wrote.

After I get my clothes put away, I deal with the note, then shut my curtains, and go down to the kitchen.

"Dude, you didn't tell me today was cinnamon roll day," Damon says, sitting at the counter, happily eating one of my mom's practically legendary rolls.

"I didn't know," I say, surprised the smell didn't wake me.

"I made some to send to college with Dani," my mom says. "And a bunch of cookies and a basketful of snacks."

Damon paws through the basket. "She'll gain her freshman twenty her first week." He laughs. Damon always finds himself hilarious.

"No, she won't," I say, standing up for her. "Dani eats super healthy and is mostly vegan."

"And they are all healthy snacks," my mom says to Damon before turning to me. "Chase, would you do me a favor and run them over?"

Uh, no, I think, I can't. But I know I need to. I want to tell her I'm sorry before she leaves.

But before I get a chance to even pick up the basket, Damon's phone buzzes with a text.

"You can give it to her outside," he says. "We're all supposed to go say goodbye now."

It was our dream.

Devaney

I HAVE A bit of a packing crisis—okay, it was more than a crisis—over a pair of shoes. Actually, I couldn't care less about the shoes. It's more that I'm not sure I want to do this. Not sure I want to leave home. Not sure I even want to go to college. And really not sure I want to go through rush. Even though both my mom and Jadyn have fond memories of being in a sorority, the idea seems antiquated in so many ways. Not to mention that you have to pay to be in one. Like I have to buy some friends to fit in. Jadyn told me what you pay is no different than joining a social club, a country club, or a business club.

Which I get. It just seems overwhelming, I guess. That starting tomorrow, I will meet hundreds of girls and have to decide which group of them I want to be friends with. Pledge my college years to.

Jadyn says to be myself. My mom told me to be a Diamond. Said that my name holds clout since my father is practically a football legend there. Even though she's married twice since she and my dad divorced, she's kept the Diamond name. She says it's for me and Damon—so we share the same last name—but she likes the prestige it brings her.

Jennifer already has the car packed and ready to roll. I need to get down there, but I also just need a moment.

I sit on my window seat and take a deep breath. Try to calm myself. My eyes do what they always do when I'm in this spot—wander to the window across from me, to Chase's room. I tilt my head in curiosity when I notice his curtains are closed and there's a white sheet of paper taped to the window.

There is just one word written in a flowing script that isn't Chase's typical handwriting.

dream

I look down at my hand. At my empty ring finger. I took off the *dream* ring he had given me the second I got home on the day things ended. The day of our fight. A fight I've never fully recovered from.

I get up, go to my jewelry box, and stare at the ring. I look at it every day. I'm not sure if it's for the hope my dream will come true or to punish myself for it not coming true.

But the sign feels like an olive branch.

I put the ring on and then trace my fingers across each letter, just like Chase did the day he gave it to me.

It was during the summer two years ago. Chase had just gotten back from quarterback camp, and I'll never forget how he took my breath away when he stepped out of the car. He looked grown-up. Still his adorable, goofy self, but the truth was, my best friend had gotten really hot.

"Dani!" I hear being yelled out, bringing me out of my reverie.

I startle and decide to leave the ring on, but then I run into my closet, pull a photo out from underneath my jewelry box, and tape it to my window before I go.

When I get downstairs, I find my entire family, all the Mackenzies, and even the dogs—Angel and Winger—waiting for me. The kids are holding balloons, the dogs have on collegiate neckerchiefs, and there's even a banner that says, *Good Luck at College.*

I get hugs and kisses from everyone, but when it's Chase's turn, I just stand there, frozen, looking up into his eyes, my emotions ping-ponging between sadness from the way he yelled at me yesterday to happiness from the sweet sign today.

He shocks me when he takes both my hands in his and says, "Good luck." But he stops when his finger touches the ring. He doesn't pull my hand up to look at it. He already knows what it says. "You haven't worn that since—did you see my sign?"

I'm standing completely still, staring into his gaze. "Yes. And thank you," I say as tears prickle my eyes.

He pulls me into a hug. Which doesn't help. He hasn't hugged me like this in what feels like forever. And I've missed it. "You'll have so much fun at college; I know you will. Scope things out, get the lay of the land, and then your brother and I will be there with you soon."

"You're coming to Nebraska?" I ask. "Like, for sure?"

"Of course. It was our dream. Well, I mean, individually anyway," he says, putting his head down.

Individually, not as a couple, is what he means. His dream, my dream, which is not the same as *our* dream.

Still, the hug, like the sign in the window, makes me feel like maybe, someday, we could be friends again. And when he unwraps his arms from around me, I'm not ready for him to let go.

"Take care of yourself, Dani."

Those are the last words I remember hearing even though I got numerous well wishes and good-byes before I was loaded into the car. I turn to Jennifer, who is in the passenger seat next to me. She's taking me to the airport, but both my parents are going to help me move in. Dad drove my car up to Lincoln yesterday and had a get-together last night with some old teammates. He'll be meeting me and my mom there before flying back home with her.

"You feel like driving?" I ask Jennifer.

"Of course," she says. She loves to drive.

Everyone has dispersed from the driveway, but Chase is still standing there with my brother and Haley, watching us.

When we get out of the car to switch sides, I can't help myself.

I rush toward Haley, throwing my arms around her, then Damon, and Chase, like I'm never going to see them again.

A package deal.

Chase

"WOW," HALEY SAYS as we watch the car pull out of the driveway. "Dani hasn't hugged me like that since …" She stops talking.

We don't talk about that summer. Damon and my sister know what happened. Why everything changed.

"That summer," I say. "It's okay. We should be able to talk about it. We had a lot of fun together."

"We did," my sister says, frowning. "I tried. Like, for me and her to be close even though she and you weren't. It's like we're a package deal or something."

"And right now, we ain't part of the package," Damon drawls. "My sister is a smart girl, but sometimes, she can be really dumb. And as I always say, you can't fix stupid."

"But she hugged you, Chase," Haley says, "not just then, but also before when everyone was saying goodbye. She hasn't done that either."

"I know," I say. "Maybe …"

"Maybe what? Did something happen between you two?" Damon asks.

"No, we got into a fight yesterday. I yelled at her. That's why Mom made me go to my room and told everyone to leave. But today, I don't know … maybe the ice thawed a little."

"It needs to melt," Haley says. She wraps her arms around me and Damon. "Next year, when you two go off to college, I'll be bawling. Seriously, I don't know what I will do without you jerks around."

Let go of it all.

Devaney

WHEN JENNIFER PULLS out onto the tarmac, I see that my mother has already arrived. Once we get my bags out of the car and loaded onto the plane, Jennifer gives me a big hug.

"I'm going to miss you," I say sincerely. "And the babies."

"We'll miss you, too. Enjoy rush and college."

What she says makes me feel hopeful, but then I turn and greet my mother—the woman who has so many expectations of me. Of how I need to look. How I need to behave. And not because *I want* to act or look a certain way, but to impress those she deems worthy.

"Devaney, take a seat," my mother says. "We aren't due to take off for a bit, and I brought you here early, so we could have a chat."

Oh boy. What did I do wrong now?

I sit as told and then really look at my mom. "Did you change your hair color?" I ask her.

Something about her looks … different. She looks softer somehow. Her hair is in loose curls that don't seem to be held in place by a bottle of hair spray. Her makeup is a little less severe. Her clothes are obviously still designer, but she's wearing a flowing dress that makes her look … well, more like me.

She grins at me. "I have a lot I need to tell you, sweetheart."

When was the last time she called me that?

"Uh, okay," I mumble out.

"First of all, yes, my hair is a different shade. More like our natural strawberry-blonde."

"It's pretty," I tell her.

"Thank you." She takes a deep breath. "Okay, here goes. Van," she says, referring to her third husband—who is not just a friend of the billionaire Tripp Archibald, like I first thought, but he's also his brother—"has been really good for me. He's incredibly honest and humble, and because of him, I have been in counseling for about six months."

My eyes get huge. "Counseling for what?"

"Me," she says simply. "Van overheard me speaking to you one day and talked to me about it. He loves me, but he loves his family more than anything. The Archibald family, for all their money, have managed to stay incredibly close. He said it's because their parents taught them to treat each other with respect. He felt that what I told you that day was not only disrespectful, but also possibly detrimental to you."

"What did you say?" I ask, trying to figure out where this is all coming from.

"It doesn't matter at this point, but I realized he was right. Since then, I've come to discover a lot about myself. The biggest thing is that I was—am—insecure when it comes to love. I loved your father so much when I married him, but before I'd met him, I'd had my own dreams. Dreams that, honestly, weren't even mine. They were what my parents had told me I needed to do to succeed. When you hear something over and over, it becomes part of you. And it morphed into what I thought I wanted out of life.

"You might find it both funny and ironic that my parents were hard on me. They preached to me about getting excellent grades, going to medical school, becoming a doctor, and of course, marrying one. That was literally my life plan, all spelled out.

"My parents never went to college, but my father was smart

and moved up in his company. My mother very much tried to keep up with the Joneses, and she always worried about what people would think of her. And, well, me.

"My first few years in college, I worked hard. I chose my sorority based on their grade point average and didn't get involved with it any more than required. I didn't like Jadyn and thought she was slutty because she hung out with so many guys. In some respects, she was the girl I wished I could be. No parents to tell her what to do. Crazy, carefree, and popular. Eventually, we became friends. And then she bribed me into going on a date with her best friend. Your father. I tried to resist his charm because I didn't think marrying an athlete was in the cards for me. But I fell in love with him. We married. I got pregnant quickly. It was easy to get caught up in all things Danny Diamond."

She pauses for a moment to take a sip of water. And it shocks me to see tears glistening in her eyes when she speaks about being in love with my dad.

"Things were great for a while, but then … your dad was famous. Girls cheered his name. I was jealous. Even of Jadyn. Your father and Jadyn were so close, and when I was pregnant, those insecurities rose to the surface. And when you were born, I was scared to death. I had always wanted to be a doctor, but being a mother seemed so foreign. I thought it was supposed to be natural, and when it wasn't, I got rigid, trying to maintain a sense of control when, in reality, I had none. It led me to cheat on your father because I was searching for something.

"The counseling has made me realize that what I was searching for was me. I've never had a strong sense of self. I simply kept trying to fit myself into other people's expectations. And that is hard."

She smiles at me. "I'm still a work in progress, but it was really important for me to tell you all this today, before you go to college. I want you to try to forget any expectations you think I have. I promise you, starting today, you'll get no more pressure or judgment from me. If you decide you don't want to rush and you'd rather, I don't know, join the Peace Corps, you'll have my full support. What I'm trying to say is that I don't want you to carry the burden of family expectations with you to school."

I throw my arms around my mom—something I haven't done since before the divorce—and start crying. What a relief it would be if what she is saying is true.

"I had a meltdown over a pair of shoes," I admit, trying to lighten the mood.

"Devaney, you're an incredible young woman. Smart and sweet, and you've always had such spunk. I know the divorce was hard on you, and I know I've gone overboard in worrying about what others think. I know that's affected you and possibly even your love life. Or so I've been told," she says with another grin.

"By who?"

My mom glances at her phone. "Maybe I'll let them tell you." She gets up, goes to the plane's door, and seems to motion to someone.

I'm shocked when Jennifer, who I thought was already well on her way home by now, and Jadyn, who I just said goodbye to at the house, come on board.

"*They* told you?" I practically stutter out. "But you don't really like them."

When I watch Jadyn and my mother hug though, it feels ... genuine. Jadyn smiles, and the usual tension in her jaw when my mom's around is gone.

"We're all BFFs now," Jennifer says, throwing her arm around my shoulders.

"What?" I say in shock.

My mother has tried to break Jennifer and my dad up on more than one occasion.

How could this possibly be?

Jadyn nods in agreement, and while I know she wouldn't lie to me, I still stand here with my mouth hanging open.

"During my counseling," my mother explains, "I examined past relationships. My insecurity, especially regarding Jadyn and Danny's friendship, is what undermined my relationship with them both. We were all so close in college, and I hope, someday, we will be again."

"And you forgave her?" I ask Jadyn. Because I don't know if I can handle all this change at once.

Jadyn sits down next to me and pats my hand. It's as comforting as always. "We had a few phone conversations, and then I went to her house for lunch. Five hours and a whole lot of tears and laughter later, it was healing—for both of us."

Jennifer sits on the other side of me. "Similar deal. Only dinner. First with me and then with both your father and me. I'm a huge believer that when children are involved, no matter how old they are, coparenting is important. I've always wanted us all to get along. It makes life so much nicer. Happier."

"One of the questions my counselor asked me," Mom says, "was for the names of the two strongest women I personally knew. These two are who I immediately thought of. And thanks to Van believing in me and helping me on this path, I feel secure in a relationship for the first time in my life. It's something I never felt with your father—or Richard for that matter. And this sounds crazy for someone who is taking her daughter to college today to say, but I feel like I've finally grown up."

I stand up suddenly and hug my mother, tears falling again—this time not over the hurt she's caused me, but from relief. "So, you're not mad I'm not going to an Ivy League school?" I ask, still not quite able to believe this is happening.

"Nope. Your life is officially yours to live, and from now on, I'm going to support all your choices because I love you and don't want you to turn out like me."

This makes me cry harder.

"In fact, that's why Jadyn and Jennifer are here. The three of us—*together*—with input from your roommate, designed your dorm room with love. And we want to be there with you when you move in."

"And we hope you'll love it!" Jennifer says.

"It's our gift to you," Jadyn says.

I hug them all again. I'm so overwhelmed, but I feel happy and loved.

I LIE IN my bed, staring up at my dorm room ceiling after everyone has left, and think about a lot of things.

The people I met during move-in. The ones I'll meet during rush.

And about life.

My life specifically. How since my parents got divorced, I've sometimes felt like a rag doll, stuck in the middle of two kids, each pulling on an arm.

Could that really be over? Part of me isn't sure how to handle this news. *How do I just let go of it all?*

I consider calling my brother, but he's like a duck, conflict rolling off his back like water.

I touch the *dream* ring on my finger and picture Chase's handsome face. He looked so good today.

And I can't believe I'm going to do this tonight of all nights.

But I need to know.

Know if I deserve all the blame I have put on myself.

I scroll back in my phone and start to watch the video my friend took because she was so sure it was a moment I'd want to remember forever.

The day Hunter Lansford asked me to Homecoming.

I watch the first thirty seconds, and then I pause it and focus on what happened after.

And as I replay it all in my mind, I realize that, like my mother, I need to work on my own insecurities. I know confidence is in me. At cheer competitions when I was younger, I was the teammate who was never nervous, who was ready to face any challenge. Who didn't fall apart when a routine wasn't done to perfection. I could react on the fly, without a second thought.

It's like I just lost it somehow.

I think about what my mom said earlier today about the most confident people she knew.

A memory immediately pops into my brain, and I see three smiling faces planning what was supposed to be our future together that summer in the Ozarks.

A place I've never been back to since.

It's late, but I text her anyway.

Me: *You still up?*

Haley: *Yeah. How's your dorm? You get all settled?*

I don't reply. There's too much to type, so I call her and tell her everything that happened today with my mom.

When I finish, she goes, "Wow. That's a lot to digest. But it's good, right? Probably weird though because I know you've always gotten a lot of pressure from her. And now, that's all just supposed to be gone? I think that would feel a little weird, like a joke almost. Was it weird? Did she seem genuine? Like, with my mom and Jennifer?"

"Yeah, it did. And that is *exactly* how I'm feeling. I am not sure *what* to feel."

"Well, the good thing is, you can go through rush with no pressure or family expectations, right?"

"Yeah," I say, although somehow, I'm not convinced.

"Dani, I always looked up to you when we were kids. Actually, I wanted to be you. Never afraid. A fierce competitor. When your parents divorced—"

"It affected me," I say, realizing now just how much.

"Which is understandable, but—"

"If my mom can find herself after being lost for twenty-some years, I ought to be able to do it, too."

"Exactly," Haley says.

"Truth," I tell her, "the reason I called you is because my mom said that her counselor asked her to think of the strongest women she knew. She thought of your mom and Jennifer, but I thought of you. And Chase and Damon. All of us when we were on that trip in the Ozarks. Remember how we talked about running a business together? And you were all so sure. I wanted it, but I wasn't confident about it the way you all were."

"We were sure, yes. But that doesn't mean we aren't a little scared it might not work. That's normal. Being scared isn't a fault. Not recognizing it and letting it keep you from something you want, might be. What do you want, Devaney Diamond? And what kind of person do you want to be?"

"I don't know, but I'd better figure it out quick."

"Yeah, because I've really missed you."

"Oh, Haley," I say, feeling emotional for the thousandth time today.

"And I'm pretty comfortable with saying that goes for my brother, too. And just so you know, you don't have to be dating Chase for us to all be friends again. The two of you just, well, you need to fix things—together."

"Do you think that we could be best friends again?"

"I definitely do," she says.

After saying goodbye, I hang up and go to sleep with a smile on my face.

Would hurt less.

Chase

I'M DOWN IN the kitchen, making a smoothie before bed.

"Say good night to Chase," Mom says, walking by me with my baby sister in her arms.

"Nighty-nighty!" Emersyn says, leaning down to give me a kiss.

"Sleep tight." I give her side a little tickle.

"Time for a tickle fight!" she yells back.

Dad comes in the room, swoops Emersyn out of Mom's arms, and then whisks her off to bed. She's shrill-laughing as he continues to tickle her.

"And don't forget to turn out the light!" Mom yells as they leave.

I roll my eyes but can't help but smile. My parents have had the same bedtime routine for us kids since, well, we were kids.

"Kinda sucks no one tucks me in anymore," I say teasingly to my mom as I sit down at the table and move the slightly skewed place mat back into its proper place. I stop in my tracks, my grin immediately fading. "What's this?"

"I had Dani sign the table," Mom says simply, barely looking up from whatever she's reading.

"But she already signed it."

Mom glances up at me. "Yes, she did. When she was *five*. Her signature has changed a little since then. I thought I'd have all you kids sign it again when you turned eighteen, but then I decided to wait until you went off to college. She's the first one."

I look down at Devaney's name scrolled beautifully above my place mat. "Why did she sign it here?"

Mom looks up at me again, her eyes narrowed. "I assume because there was space."

"But this is where *I* always sit."

"If it's a problem, Chase, sit somewhere else."

Instead of moving, I run my fingers over each letter. *D-E-V-A-N-E-Y.*

"You should have just let her carve it into my chest. Probably would have hurt less," I mutter, letting out a huge breath of air.

"Oh, for goodness' sake, Chase. Don't be so dramatic. If you want to be friends with Dani again, you're going to have to get over what happened in the past and at least meet her halfway."

WEDNESDAY, AUGUST 21ST

A chance.

Devaney

THE FIRST FEW days of rush have been a whirlwind. On Monday, we were split into groups, listened to presentations about Greek life, had lunch, and then spent four hours touring sorority houses, followed by dinner.

My roommate, Alyssa, and I weren't in the same group, so at the end of the day, we talked about our initial impressions. We unanimously agreed, before falling asleep early, that rush was exhausting. And I was very glad I'd listened to everyone about needing comfortable shoes. We'd walked a ton.

Yesterday was more of the same.

We started at nine in the morning and had six hours of open houses and a lunch break. One thing I really thought was fun were the cheers, chants, and songs each house did. Something about that added to the revelry of it all.

Dinner was on our own, followed by a group event.

I have met a whole lot of people in a very short time. It's been exciting though, and I've started to notice how each house varies.

The hardest part came after the end of our first two days—or round one—when we had to rank each house according to our preference. I was glad that I had talked to Jadyn about the process so that I understood that the houses would all be doing the same by narrowing the field.

But I'm worried for today because I also know that, as a legacy, this might be when my mom's sorority will cut me. Jadyn said that if, for some reason, they didn't think we had a chance for a final match, they would often cut legacies loose to give them the ability to focus on other options.

Either way, as I lie in my bed this morning, I can't help but wonder which houses I will get invitations to today. Ten is the maximum number we can visit, and we'll spend thirty minutes at each, getting to meet more of the members and learning about their history and philanthropy. Because the first couple of days were so long and very informal, our clothing was casual. Today, things change to semi-casual, and I'm excited to put on the pretty sundress and sandals I brought.

I take a moment to look around at the room that is mine for the next year. Alyssa is still asleep.

She's from a small town in Nebraska, the youngest of five with four older brothers; she loves sports and is a former cheerleader. We met through the school's roommate-matching portal and seemed to be a good fit.

Apparently, my mother or Jadyn spoke to her about their plan for decorating our dorm room because she was fully on board with the concept they surprised me with. And it really was amazing to know that my mother, Jennifer, and Jadyn had worked together to do this.

Our room looked so bleak and institutional when I first walked in, but it's incredible what some fabric and removable wallpaper can do. The room now has a slight boho vibe. The walls are covered in a pretty white paper with soft gray splashes that make the room look bigger and brighter. Curtains frame the windows. Our bedding has pale shades of pinks, grays, and teal with lots of texture added by a wide array of pillows. A console table doubles as a nightstand for both of us, and underneath sits upholstered storage cubes that can be pulled out for extra seating. The wooden closet doors and desks got makeovers with coordinating wallpaper. The whole thing just feels cozy and chic. We love it.

I don't want to wake Alyssa, so I'm quiet when I sit up in bed and grab my phone from the console table. And I actually sort of surprise myself when I text a person I wouldn't normally ask for advice.

Me: *Are you up?*

Mom: *Of course. You know I start my day at six with a cup of coffee before I work out with my trainer.*

Me: *I didn't know if the new you still had the same routine.*

Mom: *She does but is working on being more flexible. How are you? How is rush? What do you think? Are you nervous for today? It had to be so hard to narrow it down to your top ten.*

Me: *That's how I'm feeling. Excited but hoping I get some invites.*

Mom: *You will, for sure. Most cuts during this time are simply due to basic qualifications, like if a recruit's GPA doesn't meet the house's standard.*

Me: *I know. But still.*

Mom: *You're smart and a beautiful person inside and out.*

Me: *Do you really think that I'm beautiful inside?*

My phone buzzes in my hand. I refuse the call but then grab my key, quietly get out of bed, go out into the hall, sit on the floor, and call her back.

"Hi. Sorry. Alyssa is still asleep. I didn't want to wake her."

"And I wanted to tell you, yes, I think you're beautiful inside. You have so much of your father in you, Devaney. Probably why you and I have clashed so much."

"You think Dad is a good man?"

Mom actually lets out a laugh. "Of course I do. Do you think that I don't?"

"Um, well, it was kind of traumatic for me the day you stormed into our house when you got back from Bermuda."

"And what did I do?"

"You were mad about the cheer sleepover that had turned into a party. You called my friendship with Chase stupid and said I couldn't see him anymore. And then when Jennifer tried to explain what happened, you called her a husband-stealing whore. And when Dad came in the house a few minutes later, you called him some not-so-nice things."

"I hadn't expected Jennifer to be there, and I reacted. Badly. I apologize for that. I was hurt, upset, and worried about you."

"But you left us," I say softly, tears filling my eyes.

"Devaney, I'm sorry. I've told you so many things that were wrong. I pray—literally—every night that whatever issues I might have given you or that the hits your confidence took because of me will not be permanent.

"Do you remember Maggie from your fourth-grade class? She was so smart but got picked on. Remember how you stood up for her? How you became friends with her? In grade school, I was a Maggie. But no one stood up for me."

"I'm sorry, Mom."

"My point is, when I went to college, I tried to throw away all that emotional baggage. And because of my experiences as a kid, I focused a lot on the outside of me. The way I looked.

"I'd never really done that before because I didn't care what I looked like. I was too busy studying. I never wore makeup. Didn't wear stylish clothing. I'd told myself I was above it all because I had lofty goals.

"But when I studied up on rush, I somehow found this old

research paper that talked about salespeople and how those who were better groomed and more attractive sold more than those who weren't. And I was smart enough to put two and two together. I knew that if I wanted to rush into a top sorority, I needed more than just the résumé and grades. I needed to look the part.

"And as your dad was thrust into the spotlight when he went pro, so was I. And, again, I knew I had to look the part. It became almost an obsession.

"I'm not trying to make excuses for myself. I own up to how I was. My point is this—I think your father is a wonderful man. He put up with me for a long time, mostly because of you and Damon, and when it came time to end our marriage, I truly believe he would have given me all of his worldly possessions for custody of you two. That, in and of itself, says more than I ever could.

"You are like your father. You always have been. You have a good, loving soul. And I'm very proud of you."

"And what do you think of Chase?"

"I thought you weren't friends anymore?"

"We aren't, but I wish we still were."

"Who you are friends with is totally up to you."

"And what if, say, I wanted to marry someone like Chase? Would you still tell me I could do better?"

"Here's the thing, Devaney. You are an adult. Your life is now yours. When I told you on the plane that I would support all your decisions, I meant it. You'll probably make some bad decisions. But that's okay. We all do. It's part of the growing and learning process."

"What if I screw things up beyond repair and am left with nothing?"

"I'll help you pick up the pieces," she says.

"I'm in pieces now, Mom. I broke things with Chase. I miss

him terribly. And I might possibly even be a little in love with him."

"I think you always have been a little in love with him, Devaney. And if you feel that way, you should follow in your mother's footsteps and ask for forgiveness. Make things right. It might take some time for you both to heal, but that's the first step."

I nod my head, knowing that she's right. "Thanks, Mom."

"You're welcome. And keep me posted on how it goes today. And tomorrow. Even if it's just a quick text. And you might want to include Jadyn and Jennifer. I know they are thinking about you, too."

I agree to do so and then hang up the phone.

I sit here.

And before I lose my nerve, I call his number.

"Hey, Dani," Chase says, his voice sounding gravelly.

"Sorry if I woke you."

"Are you okay?" he asks.

"I'm fine. Actually, that's not true. I haven't been fine since that day. And I wanted to tell you I'm sorry. For everything. And that I hope, someday, you might forgive me. Because I need you to be my friend. I know you're with Lacey and everything, but we were best friends. And I miss you."

"I miss you, too," he says.

"So, you think there's a chance?"

"Hmm," he says, a playful tone in his voice now. "I don't know. You are my best friend's older sister. Like, you are a whole five months older than me. That might be a problem."

"You're silly," I say, letting out a laugh.

"Dani," he says, his voice turning serious again, "are you still wearing the ring?"

I look down at my finger and smile. "Yes, I am."

"And how is rush going so far?"

"Busy. Exhausting. Today, I'll find out if I got invited back to any of the houses I put in my top ten."

"You know that I'm kind of lucky."

"Are lucky or *get* lucky?" I tease.

"With you, it used to be both," he fires back. "Just know that I infused some of my luck in that ring before I gave it to you."

"Oh, did you now?" I flirt.

"Yes, I did. Which means, I predict you will get ten invites today and six tomorrow."

"How do you know how many I could get each day?"

"I've had to listen to my mom talk with Jennifer about it every night. I'm practically a rush expert. So, you need any advice, just call me."

"I actually just called my mom. She told me that she's been getting counseling, that she's friendly with your mom and Jennifer now. And it really seems like she's changed. She even told me to text her, Jennifer, and your mom this morning when I find out. That they are all thinking about me."

"She's right about that. But I'd be willing to bet that I've been thinking about you more."

"That means a lot, Chase. Thank you. I have to go now though. Get ready for today."

"Question for you," he says, "before you go."

"Okay."

"How are you going to decide which house you want to be in?"

"I have no idea. When I figure it out, I'll let you know."

"And you'll text me?"

"I will."

"Good. Bye, Dani," he says and then hangs up.

I hold my phone to my chest and let out a relieved sigh, feeling like I can fully breathe for the first time in two years.

I GO BACK in my room to find Alyssa awake. We get ready, have some breakfast, and then go pick up our invites.

> **Group text to Jennifer, Auntie Jay, Mom:** *I got invites to my top ten!!! And, yes, one of them is where I'm a legacy.*
>
> **Jennifer:** *Woohoo! Congrats!!!*
>
> **Auntie Jay:** *Just be your amazing self today, Dani. I know it's stressful, but the rush process has changed a lot since your mom and I went through it. And it seems like a much smarter way of doing things. We just visited all the houses and prayed that the one we wanted would take us. Now, you keep cutting a little bit each day so that you know who is as interested in you as you are in them.*
>
> **Mom:** *That's awesome, Devaney. And I agree with the above sentiments and would add to really focus on what the sorority would offer you, not the other way around.*
>
> **Me:** *Thank you!<3*

I know Chase wanted to be included, but I send him a separate text. I don't expect him to answer since he's at school, but I send it anyway.

> **Me:** *I guess you are lucky. Ten out of ten.*
>
> **Chase:** *Told ya. ;)*
>
> **Me:** *Aren't you in class?*
>
> **Chase:** *Yeah, but I'd take a detention before not replying to you. I gotta put my phone away now though cause Coach wouldn't be too thrilled if I missed practice.*

I hold my phone to my chest again and sigh.

"What's that dreamy look for?" Alyssa asks me.

"Oh, was just texting my moms and aunt to let them know about the invites."

"No," she says, "you were texting a boy. I thought you said

39

you didn't have a boy back home. And if you don't, how have you already met someone here?"

"Fine. Boy from home, but it's a friend thing," I say.

"That's good because we are in college now. And I, for one, am ready to meet some college boys."

"You do realize that the freshmen here are the same boys we went to high school with last year, right?"

"Maybe for you, but there was a total of fifty-two boys in my senior class. I'm looking forward to a bigger pond to fish from."

Which makes me laugh out loud. Because I realize that's what I was in high school. A big fish in a little pond. Here, I'm just a fish, trying to navigate a really big lake.

And I think I'm okay with that.

THURSDAY, AUGUST 22ND

I would kiss that.

Devaney

LAST NIGHT, I had to narrow my choices from ten to six. And like yesterday, we'll get to spend a little longer at each house. If we get six invites, we will be going from nine until dinner at seven with just an hour for lunch.

Jadyn suggested that I should make my own decisions and not be swayed by other girls rushing. And Alyssa and I discussed early in the process that it didn't matter where we ended up; we'd be roommates and friends regardless.

When she shows me her six invites though, I do find it interesting how much they vary from mine.

"We only share one," she says to me. "I figured we would have more overlap."

"Me, too," I tell her. "What are you looking for in a group?"

"Well, I definitely want all the girls to be pretty. The prettier they are, the hotter guys I'll meet, right?"

Alyssa is a pretty girl. She's a brunette with curves in all the right places. Based on the photos she showed me, I think she was a lot like me, just in a smaller school. Captain of her cheer squad. Homecoming queen. She was in a few more activities than me and had a slightly lower GPA, but on paper, we're pretty similar.

"That, or you will have a lot of gorgeous competition," I tease.

"Oh my God, I never thought of it that way." Her eyes get big, and I realize she is taking me seriously.

"I'm just joking," I tell her.

"And how are you choosing?"

"Honestly, I have no idea. I'm trying not to think too hard about it and go with my gut. Where I feel most comfortable."

"Well, if that were the case, we'd all be in ..." She whispers the name of a sorority. "They need to watch a few makeup tutorials and work out occasionally, if you know what I mean."

I give her a curt smile, not loving the catty way she sounds while at the same time knowing those very words could have come out of the mouths of any one of my high school friends.

Group text to Jennifer, Auntie Jay, Mom: *I got invites to my top sex!!! And, yes, one of them is where I'm a legacy.*

Jennifer: *Top sex, huh? What really goes on at rush?*

Auntie Jay: *OMG. LMAO. Top sex. Well, if you have to be the best at something...*

Mom: *I guess the selection process really has changed since we went through it.*

Jennifer: *Although that's what college is all about, right? Lots of education that doesn't take place in the classroom, if you know what I mean. ;)*

Me: *I meant, TOP SIX sororities.*

Jennifer: *LOL. I think we knew that. Hope your visits are great!*

I'm getting ready to text Chase next, but before I can, he sends me a screenshot of the group text with our moms. His mom must have sent it to him.

Chase: *So, top sex today and then what?*

Me: *Very funny.*

Chase: *The comments after are golden. I forwarded it to Damon. I think he's already shared it with half the school. We're DYING!*

Me: *OMG! Please, the fire jokes in the Ozarks were bad enough. Please. Please. Don't send it to the grandparents.*

Chase: *Uh …*

Me: *Do you want to hear about what's happening today?*

Chase: *Yes.*

Me: *Okay. Today, we keep narrowing down our options, so we can spend more time getting to know the sororities we are most interested in. Tonight is going to be the hardest. We have to chose our top two and then stack rank the rest. Tomorrow, we can get a maximum of two invitations.*

Chase: *Wow, that's a big jump. And you'll for sure get one of those two on Bid Day?*

Me: *Hopefully, yes.*

Chase: *And what's your criteria for narrowing?*

Me: *Are you going to get in trouble? Aren't you in class?*

Chase: *I got a pass from Coach. I'm currently sitting in the whirlpool.*

Me: *Did you get hurt?!*

Chase: *Not really. It's just a bruise, but Coach was pissed. A sophomore defensive end decided to tackle his own quarterback during practice.*

Me: *What an idiot. Where does it hurt?*

Chase: *Why? You want to kiss it and make it feel better?*

Me: *I did that more times than I can count when we were kids. What hurts now?*

Chase: *Oh, trust me, I remember. Probably why I never*

minded getting scraped up a bit.

Me: *Are you flirting with me?*

Chase: *What do you want my answer to be?*

Me: *Is it bad if I say that I kind of hope you are?*

Chase: *Not as far as I'm concerned. Did I mention that I'm naked?*

Me: *Really?*

Chase: *No, not really, silly. I was attempting to use one of your brother's typical lines on you, hoping you'd say something like—Oh, send me a picture.*

Me: *Chase Mackenzie, you'd better not be sending dick pics to anyone. You know better than that. It could come back to haunt you when you turn pro. Or anytime really.*

Chase: *Thanks for the talk, Mom.*

Me: *I have to go to my first visit. Tell me what really hurts. And don't mention any boy parts.*

Chase: *Even if that's what needs kissed?*

Me: *…*

Chase: *Bruised my elbow when I hit the ground.*

Me: *I would kiss that.*

FRIDAY, AUGUST 23RD

Skip memory lane.

Devaney

I GET BACK to my room and flop on my bed, exhausted. I already talked to my mom and Jennifer earlier about what I thought of each of the houses I'd visited today, how I was starting to feel comfortable in them, and discussed the pros and cons of each in a very methodical way. I turned in my preference card, and now, I just have to wait and see what happens.

Today, we had more free time. I hung out with some of the girls. We got coffee and had a lot of nervous discussions about tomorrow. Everyone shared who they thought their two hopefuls would be. And we talked about what happens next.

I glance at the clock, not able to believe it's nearly ten.

A bunch of the girls, including Alyssa, went out, but I didn't go. I feel like I just need some time. To reflect on my decision. To relax.

To take some time for me.

But what I really want to do is talk to Chase. Yesterday was the last day of his preseason training, and I know tonight was the school's annual red and blue scrimmage between the varsity and JV teams.

I decide to text him before calling in case he went out after.

Me: *If you are home from the scrimmage, give me a call.*

My phone rings almost immediately.

"Hey," he says when I answer.

I can honestly say that I've missed hearing his voice over the phone on a regular basis.

"How was the game tonight? How's your elbow?"

"It was fine. I only played the first quarter."

"Because your elbow is bothering you?"

"No, because I don't want to get hurt in a stupid scrimmage because some freshman is trying to show off."

"I wouldn't want that for you either," I tell him.

"I heard you talked to my mom today. I'm a little disappointed you didn't call me."

"I wanted to wait and call you now. Once the day was over."

"Like back in the good old days?" he says.

"Yeah, even if we'd hung out all day or if I had just left your house, yours was usually the last voice I heard before I went to sleep every night."

"That was one of the hardest things to get used to. Not picking up my phone to call you when I got into bed."

"It was for me, too," I tell him.

He breathes in deeply, and I can hear him exhale. Like he's trying not to sigh at me or that I'm testing his patience. Not sure which. Either way, he goes, "So, you made your final choices today, right? Mom said you were having a hard time with deciding between three of them."

"Actually, I didn't really tell her or my mom, but I knew which was my number one. What I couldn't decide was which would be number two."

"That must mean you have a favorite?"

"I do. And don't laugh at me."

"You always say that, but you know I never do," he sasses

back.

"That's mostly true," I say, "but there was that one time—"

"Let's skip memory lane for now and talk about the thing that happened that you don't want me to laugh about."

"You know how I'm not super emotional typically, like I've never been a crier unless I'm really sad?"

"Of course."

"I can't even believe I'm saying this, let alone the fact that it happened. And I'm not sure if it was the stress. Or the fact that this process was almost over. Or that I was exhausted. Or that I barely had a voice left from all the talking I'd done this week. But when I walked into one of the houses, I started crying because I just couldn't imagine being anywhere else."

"That's great though. If it made you that emotional, it has to be the right place for you."

"And the real shocker of it all—"

"Are you kidding?" He says this like he already knows what I was going to say. "Your favorite was our moms' sorority, wasn't it?"

"It was. Seriously, just because it was theirs, I'd sort of put it at the bottom of my list. I didn't want to be selected just because I was a legacy and they had to take me. But they didn't cut me early, which supposedly means that's not the case. And I hope it isn't. And I really, really hope it's where I end up."

"Why did you choose it?" he asks me.

"You know how my dad always says that in high school, he was a big fish in a little pond?"

"And when he went to college, the pond got bigger?" Chase confirms.

"Exactly. I was popular in high school. Considered pretty. Was homecoming queen and all that. But I've realized, at college, I'm just a little fish. Half the girls who went through rush were like me in that way."

"And the other half?" he asks.

"My first few days, I was drawn to certain sororities that I was convinced would be my top picks. The girls in them were all sort of similar and a lot like high-school Devaney. But as the week continued, I noticed that in the sorority I liked the best, all the girls weren't the same. They were more diverse. Their personalities, their interests, their styles, their looks. I didn't feel like a clone there. I felt like an individual. Like we were *all* individuals. And that felt—freeing. Because I don't want to play the high school game in college. These girls seem to accept me for exactly who I am—or maybe for who I could be someday."

"Dani, you weren't the most popular girl in high school your freshman year either. You're starting over. Heck, you could go all emo if you wanted. Although that'd be hard with hair like yours."

"What do you mean?"

"Your hair is like sunshine. It'd be impossible to feel dark around you when you're so bright."

I let out a little chuckle. "Is that the line you use when you and Damon go out? I see all his private photos. How do you even get into clubs anyway?"

"Damon got us fake IDs, but I won't let him use them. Either the club lets us in without them or they don't. And we don't drink when we get in even though we probably could."

"I suppose when you're driving an exotic car with *Diamond* on the plates, they don't question you."

"That is correct. And I know it sounds reckless, but I make sure it's not. Damon just likes the attention. *College girls are way more fun than high school girls, I'm just saying*, is what he says."

"You sound more like my dad than Damon."

"Did having the name Diamond help you during rush?"

"I honestly don't think so," I tell him.

"I'm proud of you, Dani."

"For getting chosen?"

"No, for the reasons you chose."

"Well, I hope it works out the way I want when I open my bid tomorrow."

"Well, it's not pizza after a game," he says, "but I'm really glad I got to talk to you tonight."

"I'm really glad, too, Chase. Good night."

I'm about to end the call, but he says, "Don't you mean, nighty-night?"

I laugh. "If only I were there for the tickle fight."

"If only," he says sexily. "Don't forget to turn out the light."

SATURDAY, AUGUST 24TH

Make another wish.

Devaney

IT'S BID DAY!

I slept in until nearly nine this morning, got ready, and went to brunch with some of the girls.

Then, it was back to our meeting room for an informational meeting, which was really fun because we got to find out which sororities all our advisors are in.

When three o'clock rolls around, you can feel the excitement in the air. We meet up with our group leader and each get handed an envelope. The good news is, we have the bid in our hands. The bad news is, we can't open it yet.

We're taken to the nearby soccer field, where we find all the sororities wrapped around the edges of the field in groups. They are all dressed up, their Greek letters held up to make it easy for us to find them, and all are wearing their colors. I've already spotted where my top two are, but my eyes keep going back to my top choice.

Pretty much all of us are vibrating with excitement. Especially when they start the countdown. When we get to one, we will open our envelopes at the same time.

"Ten! Nine! Eight! Seven! Six! Five! Four! Three! Two! One!"

I feel like it's New Year's Eve as I watch the girls tear into their envelopes. I take a moment, close my eyes, and make another wish, and then I gently open the flap and pull out the card inside.

The girls around me have opened their cards and are all screaming and hugging each other.

The first thing I see is a seal in the colors I was hoping to see, followed by the letters I wanted.

"Ahhh!" I yell out.

Alyssa comes over and hugs me. She's thrilled because she got her favorite, too. We jump up and down and scream, hug each other, and share our bids with those in our groups. The sororities around us are hooting and hollering.

"All right, ladies, it's time to go home!" our advisor yells out.

We take off running toward the sororities we got. It reminds me of being on a football field before a big game. I'm greeted with hugs and screeches from some of the girls I got to know during rush. Very quickly, we're being paraded to Sorority Row. And by paraded, I literally mean that. Our route is lined with fraternity guys all cheering and high-fiving us as we go by.

In what feels like a blur in time, we're at the house. There's a huge sign welcoming us, balloon arches, and a *Welcome Home* banner over the door. Once inside, we're given sorority tees to put on, accessorized with boas and sunglasses, and gold glitter is brushed onto our faces. It sort of reminds me of—although on a much larger scale here—how we used to dress up the new cheer squad members after tryouts to let everyone at school know they'd made the team.

We hug more people, get introduced to all the girls in our pledge class, and make our way back outside for photos and fun. And it's really cool to look down the street and see the happy celebrations going on at each house.

Later, we're taken on a bus to a pretty house on a lake for

swimming, food, fun, and lots of bonding.

And as the night winds down, I realize another reason why I feel so comfortable here. The lake reminds me of home.

FRIDAY, AUGUST 30TH

Together forever.

Chase

"I KNOW YOUR mother was all misty about you having your last first day of high school, and I teased her about it, but I will admit, knowing tonight is the start of your last year of high school football has me feeling the same way," my dad says, sitting down next to me at the kitchen table, where I'm eating my pregame meal after school.

Tonight, Mom made one of my favorites—a steaming cup of bone broth to start, followed by chicken pesto pasta, loaded down with sautéed veggies.

"It's crazy to think that in January, less than five months from now, you could be starting your college career."

I nod at him. With my AP classes and dual enrollment, I have enough credits to graduate in December, will start college academically as a sophomore, and will be able to graduate with my degree in two and a half years. I'd have four full years of football eligibility, but if warranted, I could enter the professional draft at the end of my third football season as a college graduate.

"I know you haven't decided for sure, but have you told Damon you're considering it yet?" Dad asks me.

It's hard for me not to sigh. Damon gets good grades and is

smart, but he doesn't want to deal with the extra work. And there have been numerous times over the past few years when I wished I had chosen to just coast a little academically. Those times mostly occurred when I was studying instead of hanging out with him and our friends.

"I haven't," I reply, feeling bad for lying to my best friend. Well, not a lie really, more of an omission of the truth. "He's already been talking about prom, the graduation parties. I'm sure it's just because it's the start of our senior year. Everyone is counting down the days until we're out of there."

"It's smart that you have applied for spring admission to the schools you're most interested in playing football at. There are so many advantages—"

"I know, Dad." I repeat the spiel, "I'll get a jump on getting accustomed to college life and, most importantly, get to be part of the team practices and strength training for a full semester before fall camp begins. Participating in the spring and playing in the spring game will hopefully allow me to prove myself and be ahead of the curve when the other players come in for fall camp."

"Right," Dad says with a grin. "Which is good since your goal is to be the starter your first season." He cocks his head and studies my face. "Unless that's not what you want. You're a great player, Chase. This isn't something you have to do."

"It's what I want to do," I say firmly. "It's what's best for me. My career. And although I want to go to college with Damon, do you think that is what's best for us? We've both been heavily recruited, oftentimes from different schools, but pretty early on, we let them know we were a package deal, and if one of us wasn't a fit, neither of us was an option. It's not the way it's typically done, and many times throughout the process, we've been told it's a foolish decision. That we should choose the school where we'd make the most impact, especially if we want to play pro."

"Is the pressure getting to you?"

"Maybe a little," I admit. "Actually, no. It's really not. It's more that I want to make the right decision. You know that we both wanted to unofficially commit to Nebraska last year, but everyone convinced us to wait. To take our official visits this fall and consider our options carefully before signing."

"I heard Damon wants you to go on all five of the official recruiting visits you are eligible for. That will be a lot."

"Yeah, we'll be playing Friday night and then spending the rest of the weekend traveling and visiting different campuses."

"Is Lacey worried it will cut into your social life too much?" Dad asks with a touch of concern.

I roll my eyes. "Let's keep her out of this conversation for now. I know that players can pay for their own flights, so we'll be able to use the plane, right? That would make it easier at least."

"Of course. You can go straight from your game to the airport. Just let us know if you want us to accompany you on any of them, so we can make plans."

"Okay." I set down my fork and get to the heart of the matter. The question that has been gnawing at my brain since the second Dani left for school. What I really want to ask is if it would be stupid of me to go to the college the girl I love is at, hoping that, eventually, we'd work it out even though their team isn't even close to being in the top ten. But what I say is, "Would it be stupid to choose to play for the college I've wanted to go to my whole life when they haven't been winning?"

Dad smiles as my mom walks into the room. She's already all decked out in our school gear.

"I heard that," she says. "Can I answer?"

"Of course," Dad and I reply at the same time.

"I think you should follow your heart. Your heart is the reason you are such a good player. It always has been. Go on your visits. Soak up the atmosphere at each stadium. Imagine what it would be like to live in each town."

"Well, that, plus, you'll need to consider the team's record and who your position coach would be," Dad says. "Determine who would be ahead of you in the lineup, how you'd fit into the team's current offense."

My mom rolls her eyes at him. "Chase knows all that," she says. "I say, let your mind fill with all the pros and cons, but in the end, it's not about that. It's ultimately which place feels like it fits your vision for the future. In other words, *your* dream."

When she says the word *dream*, my thoughts immediately go to Dani.

I shove a last bite in my mouth and politely excuse myself before heading up to my room.

I sit at my desk and flip through a calendar hanging on the wall. One date has been circled in red since I hung the Christmas gift up. *December 18th.* National Letter of Intent day. Nothing is considered official until I've signed on the dotted line that will legally bind me to one year at that university. It's supposed to be the beginning of my future.

My phone buzzes with a text from Lacey, letting me know she's almost here.

I don't bother to reply because I'm drawn to my window. Since Dani left for college, I've kept the curtains closed. I knew it would be too hard, looking out and knowing she wasn't there anymore.

I take a deep breath, knowing I'm being ridiculous, and pull open the curtains, letting daylight flood into the room. I remove the piece of paper from the window and look at the word I wrote in a flowing script, trying to mimic her ring. The cool thing is, she understood and even wore the ring to school. I carefully fold the paper up and put it into my duffel as I hear Lacey's car pull into the drive.

I dare a glance at Dani's window, and it's then when I spot it. Hanging in her window is a photo. A photo that means everything to me. *To us.*

Or at least, it did.

I punch my fist into the window frame and yank the fabric shut just as Lacey walks in my room and locks the door behind her. She gives me a wicked grin and looks me up and down.

"You look stressed, baby," she says, patting the bed. "Let me help you with that."

I'M PULLING MY pants back up when she glances at her phone.

"You don't have to go yet."

"It's the first game, Lace. I know you heard Damon's car leave."

"Everyone in the neighborhood can hear Damon's car when he leaves," she says with a laugh, but then she eyes me seriously. "Why don't *you* ask for an exotic car like his for your birthday? You're turning eighteen. That's a big deal."

On Damon's seventeenth birthday this summer, he got surprised with what he calls his *Outrageous Orange Baby*, a Lamborghini Murciélago LP640 that Jennifer had totally picked out for him. She has a passion for exotic cars and a garage full of them in LA. Orange is both of their favorite colors, and this one is more toward yellow than pumpkin. Girls love it. Actually, girls love Damon—hot car or not. He's got the gift of gab, my dad says, and he can talk to anyone.

I assume he left early to stop by his latest fling's house for a little pre-game action.

"Not really my style," I tell Lacey, although you'd think by now, she'd have figured it out. "I love my truck."

What I should really say is that I have a love-hate relationship with my truck. Mostly because every single time I get in it, I'm reminded of the first time I did. It was in the driveway the day we arrived back from our trip to the Ozarks. My parents told me it was for me. For my sixteenth birthday.

Jennifer then went on to explain how it started out as a regular, new black Ford Raptor. How they took it to the guys who modify her cars, who added a higher-flow three-inch exhaust and a cold air intake. Added to that was a performance pack engine upgrade that makes it faster than the already-powerful motor, a massive windshield logo, new grill, industrial-looking off-road lights atop a custom-designed bar, body moldings, and some sweet wheels under a three-inch lift kit. The interior is equally awesome. Embroidered headrests and handmade seats with an impressive sound system. I got to drive it that day with my parents in the car since I still only had my permit, but later that night, I asked Dani to take me for a ride. We went parking, and I just knew we'd be together forever.

Until we weren't.

And she's still the only girl I've ever let drive it.

"I know you do," Lacey says, bringing me back to the present.

I pull on my suit jacket, tighten my tie back up, and then grab my duffel, tossing it over my shoulder.

"You look so handsome," Lacey says, running her hand across my chest.

It makes me feel guilty, knowing I was just thinking about someone else after our intimate moment.

I like Lacey—I do. I'll never love her, but I also can't live in the past.

I give her a kiss before making my way to the door. "And you're the prettiest girl at school."

She rolls her eyes. "I bet you say that to all the girls."

"Lacey, I don't have time for this right now." I can't deal with her jealousy when there's nothing to be jealous of. At least, with no one at our school.

"We're seniors, Chase. We've been dating since last year's Homecoming, but we aren't in a relationship. Don't you think that's kind of weird? My friends certainly do."

"I don't care what your friends think. And if you aren't cool with the way things are—"

"Yeah, yeah, I know. There are plenty of other girls dying to take my place."

"That's not *at all* what I meant. If you aren't happy with the way things are and don't understand why I can't be in a committed relationship, then you can get out. No harm—"

"No foul," she finishes.

"Exactly. I really gotta go."

She takes my hand and pulls me back on the bed with her.

Ugh. I don't have time for this conversation right now, but I still say, "You know I like you, Lacey."

"You mean, you like *having sex* with me," she fires back.

"This moment—right here, right now—is *exactly* why I don't want to be in a relationship. I have a big game tonight. I have a lot to prove out there. Scouts will be there. They will be at *every* game this season, and instead of focusing on that—"

"Why do you think we do what we just did before your games? I'm helping you. Relaxing you. So you can play better."

"It's very nice, Lacey, but it's not what makes me play well. I was winning games long before you started this little routine."

"But I'm—can you at least go out with me tonight after the game?"

"Not tonight, okay? I'll be tired. We have to get up early to head to Lincoln for the home opener."

"We should go out after the games. *Everyone* goes out after the games, and I'm always alone. You're just no fun anymore."

I take a deep breath, trying to stay calm. "I really have to go."

"Can I come to the game with you tomorrow?"

"If my parents didn't invite you, the answer would be no because they only have so many tickets."

"We had so much fun this summer, Chase."

"Sure we did, Lace. We also had *time* to have fun."

"It's our senior year. It's supposed to be the best year of our lives. I've got so many—"

"Plans?"

"Yeah," she says with a frown.

"I'm really sorry I'm disappointing you," I say, feeling bad.

She leans in, puts her mouth close to my lips, and says, "I love you, Chase."

I back away. "Oh."

"I tell you I love you, and all you say is *oh*?" she says, her voice rising. "Do you even care about me?"

"Of course I do."

"Well, you're not acting like it right now."

I run my hand across her shoulder. "What's going on? What started all this? If you are unhappy, I understand. We can end things amicably."

"Football started all this," she says.

A half-smile, half-frown forms on my face, and I hold my hands up in the air, like, *What do you want me to do about it?*

She smiles and smacks me playfully. "Shut up."

"I didn't say anything," I say as my smile grows along with hers.

"Have you decided where you're committing to yet? Are you considering Auburn? At all?" She visited the school along with a few others, and it was by far her favorite.

"I got an offer from them, but Damon and I are going to sit down on Sunday with our parents and plan out our recruiting trips. And you should know, that is going to take up a ton of my free time. For five weekends, we'll leave straight after our game on Friday night and then go to different campuses for the entire weekend."

"But once all that's over, we'll have an amazing spring, right?" she asks. "You'll commit, and then all the pressure will be off. We'll have winter formal, prom, graduation. It will be so much fun!"

I know I should tell her I probably won't be here for all of that, but I can't bring myself to do it. No need to rock the boat when I haven't made a decision yet.

She plants another kiss on my lips. "I do love you, Chase."

"And I really do have to go," I tell her.

I RUSH DOWNSTAIRS, grab my keys off the rack, and run out the front door. I throw my duffel into my truck and then stop and stare up at Dani's window.

Shit.

I run up to their front door, knock once, and then open it. I don't see anyone, so I rush upstairs and into Dani's room, grab the photo off her window, and try to get the heck out of here before anyone sees me.

"What are you doing?" Damon says, coming up from behind me and scaring me half to death.

I jump, take a deep breath, and then try to look nonchalant when I turn around to face him. "I thought you'd left already?"

"Oh, you probably heard Dad leave in my car. He and Jennifer drove separately, so I could have it there after the game. I thought we should go together. Being it's the first game of our last high school season and all. So, you going to tell me why you were in my sister's room?" he asks, tilting his head at me.

"Can we talk in the car?"

"Sure," he says, picking up his duffel from the dining room floor. "Let's roll."

As we go out the door, I see Lacey getting into her car, and feeling like I was just busted again, I mutter, "Oh shit," before realizing it's okay because Damon is with me.

Damon talks out of the corner of his mouth as we rush to my truck. "Quick getaway?"

"Yep."

Once in my truck and on our way to school, Damon turns down the blaring music and stares at me. "You can't take whatever just happened onto the field. What's up? And what's it got to do with Lacey and my sister?"

I hand him the photo I took from her window. "Remember this?"

"It's the cupcake Dani made you when we were all together in the Ozarks."

"Did you put it in her window?" I ask.

"This picture?" he asks, looking confused but then going, "Did *she* put it in the window for you? I remember you were going on and on about all the little stuff on it. Are you hot for my sister again? Shit, did Lacey see it? Does she know?"

"The day Dani left for college, you came over and told me she was freaking out. I hung up a sign in my window. We used to do that—write each other little notes. Before."

"Before," Damon says. "You know how with time periods, there is BC or AD?"

"Uh, yeah?"

"Haley and I call the period after that summer BS. Get it? It's like BS—bullshit—but then also *Before That Summer*. We feel like our lives were split into two then. We had so much fun together there, and it's been nothing but BS since."

"Agreed. But anyway, I put up a sign for her to help her calm down."

"What did it say?"

"*Dream.* You know I gave her that ring when I got home from camp. Dani and I talked a lot about our dreams that day. Our individual dreams. What she wanted out of life. What I did. The cupcake was important because it was a combination of the two. The day she left, I put up the sign, closed my curtains, and didn't open them again. Until today. She must have hung the picture up before she left."

"What are you going to do with it?"

"It's stupid. Don't give me shit, okay?"

"Okay."

"I'm going to hang it in my locker. Remind me of what I've always dreamed of."

"You mean, what you two dreamed of—together."

"Yeah, I guess."

"And you still hope that—wait, is that why you won't commit to Lacey?"

I bite my lip and nod.

"Hey, it's cool. I don't want you to commit to anyone. It's our senior year. We have campus visits to take, coeds to meet. Last thing you need is a clingy girlfriend."

"She just told me she loves me."

"Oh shit. Time to cut her loose," Damon says very seriously. "I don't know why you keep dating her. Everyone thinks you're together, and you are even though you aren't official."

"Probably because it's easy."

"You mean, she's easy." Damon laughs.

"She's not easy, Damon. She likes me. Loves me. And I know what it's like to love someone when they don't love you back."

"Reason number two why you need to cut her loose—before she gets hurt."

"She was pressuring me about it before—that's the other reason I'm stressed."

"Three strikes, and she's out. Although she told the whole cheer squad that she likes to *relieve* your stress before every game."

I run my hand through my hair as I turn into the school parking lot.

"Forget about it," Damon says. "Let's go play some ball."

"We have to figure out our recruiting visits soon. Where we're going."

Damon rubs his hands together. "It's going to be a good

freaking year, bro."

WHEN I GET into the locker room, I cut off a few pieces of athletic tape and then hang the *dream* sign and the cupcake photo way in the back of my locker, where no one but me will see them.

But what I keep thinking about is what my dad said. That in less than five months, I could be at college. What neither of us said was that I could be there with Dani.

And I don't know if that would be a good thing or a bad thing, but for the first time in a long time, I feel hopeful about it.

FRIDAY, SEPTEMBER 6TH

Before that summer.

Chase

ANOTHER FRIDAY NIGHT.

Another game.

Although our first game was kind of a gimme, this one is not. We'll be playing the team we beat last year for the district title, and there's been a lot of speculation as to whether or not I still have what it takes.

Last week, I didn't have to try very hard. My offensive line held the other team, not giving up a single sack, and I just dropped back and launched the ball. We were up by twenty-eight points before the end of the second quarter, so most of the starters sat out the whole second half.

The reporters are saying that was a mistake.

We're going to have to prove them wrong.

"I saw the papers this morning," Lacey says. She's wearing her cute little cheerleading outfit, straddling me on my bed. Very quickly, she has her top and bra off. "You're lucky I'm here—"

The room to my door flies open, and my little brother is standing there, staring at Lacey's naked chest, his eyes wide but a fat smile taking over his face.

Lacey rolls off me, lying flat on the bed to cover herself.

I get up and ask Ryder what he wants.

"I, uh … I forget."

He's in the eighth grade, and although I heard him talking with his friends about some over-the-shirt action with some girl during Seven Minutes in Heaven, I'm pretty sure he's never seen boobs up close and personal before.

Probably will run off and tell his friends.

"Then, I'm busy," I say nicely but still fling the door shut in his face and then lock it.

"That was mortifying," Lacey says.

"Maybe you shouldn't attack me the second you walk in the room," I tease. "Or at least lock the door first."

She gives me a sexy smirk in response and reaches for my belt buckle. She hasn't said she loves me since last week, and she hasn't brought up the whole commitment thing either.

"Sadly, you should probably put your clothes back on. My brother is a tattletale, and I expect my mom will be knocking on my door any minute."

"Oh, we don't want that. She likes me. At least, I think she likes me."

"I like you more," I say.

But I immediately regret it when she goes, "Oh, Chase. I know it's not an *I love you*, but"—she tosses her arms around me—"it means a lot."

"It means a lot that I like you more than my *mother* does?" *Because I'm like, What?*

She shakes her head at me. "You're impossible."

"I know," I tell her, pulling her top back over her head and then leaning in to kiss her. "I'm sorry."

"You're lucky you're so damn cute." She takes my cheeks between her hands and deepens the kiss. "I do have one thing to tell you."

"What's that?"

"This year, if you want me to be your date for Homecoming, you're going to have to ask me. *Properly.*"

"By properly, I assume you mean, *publicly*?" I let out a shaky breath as the day Hunter Lansford asked Dani comes rushing back to my brain.

"You bet I do. You don't want a commitment? That's cool. Last year, I asked you, but I won't do it again. And if someone else asks me first, I just might say yes."

I put my head down, trying to steady my breathing, which she must take as me being upset about what she said.

"Everyone thinks we're the perfect couple, Chase, but we're not even a couple."

"We sort of are," I offer. "It's not like I'm with anyone else."

She rolls her eyes and pulls me back into a hug. "What am I even going to do with you?"

"I don't know," I say honestly. "But I need to get going. Coach wants us there early tonight."

"Actually, I do know what I'm going to do. I'll be there. Cheering for you. Like always."

"Thank you," I tell her, walking her out to her car. "That means a lot to me."

"Roses," she says.

"What?"

"Roses *always* win you a homecoming date," she says before driving off.

DAMON IS STANDING by my truck, waiting for me. But I look past him to a certain car in his driveway.

"Is your sister home?" I ask, but what I want to do is run into their house immediately and tell Dani how much I've missed seeing her every day and how I look out my window at night, hoping to catch a glimpse of her and then realize she's gone. How I wish I could see that golden hair that looks like sunshine.

Although what I really want would be for her to see me, throw herself in my arms, and beg me to love her again.

"Yeah. I didn't know she was coming home this weekend. Is it for your birthday?"

"I don't know. We haven't talked much."

I don't tell him that we sort of made up, talking on the phone while she was going through rush, but since she pledged, it's only been a few random texts. I tell myself that she's just busy. Getting used to being at a new school, meeting new people, but it bothers me that she hasn't called once since. It already feels like she's moved on without me. Again.

"BS," he says.

I say what I'm thinking, "Exactly." It is bullshit. But I know he's referring to *Before That Summer*.

"It really does suck," he says, hopping into my truck. "At least we didn't let it screw up our friendship."

"No way. Can't mess up a lifetime of on-the-field chemistry."

"Lots of scouts are coming to the game tonight. More than usual," Damon says. "I overheard the coaching staff discussing it."

"Well, it's a pretty big game. At least for this early in the season."

"Reporters, too."

"Does it sometimes seem kinda crazy to you, how much attention we get?" I ask him.

"We're Shock and Awe, baby!" he yells out.

Shock and Awe are sort of my and Damon's nicknames in the press. It started when a skeptical local reporter, who thought we were only getting hype because of Damon's last name, came to see one of our games. He wrote later that he was *shocked* at my throwing technique and accuracy and *awed* by Damon's agility and ability to catch pretty much anything thrown his way.

"Well, I'm sure the fact that your last name is Diamond doesn't hurt either," I tease.

"You nervous?" he asks me.

"About the scouts? Not really." I start the car and pull out of the driveway.

"About the game?" Damon asks.

I shake my head. "No, not at all."

"Me neither. We're just gonna go out and do what we do."

I turn and give him a high five. "Score."

"Before and after the game," Damon says with a grin.

"Who is it tonight?"

"I'm not sure. I've got, like, three girls coming over. Figured we'd swim or hot tub or something."

"Sounds fun."

"Really? Because if you are done with Lacey, we could have *a lot* of fun. I know she's laid off on the commitment thing, but she's getting a bit possessive, don't you think?"

"She knows we are not in a committed relationship. I've been really honest with her about that."

"But yet she's over all the time, usually in your bedroom."

"Well," I say with a laugh, "she's persistent."

"And hot," Damon says. "One of the hottest girls at school, if you ask me."

"You think so?"

"Definitely. Do you not? Is there someone else you've got your eye on? I can make it happen tonight."

I think about the car in his driveway.

He punches me. "Shit. You didn't say no. Are you really gonna have fun? Like, party, hook up? Lots of girls would be in line. Or would be, if it wasn't for Lacey always clinging to you at school."

"And she comes over before every game."

Damon gives me another punch in the shoulder. "Maybe you should save that sexual energy for the game—get the testosterone flowing, beast mode, ya know?"

"If I were a defensive player, I might agree, but a little pregame—" I laugh. "She seems to think she's the reason I play so well. Thinks a little fun before the game calms me down."

"You've got her fooled. You've been cool as a cucumber under pressure since we were kids. Well, no reason to tell her that. She good at it?" he asks.

"Something like that," I mutter.

"Sweet. What do you say, after your birthday party tomorrow night, we go out to the farm? They're gonna have a DJ, I heard."

The farm is a place out in the country. Twenty acres of privacy with a decked-out backyard—firepits, pool, and a big screened porch that is the size of some houses and set up to entertain. Fortunately for us, the kid's parents are out of town a lot. He's got a massive field hidden from the road, where everyone can park, and there are no neighbors close enough to complain about the noise.

"Maybe," I say noncommittally, Dani still in the back of my mind.

"We could also go to a club. Take Dad's Ferrari. Use our fake IDs."

"You know I won't use a fake ID," I tell him. "Or drink at a club. So, why bother?"

"Because Diamond on the plates opens a lot of doors," Damon says and then grins at me. "You should be taking advantage of all of it with me."

WHEN WE GET to school, Lacey is waiting for me in the parking lot even though I just saw her.

"Tell her no after-game fun," Damon says. "You're mine tonight."

"I never have fun after a game. You know I always go straight home."

But what Damon doesn't know is the reason why. How, for

me, the best part of a game was after it. When it didn't matter how I'd played because I knew Dani would order pizza, meet the driver out front, and then sneak to my room with it. I remember how we would lie there and talk for hours about everything and nothing at all.

The second I get out of my truck, Lacey plants a kiss on my lips, waking me from my thoughts. "You must be thinking hard about the game. In the zone already?"

"Something like that," I tell her.

Code red sexy.

Devaney

THE LIGHTS ARE on at the stadium, the band is playing, and the cheerleaders are yelling. It's weird, not being out there on the field, lined up with my pom-poms, anxiously awaiting the team's big entrance onto the field to start the game.

Instead, I'm seated in front of an open window, in a skybox filled with family and friends.

My dad sits down next to me. "How did you think they looked in warm-ups?"

"Chase's arm looks strong, and he seems to have a slightly longer follow-through. Has he been working on that?"

"Good eye," Dad says. "He has."

"And although Damon caught everything thrown to him, he seemed a little slow on his takeoff. Is his ankle still bothering him?"

"A bit." Dad shakes his head. "I told him not to goof around on the wakeboard, but he didn't listen."

"Does he ever?" I laugh.

"The two of you got that from me." He laughs. "Don't tell Jennifer."

"I'm pretty sure she already knows. But be quiet. She's headed this way."

Actually, they *all* are. The three mother figures in my life. Chase's mom and Jennifer, who are followed into the suite by my mother and her husband, Van.

"It's good to have you back home, Devaney," my mother says, wrapping me in stiff arms.

But, hey, at least she's trying. Van, on the other hand, hugs you like he means it.

"Thanks, Mom."

"I missed you. Gosh, you look so grown-up. How did that happen? You've been at college for just a few weeks."

I shrug, looking between my mom, Jennifer, and Jadyn. Except for the player's number, all three are decked out in matching blinged-out jerseys, but they wear them so differently. Mom's hair is still softly curled, but I can tell she's gone back to being a fan of hair spray. Her makeup is on point, and she's wearing a bold red lip color. Paired with the jersey are white linen capris, silver wedges, and the massive diamond studs Dad bought for her when he won his first Super Bowl. It's one of my earliest memories. I was only three at the time, but I do remember confetti raining down on us and the roar of the crowd.

Jennifer—the youngest of the three women—has her hair straightened and is wearing a cute pair of wide-legged jeans with glittery high-top tennis shoes.

Jadyn has on fringed jean shorts with a pair of beaded sandals, her blonde hair in a messy braid. The braid, I know, will be undone and redone numerous times during the game—a nervous habit that seems to calm her. Her makeup is natural, and if you only took a quick glance, you might mistake her for a student.

My mother looks me over again. "What did you do to your shirt?" Her tone sounds much like her old judgmental self.

"Uh …"

She puts out her hand. "I mean, I love it. You look adorable."

"Thanks," I say to her. "Haley told me that I couldn't wear a shirt just like our moms."

"No, I don't suppose you could," my mom says with a laugh that sounds genuine.

"So, she snipped off the sleeves, cut the hem so it skimmed just above the waist, and added slits up the sides."

"Very fashionable and creative," Mom says, which nearly causes me to drop dead. Because it sounds like she really *has* changed. "I love how your black bralette shows through the shirt and, of course, the studded Jimmy Choo boots make it all the more special."

One thing my mom and I do share is a love of good shoes.

"Don't forget the hair and makeup," Jennifer tells her, noting my messy pony and eyes that are heavy on black eyeliner and mascara.

"Definitely can't forget that," Jadyn teases.

And it's kind of crazy. Witnessing how they are all getting along. It used to be that my mom and Richard would sit in one corner, Mom acting like she was above it all somehow. But tonight, she's joking with Jennifer. And Van is sneaking sips from a flask with Phillip.

"Crazy how things change, isn't it?" my dad says to me.

"It certainly is."

OUR TEAM WINS, and after the game, we all make our way down to the field, where I find myself congratulating Chase on a good game. He rushed for over one hundred fifty yards and threw for over three hundred. With stats like that, you'd think we won the game easily, but it was a close battle with a final score of 42-39.

"You look good, wearing my last name," he says to me, his fingers grazing my exposed skin as he flicks the edge of my shirt. His helmet is swinging from one hand, his hair wet with sweat, his shoulder pads giving bulk to his tall frame.

Admit it, Dani. He looks sexy. Freaking four-alarm, code red sexy.

I laugh internally. In high school, we judged boys on their fire scale.

My eyes trail down Chase's chest and dare to go lower.

"Surprised you didn't wear your brother's number," he continues.

I lay my hand on the number one—his number—that is blazed across my chest. "I wore yours because—"

I'm interrupted when a perky cheerleader bounces up to him, throws her arms around his neck, and kisses him. "Baby, what a great game you had!"

"Hey, Lacey," I say to her as she wraps her hand around Chase's bicep. We cheered together for years, both on a competitive squad and in school. "The cheer team looked great out there. I knew you'd make a great captain. And I love the new uniforms."

Lacey keeps hanging on to Chase.

Earlier, before the game, I saw them kiss. Chase's hands were inappropriately low on her skirt, and her hips were pushed against his, so the fact that his arm is stiff at her waist tells me he's uncomfortable right now.

And it's pretty obvious that Lacey is over here, marking her territory. I know I would if I were her.

"That jersey is so cute and sparkly. Wait, that's Chase's number, not Damon's. Why are you wearing that?" she asks pointedly, her hand now firmly placed across the number on Chase's chest.

"His mom gave it to me," I say.

"So cute." She looks up at Chase. "I'll have to ask your mom to get me one!"

Over my dead body, is the first thought that comes to mind.

"Well, good to see you, Dani," Lacey says, trying to get rid of me. "Hope college is going well. Bet you've met all sorts of hot guys." Then she turns to Chase and whispers loudly enough for me to hear, "We need to celebrate your big victory tonight." She kisses him with way too much tongue and skips away.

I roll my eyes. I can't even stop myself.

"Will I get to see you tonight?" Chase asks, acting like that train wreck didn't just occur in front of us.

"Yeah, I'll be around."

"Going to any parties tonight?" he asks.

"Nah, plenty of parties at college."

"We should hang out while you're home, Dani. It's been a long time. The hug, before you left for college—well, it made me realize how much I miss you. I really do hope we can be friends again someday."

"Yeah, me, too," I say wistfully.

"I suppose I'd better go hit the showers." He starts to leave, but then he turns back around and says, "Regardless of what Lacey just said, nothing has changed. You know I *never* go out after a game." He gives me a wink. The kind he gave me when we were best friends.

And that wink feels more intimate than if he'd kissed me in front of everyone.

From out of nowhere, Chase's dad comes racing across the field, grabs Chase's mom, and tackles her to the ground. But just when I think he's got her down, Jadyn somehow flips him over, pins him to the ground, and kisses him.

"Seems like they've done that a few times before," I say with a laugh.

"It's something we would have done as kids," Chase says.

"I'm pretty sure we did. But I don't think I ever got kissed." I let out a dreamy sigh. "That's what I want. That sort of relationship—where you have fun together, even when you're old."

"They're crazy," Chase says.

"Crazy in love still, I think," I say to him.

"Well, that's what happens when you marry your best friend," he counters. He doesn't say, *Hint, hint,* but sort of implies it by the way he looks at me.

Either way, I know exactly what I'll be doing tonight.

And I'm pretty sure I was just invited.

A cute boy.

Devaney

I DO WHAT I used to do when we were kids—feign exhaustion and then go up to my room. Once the babies are tucked in and everything is quiet, I order pizza.

I consider changing, but Chase said he liked seeing his number on me. And I know guys kind of have a thing about that. A girl wearing his number.

Chase said he wants us to be friends again. And I want that more than anything. I miss him desperately. That summer in the Ozarks changed everything for us. Not only did I lose my new love, but I also lost my friend.

And honestly, that hurt worse.

I leave my house, sit on the front porch, and wait for the delivery. Once the driver drops my order off, I'm happy to discover that the code on the Mackenzies' front door hasn't changed, so I am able to let myself in and sneak up to Chase's room. His lights are off, as usual, so everyone thinks he's asleep.

"I smell pizza," he says, lighting up his phone for just a moment and allowing me a view of him.

He's lying on his bed, his long form stretched out and covered by only a pair of athletic shorts. Most of his body is sheathed in shadows, making his cheekbones look more chiseled, his muscles more defined.

"Is that okay?" I ask, suddenly feeling nervous. "The way you said you never go out, I thought maybe this would be okay."

"Pizza is always okay," he says happily, standing up.

He takes the boxes from me and sets them on his desk, then pulls me into his arms and just holds me. He takes in a deep breath, taking in my scent. I've known him long enough to know exactly what he's doing.

But then he says, "Gosh, that pizza smells good."

I roll my eyes at my stupidity. *He has a girlfriend. He's smelling the food. Not you.*

"Let's eat then," I offer.

"You smell good, too, Dani. I can't stress enough how much I've missed you. Missed talking. Missed being friends. Missed nights like these."

He lets go of me, and we resume our old habit. He takes the blanket off the end of his bed and spreads it out on the floor. I set the pizza boxes on top of it.

"Wait," he says. "I want to go get something."

A few moments later, he's back in his room, setting up a two-man pop-up tent.

"Well, this is something new," I say with a laugh.

"I'd like to be able to see your face, Dani. But your brother isn't home yet, and if Lacey drove by and saw a light on in my room—anyway, pick up the boxes and the blanket. I have a plan."

I do as he asked and watch as he puts the tent down where we were just sitting, and then he covers the top of it with his heavy quilt bedspread. He goes out into the hall and comes back with more blankets from the linen closet then he spreads those out on the floor inside the tent and tosses all his pillows in for good measure.

"Okay," he says. "You get inside."

I take the pizza boxes with me, set them on the ground, and then lean back on a pillow.

Chase reaches inside and hands me a small battery-powered lantern. "No candles for us," he teases, referring to the night in the Ozarks when we were taking a romantic bath together and accidentally lit a robe on fire. "Turn it on. I want to see if I can see the light."

He closes me inside the tent, and a few moments later, he's in here with me, his big form filling the space.

"It's perfect," he says.

"It's cute," I tell him.

"You always said *I* was cute," he counters.

"You always were a cute boy."

"And now?"

"I think you already know that you are very handsome. If nothing else, your little modeling side gig ought to have reinforced that notion. You don't need me to tell you."

He grins at me and then motions toward the pizza. "You ordered more than you used to."

"That's because you're bigger than you used to be," I tease.

I open the boxes, and we each take a piece in our hands and then look at each other, both seeming to remember what we used to do next and wondering if we should.

I decide to go for it.

I lean in, give him a peck on the lips, and say, "You had a good game tonight, Chase." I hold my piece of pizza up in the air.

He grins at me, his white teeth practically sparkling in the dim light, as we touch our pieces together in a toast. "To many more," he says.

We each take our first bite to seal the deal.

"We were silly when we were kids, huh?" I say while we eat.

I figured Chase would inhale the pizza like he used to, but I also know this would totally be considered a cheat meal for him. He and my brother follow a pretty strict diet regime. Actually, it's one my dad created.

"I don't know about silly," he says seriously. "I mean, this tradition is pretty cool, don't you think?"

"Yeah, I guess it is."

"What were you thinking, you know, when you first started it? That first time you brought me pizza."

"Honestly," I say, rolling my eyes, "it was *maybe* slightly created out of jealousy."

"Really?" he says, a huge smile on his face. "Do tell."

"Remember Molly Baker?"

"Oh yeah."

"You must remember how she crushed on you then. Do you also remember how she invited you out for pizza after your game? *On a school night*, I might add, because in middle school, your games were on Tuesdays."

"And you were against my going out for pizza on a school night?"

"No." I grin. "I was against you having anything to do with Molly. It was also my way of showing you that no matter how much of a hotshot quarterback you became, you'd never be too cool to eat pizza. With me. On the floor."

"We always kissed as kids, but that night, you gave me what I would consider one of my first real kisses. Or maybe it was that I was old enough that my body reacted differently to it."

My eyes get huge. "Are you saying what I think you're saying?"

"That it made me hard? Yes. That's what I'm saying."

"Ohmigosh, Chase," I say, giggling.

He reaches over and covers my mouth with his hand so that I

don't wake anyone up.

"Don't laugh at me. I was both thrilled and slightly mortified." His face is close to mine, our gazes locked. "I think I was always in love with you, but that kiss, well, it did it for me."

I notice his eyes crinkle up on the sides—a sure sign that he's full-on grinning right now.

I reach my arm out and push his shoulder with my palm. He doesn't budge. Nothing on him moves, except his eyebrows, which rise, mocking me in challenge.

I roll my eyes at him again. "I get it—you're a big senior stud now, so I can't push you around anymore. Eat your damn pizza."

We both eat.

Now in a comfortable silence.

Finally, he breaks it. "So, how is college? I didn't get a chance to tell you because you've been so busy since you pledged, but Mom was excited—actually, I'm lying. My mother was ecstatic when she heard the news. Because—*not only is she your aunt, but she's also now your sister.*"

"Hmm, if she were my sister, what would that make you?"

"Your lover," he says with a grin.

"That makes no sense."

He gives me an adorable shrug. "Can't help a guy for trying."

"I thought this was about us being friends again."

"Friends who kiss, I think is a better term. That's what we were before."

"Are you saying you want to kiss me, Chase?"

"I'm just saying, if we are *really* going back to that time, we did in fact kiss."

"You didn't answer the question."

"It doesn't require an answer yet," he says cryptically even though I wish he would just grab my face and go for it. "We have a lot of catching up to do first."

"Maybe I want an answer now."

"There's plenty of time for that," he says. "Tell me how much you love college."

"Well, I wouldn't say I love it quite yet."

Even though I got to see Chase briefly at Nebraska's home opener, with all the stuff going on at the sorority house, I didn't spend more than a few minutes in the skybox with the family, so we didn't have a chance to really talk.

I fill him in on everything that's gone on. The parties, mixers, getting to know all the girls. How I've made friends but how the friendships are still so new that it's hard to know how they will play out.

"So, basically, college is good, but I miss my family and my room," I tell him.

"And I miss you *in* your room," he says. "I kept my curtains shut after you left. I couldn't imagine looking over there and not seeing you. Knowing that you'd never really be there again."

"Oh, Chase, but that means you didn't see—"

"I finally opened them before my game last week," he states, starting to look agitated.

"And how did you feel when you saw it? And do you know where it went?"

"I punched the window frame. It pissed me off, honestly."

I reach out and run my hand down his arm. "It wasn't supposed to. You wrote *dream* for me, and it really helped me calm down. I just thought the cupcake might remind you of your dreams, you know, as you started school and your senior year of football."

"Which would be great, except the cupcake meant more than that, Dani. And you know it. It wasn't just my dream or your dream; it was *our* dream. Together. As a couple. And I'm the one who took the photo. I didn't think you'd want anyone else to see it."

But all I can think is that he didn't want Lacey to look out his

JILLIAN DODD

window, see it, and ask him about it. Of course, she was one of the
cheerleaders watching the day Hunter asked me to Homecoming,
so she knows we had what my friends called a summer fling. I
want to ask him what he did with the photo because I have a
feeling, based on his attitude toward it, he threw it in the trash.

I decide to leave well enough alone and change subjects. "And
how has school been for you? It's your senior year. That's a big
deal."

"Do you want to go sit in the hot tub?" he says suddenly.

"I don't have a swimsuit on."

He shrugs.

"Sure. Why not?"

"It's a nice night," he says. "And this tent is feeling a little
small."

I know what he means. Although things are going better than
I thought they would, it's clear that certain subjects are off-limits.

He grabs a couple of towels, and we quietly make our way
outside and into the hot tub. The sky is dark, and the stars are
hidden by a thick cloud cover.

I decide to just go for it the second we get in the tub and ask
what I really want to know. "Tell me about you and Lacey. You've
been dating awhile."

"Yeah, since she asked me to Homecoming last year. Um, it's
going okay."

"I'm sure you're having sex."

He lets out a long sigh. "Damon tells me I'm honest to a fault,
but I've been lying to Lacey. Not about how I feel. I've been very
straightforward with her about that. She wants us to be official,
but I always say no. That I don't have time for a serious relationship. The other day, she finally said she doesn't care anymore—
which, really, if my sister accepted that from a guy, I'd be pissed."

"You're the quarterback, Chase. She's the head cheerleader.
Maybe it's more about the status. And based on the photos I see of

82

when you and my brother go to the farm, it's never been exclusive. So, you're like my brother? Sleeping around?"

"The pictures would indicate that, wouldn't they?" he says thoughtfully.

"Uh, yeah. You've got Lacey draped around you all week and a million different girls when you're out with my brother."

"And what about you?"

"I'm not dating anyone right now."

"First of all, just because it appears that I'm with a lot of girls, it doesn't mean that I am. You, of all people, should know that I'm not really that kind of guy. And the reason I can't commit to Lacey is not because of football. It's because I'm not in love with her. Not the way I loved you anyway. So, even though she recently told me that she loves me, I can't say it back or commit to her in that way."

The way I loved you.

"You said something when you were going through rush, about your sorority," he says, changing the subject. "About how you were tired of the high school game. That you chose a sorority where you felt you could be an individual. I'm proud of you, regarding that. Just so you know."

"Thank you," I say as his phone buzzes.

He pulls it off the edge of the tub and reads it.

"Crap. That's Damon. He, Haley, and a bunch of people are coming over to get in the hot tub. He wanted to know if I was asleep yet." We hear cars out front. "Shit. They're already here."

"Do you not want them to see us together?" I ask, suddenly feeling like the other woman.

He rolls his eyes as he gets out of the tub and extends his hand to me. "Hurry."

I get out and wrap up in a towel. Chase takes my hand, and we run toward the lake. We hit the dock, running past his family's ski boat to my dad's new pontoon. Chase somehow knows where the keys are hidden, and he quickly turns the boat on, keeping the lights off, and slowly backs out of the dock and out into the lake. Once we're around the corner and we can't be seen from our backyards, he flips on the lights and guns it all the way to the other side.

"We barely made it out in time," he says, sounding just a little breathless as he shuts off the motor and then lowers the anchor.

The way his voice sounds reminds me of hot summer nights spent tangled up in the sheets with him.

He's near the back of the boat, and I'm drawn in his direction, needing to know something with all my heart. I stand close to him, so close that our bodies are nearly touching.

Soulful music is playing softly in the background. I always hate when my dad plays it, but the track fits this moment so perfectly that I'm going to have to put it on my playlist for when I go back to school.

All of a sudden, I don't want to go back.

And I don't want to be friends with Chase again.

"When I was going through rush, I thought a lot about you," I confess. "The first few days, you are being judged on paper— your accomplishments, grades, letters of recommendation. I kept wondering when it was just going to be about me."

Serious about your abs.

Chase

WE'RE STANDING ON a boat in the middle of the lake in near-complete darkness. My heart is beating wildly, being this close to her.

I know this is supposed to be about us being friends again.

And I'm trying.

I really am.

I take her hand in mine, pretending it's a friendly gesture, and hold it gently, just so I can touch her. Feel that connection. See if it's still there.

"You, *we*, us being together that summer was something I did for me, Chase," she continues. "We were in this wonderful bubble, where there was no pressure. No expectations. Do you really think we'll be able to be friends again?"

"I hope so."

She lets go of my hand, physically backing away, and I feel like I've lost her again, but then one of her fingers touches my chest. She's got a playful grin on her face when the finger starts creeping downward. "So, you've been working out, huh?"

"That sounds like a pickup line because you know I work out all the time." I squint my eyes at her and smile. "Are you trying to pick me up, Dani?"

"I haven't decided yet," she sasses back.

And I love it. Might as well play along, see where this goes.

"You done growing yet? I heard my brother is officially taller than you now."

"I'm probably about done. But as usual, I work out with both the team as well as your brother and our dads. I've put on twenty pounds of muscle since last season, so I guess it depends on what kind of growing you're referring to."

Her hand slides down further, taunting me. "I can see that. And these abs. Damn, Chase."

"Oh, now, you're just teasing me." I laugh, assuming she's messing with me.

And I'm cool with that.

"I'm actually *very* serious about your abs, Chase. Hard not to be when you're always flaunting them in my face."

"When do I do that?"

She rolls her eyes. "Come on. You know my window is right across from yours, and *somehow*, for, like, the past *two years*, you *always* happen to be facing it when you take your shirt off?"

"Are you saying you were creeping on me?"

"Maybe. Although get this. I heard Jennifer found empty condom wrappers in Damon's jeans when she was doing the laundry, and Dad was proud. He even sees me kissing a boy, and he freaks."

"You're his little girl, no matter how *well* you've grown up." *Two can play this game. Whatever it is.*

"You think I've grown up well?" she asks, hand on her hip, almost in challenge.

"Why do you think I'm always looking at your window?"

"Oh, now, the truth comes out. Just hoping to catch a glimpse?"

"For sure. So, you said you aren't dating anyone at college. Does that mean you are just partying and hooking up?"

"Partying a little, yeah. Hooking up, not so much."

"I figured every guy there would want you," I say seriously.

"I'm not that pretty, Chase."

"Devaney, you're the prettiest girl I've ever seen."

"Like I said before, big fish, little pond."

"In that little pond, you used to like to kiss me. I'm thinking if we're going to truly become friends again, it is going to be required."

"Oh, really?" she says, but her hand moves from my abs, where it was resting, to the waistband of my swim trunks.

I reach out and push a stray piece of hair out of her face. Which causes her to shiver.

"You cold?"

"Uh, kinda," she says, but she's lying.

There's no way she could be cold when I feel like I'm on fire.

Lights me up inside.

Devaney

THE SECOND THE thought crosses my mind that I wish Chase would kiss me, he does.

I've done my fair share of making out—especially with him.

But I've never been kissed like this before.

His kiss is so soft, so tender, and so full of emotion that I almost want to cry.

Chase picks me up, and I wrap my legs around his waist, not wanting him to go anywhere. He takes a few steps backward and sits down, me in his lap.

He kisses me softly and then suddenly kisses me with more intensity than I ever knew existed.

This is definitely not the best-friend kiss.

It's the kiss that lights me up inside.

That causes my heart to race.

My blood to rush.

It's like when the gas is on for too long before you light the grill, and there's practically an audible *whoosh* as it ignites.

His hands move under the towel I have wrapped around my shoulders and push it off. Suddenly, my wet bra is gone, too.

All I can do is respond to him.

It's like my brain is on overload, and it can't quite process the way Chase's chest feels against mine after all this time. Or the way his lips blaze a trail of fire down my chest.

I resort to some kind of mimicking mode.

After he kisses my chest, I greedily run my lips down his. When he pulls me closer, I grip his waist tightly.

It's then that he makes a noise that sounds like a growl. It's a primal noise. One that turns me on.

And when he slides his hands into the back of my underwear and he lifts me up, stripping them off me and flinging them onto the deck, I push his board shorts off and move back on top of him.

I can feel his hardness against me.

And all I can think is, *Please.*

Please don't tease me anymore.

Please get closer to me.

Please be my everything again.

"Please," I say breathlessly. "Please."

Then, all I can think is, *Please, don't stop.*

Like, ever.

EVENTUALLY THOUGH, HE collapses against me.

I kiss his neck. The neck that has always been my favorite scent. And I wrap my arms around him tightly.

He runs his hands through my hair and says, "Devaney," which is the most beautiful thing I've heard in a very long time.

But at the same time, I'm also thinking, *I can't believe I just slept with Chase.*

Again.

"This might be the best night of my life," Chase says.

"Because of the sex?"

"Not just because of it," he says with a chuckle, "although that was as incredible as ever. You gave me back your friendship. At least, I hope that's what the pizza meant."

"Is that what you want? For us to be *friends*?"

"If you are asking if I want to be *just* your friend, no. But more than that, I don't want to lose you from my life again. You and I get each other. We always have. I love your brother, and there's a lot I tell him, but I've *never* been as close to anyone as I am with you. Or as honest. When we stopped being friends, I sorta felt like you'd died, but then I still had to see you. And that was almost worse."

"Like a constant reminder that you'd failed?" I ask him, totally understanding.

He leans back further, studying my face, his eyes narrowed in on me. "Is that how you feel?"

I nod.

"It's in the past," he says. "Let's focus on the present."

"Ohmigosh, Chase, speaking of presents. Happy birthday! I got you a present. I wish I had brought it with the pizza."

"Oh shit," he says, glancing at his sports watch. "It *is* my birthday. My parents are going to kill me."

"Why?"

"Because it's *after* midnight."

"That's why I'm home. Although I always used to spend the night, so I could help throw confetti and stuff on you. It was always so much fun! I remember your mom telling me that your dad, every year since they were little, would wake her up by throwing a whole bunch of stuff at her. Like candy, toys, confetti. And that's how it became a family tradition." But then I look at him in realization. "Oh, but you're not there. You're out here."

"And I left my phone on the deck."

"I don't have mine either."

"And I didn't tell anyone we were leaving."

"Shit. Are we going to be in trouble?"

"I don't know, but we'd better get back," he says.

As we come around the corner toward our cove, he says, "I was going to turn off the lights and motor and sneak in, but that would make it look like we were hiding something. So, I won't. Okay?"

"Okay," I tell him.

ALTHOUGH I WISH we could have stayed in the boat forever, I know his family is not going to be happy that he's not home. I consider going with him, but he says he'll deal with it if they are still up. He walks me to my door and gives me another really good kiss.

The kind of kiss that I missed so desperately.

"Text me when you get in bed. I'm not ready to tell you good night just yet."

And, yes, I swoon. "Okay," I say happily, practically skipping through the front door.

"Where have you been, young lady?" my dad's deep voice says sternly.

"Uh, out."

"Just because you're in college and you can do whatever you want there doesn't mean when you come home, you don't have to let us know where you are. We've been worried sick. Gosh, I hate when you make me sound like my mother," he says, which causes Jennifer, who is sitting on the couch next to him, to chuckle.

She comes over and gives me a big hug. "Everything okay?"

"Yeah. I was just next door. I took pizza over after the game, and then Chase and I took the pontoon out. I'm sorry you were worried."

"We've been calling your cell," my dad says.

"I didn't plan on being gone long." I point toward the ceiling. "It's up in my room. I just—" *What the heck am I even supposed to say?* I want to go up in my room, lie in my bed, and relive what it felt like to be back in Chase's arms.

And text him.

"Did you two make up?" Jennifer asks, studying me closely.

I know my clothes are all wrinkled and wet, and I suppose my hair is a mess, and my lips are probably red from so much kissing, but I could look this way if I'd been out in the boat. *Right?*

I nod. "Kind of. Yeah."

"Are you ever going to tell us what happened that summer?" my dad asks. "Why you stopped being best friends?"

I let out a controlled breath and seriously consider just spilling my guts. Instead, I ask him a question I already know the answer to. "Was it tricky when you and Phillip and Jadyn were growing up? Like when Jadyn would date other guys?"

My dad cocks his head, narrows his eyes, and nods. "It was for Phillip. And for me sometimes. Even though I didn't like her the way Phillip did, we knew she could do better."

"And by *better*, you meant Phillip?"

Dad sits down. "Are you saying that being friends with Chase got complicated because you were dating other people?"

"Yes, basically," I admit, although it's not exactly right.

"And that's why things have been different?" Dad asks again.

"Yes."

"We knew something had happened in the Ozarks, Dani," Jennifer says. "I wouldn't let your dad pry, but—"

"Chase and I got closer during that trip—romantically, I guess you could say. We actually decided to try dating each other. Chase wanted to talk to you about it first, Dad, sort of to get your approval, which is so ridiculously old-fashioned."

"But is very Chase," my dad states.

"Anyway, when we were on vacation, there was no—how can I put this? Outside pressure. No one telling me I shouldn't date a younger guy. That kind of thing. And we thought it might work."

"But then you went to school, and Hunter asked you to Homecoming," Jennifer says astutely, and I realize her capacity for memorizing lines of scripts translates into real-life data.

"Exactly, and even though I never told Hunter yes, he grabbed me and kissed me, and understandably, Chase got upset." I let out a sigh. "The whole thing was a mess."

"Well, we knew the part about what Hunter had said to you and how he kissed you since your brother and Chase punched him and the coach got involved."

"And things haven't been the same since."

"But tonight, you made up?" When Jennifer sees me blush in response, she seems to know *exactly* what kind of making up we did. She glances at my dad and then goes, "Like, you'll be friends again?"

"Yeah, I think so," I say.

"That's good to hear, Devaney." Dad gives me a hug and heads toward his room, saying, "I gotta get some sleep."

"I'm sorry I kept you awake," I tell Jennifer once he's in their room.

"Do you want to talk about it?" she whispers. "I have a feeling there's a lot more to the story."

"There probably is. I just don't know what it means yet."

Supposed rebellion.

Chase

"CHASE," MY MOM says the second I come through the front door. "Well, if this were your last night on earth, at least we'd know that you'd camped in your room and had some pizza."

"Not funny," I say even though I laugh because it is.

She studies me the way moms do. "Did Dani come over with pizza tonight? After your game?"

"Yeah."

"It's been a while."

"You knew?"

"That she used to sneak in with pizza after your games? Yes, Chase, we knew."

"But—"

"You weren't doing anything wrong. Although I'm sure it

made you feel like you were being sneaky."

"Hmm," I say.

"You just wiped years of supposed rebellion from him, princess," my dad says to my mom from the study.

I didn't know he was up, too.

"Look, it's your birthday. You should be able to do what you want on it but know we were all pretty disappointed you weren't home at midnight for the confetti toss."

"I'm sorry."

"Just be ready to be woken up very early and be happy about it."

"Yes, ma'am."

"You can go on up to bed now. And, Chase?"

"Yeah?"

"Happy birthday, sweetheart."

"Thanks, Mom."

She gives me a big hug. "I can't believe my first baby is eighteen."

Dad comes and joins us, giving me a hug, too. "Where were you?"

"Out on the pontoon boat with Dani," I answer truthfully. No reason to lie about it. Not that I really have to lie to my parents about anything.

"You two make up?" he asks.

I let out a sigh. *Is that what you call what we did, making up?* Not sure. But either way, I answer honestly, "I sure hope so."

Mad at you.

Devaney

THE SECOND I see his room light flick on, I call him.

"Ohmigosh, my dad totally freaked out. Were your parents pissed?" I say when he answers.

"They wish I had told them. But they saw the pizza boxes in my room and assumed I was with you. So, not too worried, just a little irritated when I wasn't here at midnight."

"How did they know you were with me?"

"Let's just say, as kids, we weren't quite as sneaky as we thought," he says with a chuckle.

"Figures," I say, laughing, too.

"Apparently, the throwing of things—the confetti toss—is set to commence first thing in the morning. Want to have a slumber party tonight? Like we used to? That way, you're here for it then?"

"Um, I'd love to. I guess as long as I leave Dad and Jennifer a note, it would be okay."

"I'm sure it will be. Damon and Haley and a few other people are crashed in the movie room. You can sleep in the tent. Or on the couch. Or in my bed, and we can set an alarm," he offers, totally leaving it open.

I know exactly which one I will choose. "I'll be right over," I tell him.

"Don't forget to leave the note."

"I won't."

I hang up and then take a moment to look at myself in the mirror. I'm a hot mess. The ends of my hair are wet from the hot tub. Makeup is basically a disaster. *Whatever.*

I grab a washcloth, wash my face, and then put my hair in a

French braid. I'll be able to sleep on it, and my hair will look decent in the morning. I throw on a pair of dry underwear and some sweats and then a tie-dye tank, sans bra.

But before I leave, I pick up the bag of stuff I brought home with me for the confetti toss. I smile at the sack full of little foam footballs, red and black confetti, and gold chocolate coins. I figure they do a coin flip at the start of each game, so it all fits.

I LEAVE THE supplies on the dining room table and then go up to Chase's room, finding him eating a cold breadstick.

"I didn't want the night to end," he tells me, pulling me into one arm while wagging the bread in front of my face.

I take a bite. "I didn't either."

Once he's full of cold pizza and breadsticks, he lies on his bed and holds his arm out for me to snuggle up next to him.

Then he kisses me.

And I don't know why, but I start crying. Not like sobbing or anything. It's just that tears keep rolling down my face. And I can't stop them.

"What's wrong?" he asks, pulling his lips away from me and trying to wipe my tears away.

"Do you hate me, Chase?"

"I was mad at you, yes, but I could never hate you."

"Don't get mad at me now for saying this, but in spite of it all, I still love you. I never stopped, and that's why it hurts so much. You've been my best friend my whole life, and I feel like a huge part of me is missing. And I know we probably shouldn't have slept together, but—"

"Don't regret it, Dani," he says. "And just for the record, I feel the same way."

"Promise you do?"

"I promise."

I start sobbing with relief.

He kisses me and holds me tight, and at some point, right before I fall asleep, he murmurs in my ear, "Best birthday ever."

SATURDAY, SEPTEMBER 7TH

After we ended.

Devaney

EVEN THOUGH I usually sleep like a rock when I'm near Chase, I don't sleep well. I keep waking up every hour to check the clock, my brain counting down to the confetti toss.

Finally, at six thirty, I hear movement downstairs, so I go to the kitchen, where I find Phillip making coffee.

"Hey, Dani," he says, pouring me a cup and placing it in front of me. "You here for the birthday throwdown?"

"Yeah. Sorry we missed midnight."

"So, you and Chase are friends again, huh?"

I smile. Nod. "I hope so."

"A morning throwdown will be just fine then. Chase isn't the only one who has missed you."

I suck in a breath. "What do you mean? I'm still always around."

"Yeah, but it's been different, having that tension, I guess. And just so you know, you're not the only one who has had to navigate staying best friends while dating other people. It's tricky at best. And can be downright heartbreaking at its worst."

"Was it hard for you when Jadyn dated other people?"

"Well, I certainly wasn't a big fan of any of her boyfriends.

Obviously, I was jealous, but at the time, I don't think I realized it. We never explored our feelings at a younger age, like you and Chase, so I can't at all judge you for how you reacted. Or for the aftermath."

"It's been difficult for me. Like, I'm here, but I don't quite fit the space anymore. And knowing I caused it all, let's just say, I have plenty of guilt."

"Chase loves you, Dani, and I'm not referring to the romantic kind right now."

"I know. I love him, too." I notice a large black leather binder on the island. "What's that?"

"Chase's modeling portfolio. The agency added some photos from more recent shoots."

"Will he be able to keep modeling if he plays football in college? Aren't there eligibility rules about earning money?" I ask, but I'm just making conversation while I'm drooling over Chase's photos.

"There are. But Chase signed with the agency a few years ago, and as long as they don't mention his involvement in college sports in any ad, it's okay. And since it's a freelance situation, meaning he can work when it fits into his schedule, it's one of the few jobs that he can do right now."

I flip from one picture to the next. The photos seem to go in chronological order. The first shots are from his past work for classic, preppy American brands. Newer ones showcase athletic gear. He looks handsome, of course. Sure, his hair is perfectly, artfully pushed back and probably has a lot of product in it, but his grin is what makes him so attractive. He looks genuinely happy, like the hot boy next door who doesn't have a care in the world.

But as I keep flipping through the pages, I start to see a different Chase.

One who looks a little more guarded. A little more worldly.

His jaw has gotten more chiseled as he's aged, but there's a tightness that wasn't there before.

While part of me knows it makes him look even more handsome and grown-up—especially the photo where his hair is slicked back and he's wearing a slim-fit European suit—I can't help but wonder about the change.

His dad is still talking, going on about Chase's passing coach.

"He's already a good passer," I mumble out, trying to keep up, when the realization hits me. I check the date on the photo.

After we ended.

The reason Chase looks guarded and worldly is because I made him that way. When I broke his heart.

"He wants to keep getting better," Phillip says.

I flip to a photo of Chase, shirtless, on a beach somewhere, low-slung board shorts on his tall frame.

And then him in nothing but a pair of jeans.

"He's shirtless in a lot of these," I say.

"He used to not be comfortable with being shirtless, but when I offered to take his place, they turned me down," his dad says with a laugh. "Something about being too old."

I laugh along with him.

I do think Chase and I are going to be friends again.

And I'm okay with that.

Especially if we're going to be the kind of friends who kiss.

"He's grown up a lot. Hard to believe he's eighteen today. My son is officially a man."

I'll say he is, I think, remembering how Chase held me last night, how amazing he made me feel. How I felt the same intense emotion as I did that summer, but how it was even better physically. I fully agree with Chase's dad. The boy I know and love has *definitely* become a man.

"So, how's college life?" Phillip says, changing the subject even though I'd just as soon scroll through this book a few thousand more times. "You're away from home. No parents telling you what to do."

I shrug. "It's different. A lot of people around all the time, but it can be lonely in a way."

"Do you like your sorority?"

"I actually really do."

Jadyn strolls into the room, wrapped tightly in a robe. "And what about all the owl stuff I sent you?"

"You and Mom both totally spoiled me. It's practically a new theme in my room."

Jadyn walks past me and grabs a folder off the counter. "This is what we're showering Chase with today. One hundred and eighty photos. And I hope it's not awkward, but it was hard to find a photo of him through the years that you weren't in," she says, dropping the folder in front of me.

"I'm not in this one," I tease, flashing her a photo of her and my mom, both pregnant, holding a sign that says, *Future BFFs.*

Phillip chuckles as he pours Jadyn a cup of coffee and hands it to her. She sits at the bar next to me.

"It came true," Jadyn says. "Even though you stopped being as close as you once were, you've never missed a birthday toss. Ever."

"I couldn't miss that."

"What did you bring this year?"

I run and grab my bag from the dining room, take it to the kitchen, and show them.

"Oh, good choices," Phillip says.

"And how's college life?" Jadyn asks the same question Phillip asked me earlier.

I don't get to answer her because he goes, "Maybe I'd watched too many raunchy movies, but I expected college to be a nonstop party."

"I didn't think you were a partier?" I say.

"I just mean that my reality wasn't exactly what I had envisioned—especially being in a frat. My point is that, at first, college didn't live up to my expectations. It was a big transition for me, I guess. To Jadyn and your dad, it was all one big adventure while I was still trying to figure out what kind of adventure I wanted to go on. If that makes sense."

"Actually, it does. I feel like that, too. If it wasn't for my roommate, no one would ever know if I went missing. And that's a weird thing."

"All that freedom," Phillip says, "is a little overwhelming. My mother told me that it was a part of growing up. I rolled my eyes at her back then, but now, I get what she was saying. Because for the first time ever, I had no one to answer to but me. No one to check in with. No real curfew."

"And when you're not sure what you want to do or be, that can be a challenge," Jadyn adds.

"So, what's your advice then?" I ask Phillip.

"My advice is that you have four years to figure it out," he says.

"Wow. That's almost profound."

He grins at me. "I don't know about that, but it's true. And I swear, your first semester will fly by, and you'll be back home for Christmas before you know it. So, enjoy it. Let life unfold." He stops and grins at his wife. "Clearly, we've been married too long. I'm starting to sound like you."

"Maybe you should tell her to try to control the unfolding. That sounds more like the Phillip I know," Jadyn says with a hearty laugh, poking fun at him.

"Hmm," I say. "Maybe it should be considered a *thoughtful* unfolding. Being aware but not totally planning everything."

"I like that," Jadyn says.

"Either way, it's good to have you here, Dani," Phillip says. "It really is."

"Thank you. That means a lot."

"So, you want to do the honors this year," Jadyn asks, "and go wake up all the kids?"

"Are you kidding me?! Of course I do. It's like Christmas morning."

Two minutes of torture.

Chase

AFTER THE EARLY morning confetti toss and a birthday breakfast, Dani, Damon, and I head over to their house to work out. Dani goes up to change, so it's just Damon and me down here right now.

"I heard about you and Lacey getting interrupted before the game," he says as he loads weights onto the barbell.

I nod and then pull off my shirt.

"Damn," Damon says. "I guess, not soon enough?"

"What do you mean?" I ask him, wondering what he's referring to.

Obviously, he and Haley were gossiping about how Ryder had walked in on us.

"Dude"—he chuckles—"look at your chest."

I glance down and notice the love bites—ones that are in the exact shape of Dani's mouth. I quickly pull my shirt back on.

"Also heard sis got in trouble for being out with you last night. Those had better not be from her."

I laugh easily because the thought of Dani anywhere near me again still seems laughable.

"Your sister hates me," I say.

"While it's true that she used to, it doesn't seem like it anymore." He pauses and then goes, "Speaking of that."

I follow his eyes to see Dani coming into the workout room, wearing a pair of spandex shorts that must have been created by God himself—her ass filling them to perfection. The boobs I had my lips all over last night are pushed up tightly in a sports bra.

The girl is practically naked, and I fight the urge to cover her with a towel. She gets on one of the elliptical machines, like she always does, for two minutes of torture—for me, not her. She barely breaks a sweat.

After she's warmed up, she likes to stretch. I watch that, too. Her hair is still in a braid, and I spot a tiny hickey and pray her brother doesn't notice. I look closer and see another one, mostly hidden by makeup, just under her right ear. The spot my lips stayed at for what felt like an eternity.

When she turns around and touches her toes, I get a showcased view of her incredible ass.

I feel myself start to get hard. *Shit.*

Damon turns to me and goes, "Dude," then looks at his sister. "That's just wrong."

I punch him in the shoulder. "I wasn't thinking about her," I whisper. "You brought up all the hickeys, which made me think about last night."

When Damon turns his attention to a rack of kettlebells, I catch Dani's eye. She gives me the kind of sexy grin that makes me want to push her brother—who wants details—out of the way and pounce on her.

Her grin makes me harder.

Shit. I cannot have a boner when her dad comes down.

There we go. The thought of Danny seeing me lust after his daughter has me calming down. He'd probably punch me.

Down, boy, I think, speaking to my dick.

"So, tell me more about what happened with Lacey," Damon says.

"She forgot to lock the door when she got there. Ryder walked in on us. She was shirtless. So, he saw some boobs."

"Probably the thrill of his life so far," Damon says with a chuckle. "Boobs were all I thought about when I was his age. Hell," he says with a grin as he does a set of curls, "I'm still into them."

"It seems to be the first thing you notice about a girl," I say with a laugh, knowing it's totally true.

Damon sets the weight down and whispers to me, "Tonight, we're going out. To the *you know where* in the *you know what.*"

"You don't have to pretend in front of me," Dani says. She's obviously overheard everything her brother said. "It's not like I don't see the pictures."

"You're part of my private group on social media?" he asks her, looking horrified.

It makes me wonder exactly what kind of photos he's been posting. I'll be honest; I'm not on social media much. Really, the only person's profile that I creep on is the girl who is now doing yoga moves in front of me.

"So, you in?" Damon asks me.

"Nah, I don't think so. It's going to be a busy day, and I'll probably be tired."

He looks from me to his sister and frowns. "Sure you will."

Adding to the devastation.

Devaney

DAMON FINISHED WORKING out and then went upstairs to shower and get ready for the rest of the day's festivities.

"Do you have plans for today?" Chase asks me. He's sweaty, and there's a towel wrapped around his neck.

I strut over to him, taking the ends of the towel in my hands and pulling him toward me. "Only ones that involve you. I came home for your birthday, Chase."

"But why?"

"I've never missed your confetti toss. I wasn't going to start now," I say but realize that might not be what he's referring to. "I meant to talk to you about this when I got here, but then—"

"We had pizza," he says with a smirk.

"Yes, we did. Anyway, I want to apologize for basically blowing you off since Bid Day. It's been so busy, and everything is new. It's overwhelming. I thought I knew the campus fairly well from going to games, but I didn't have a clue really where the classrooms were. Add to that, trying to figure out where to eat anything slightly healthy. Dealing with a new roommate. A new sorority. I have been so busy every second of every day. The sorority was actually kind of pissed I was coming home this weekend, but I didn't care. I needed to be here. I wanted to see you. I've wanted it since we talked."

"I've wanted it, too," he says.

"You could have messaged me, you know."

"I could have," he says, hanging his head, "but I didn't. I figured if you wanted to talk to me, you would reach out. And it would have been hard for me if I had messaged you and you didn't reply."

"That's part of why I haven't. If I'm going to talk to you, Chase, I want it to mean something. And random texts couldn't say what I was feeling. But trust me, I think about calling you every single night."

He nods, but I can see the hurt in his eyes.

"I realize now that surprising you for your birthday might not have been that smart. I'm assuming there's a party and that you have plans with Lacey today." Something I didn't think about when I jumped in my car with my sack of things and drove off.

He gives me a grin. "I am having a little celebration"—he glances at his watch—"and we're leaving in about thirty minutes."

"What kind of celebration?"

"Golf, followed by dinner at the club."

"With all your friends?" Somehow, I just can't picture that.

"Nah. I just wanted something low-key. I get more than enough time with my friends between football and school. With the little kids, we don't get a lot of one-on-one time with our parents, so I thought it would be fun if it was just my mom and dad, your dad and Jennifer, me, Haley, and Damon. Really, it's perfect that you're here because you'll round out our foursome."

"Lacey isn't joining you?"

"She has a cheer competition and is out of town all day."

"Bet she wasn't too happy about that," I say even though I. Am. Thrilled.

"She wasn't, but it helped that I wasn't having a party or anything. So, will you join us?"

I kiss him in reply.

He leans back and grins at me. "I take it, that's a yes?"

"It is. But I have to run upstairs and get ready. See you in a few, birthday boy."

I SHOWER OFF, thankful for the braid last night, and brush out my waves. I throw on a little makeup, put on a golf skirt and polo, pack a dress to change into for dinner, and grab my golf shoes.

I'm over at the Mackenzie house with five minutes to spare.

When I get there, I find my dad and Phillip sitting at the kitchen table, chatting, and see that Chase is just coming down the stairs.

And it's like he dressed just to torture me, wearing full-on black. Black golf polo and black shorts. The only color on him is from the neon green on the golf shoes in his hand and the logo on his polo.

I'm transported back to that summer.

Damon and Chase came in through the deck doors. Both were dressed up. My brother had his bangs flipped over to the side, and he looked cute, wearing a white button-down and a pair of khaki shorts with loafers. Chase, on the other hand, did not look cute. He looked scorchingly hot.

His long bangs were pushed up in the kind of artful mess of hair that made a girl want to run her hands through it.

His tall frame was encased in a black T-shirt that hung in a way that only high-quality cotton could. Black shorts covered the important parts with a black belt and black shoes finishing the look.

I had never, ever, ever—wait, maybe once at Halloween when he was nine and decided to dress like a vampire—seen Chase in all black.

And it was devastating.

He didn't look like my best friend anymore. He looked—dare I say—a little bit bad. Like he'd gotten an edge.

And my goodness, was it working.

And it's still working. Possibly even more so now. Because Chase is taller, broader, and older. And I think that he hasn't shaved because there's just a light scruff on his face that is only adding to the devastation in my heart.

I literally might pass out.

"Chase," my dad says as he approaches the table, "your father and I want you to come downstairs with us."

I look at them.

"You can come, too, Dani," Phillip says.

My dad and Phillip go down the stairs first, and as we follow, Chase touches the small of my back and whispers, "You look cute."

I blush and tell him, "Thank you."

We're led toward the bar, specifically to a humidor made of shiny burled wood that has sat in that same spot for as long as I can remember.

"We thought it would be fun to share a cigar on the course today," my dad says, cuffing Chase on the shoulder, and I can see the love and respect they share.

"Since you're legal and all," Chase's dad adds, tossing Chase a key. He tosses it like it's no big deal, but I can tell, it totally is.

I want to ask if I can have one, too, since I've been legal for a while, but I get the impression this is sort of a rite of passage that they want to share with him. Celebrating his transition into manhood or something, so I keep my mouth shut and just watch. Our dads are beaming with pride as Chase puts the key in the lock and opens the box.

I've never seen inside of it, and Chase must not have either because he reads aloud the engraving on the gold plaque inside, *"Phillip and Jadyn. Our love is worth celebrating. January the 13th."*

"A little background before you choose a cigar," his dad says. "This humidor was your mother's gift to me on our wedding day. I think you've heard stories, and you know that your mom's parents, Danny's parents, and my parents were all good friends. They did a lot of the things we do today to celebrate life—eating meals together, having a few beers, and talking. And Jadyn's dad used to say he was celebrating something when he smoked cigars, mostly so his wife wouldn't complain about the smoke."

"What they taught us," my dad says to Chase, "is what your mom had inscribed. That love and life are worth celebrating. Even everyday life."

"And it's what we've been trying to teach you kids," Phillip says, "and what we hope you teach yours. It's not about the possessions; it's about the people you love. Your family, your friends, the people who make your life a little brighter. Because just being with them is reason to celebrate."

I was getting choked up, just watching their exchange, but when Phillip says that, the tears I've been holding back fall from my eyes, and I realize that although they've definitely led by example, I've been doing life all wrong for a while now. I've been focusing more on impressing the people I don't care about rather than the people I do.

Chase nods solemnly in understanding and is rewarded with hugs from them both. When Chase turns toward me, his face is filled with emotion. He reaches his hand out to me and says, "I think one of those people needs to help me choose my birthday cigar."

As I take Chase's hand, our eyes lock, and I can picture this very scene someday in the future—him and Damon passing on the tradition to one of our children.

"How am I supposed to choose?" I finally say.

"I'd suggest a lighter-colored cigar," my dad replies. "They tend to be milder."

I point out a few, and Chase picks one up and sets it on the counter.

His dad says, "Grab four. One for you, Dani, Jennifer, and your mom."

"Mom is going to smoke a cigar?" Chase says with a laugh.

"You really think she's going to miss out on a moment like this?" my dad replies.

"Oh, probably not. But what about you two?"

His dad smiles and then lifts up the shelf, revealing another layer of cigars. "Your mom had this box filled when we got married. Danny and I have celebrated quite a bit since then, but these are some of the originals, and we only smoke them on very special occasions."

"What kind of occasions?" Chase asks.

"The births of our children," my dad says.

"Three championship wins," his dad says. "Angel's passing, to celebrate her life."

"The day Phillip sold his company," my dad adds.

"And the night Danny married Jennifer," his dad says. "And today, as our oldest son turns eighteen."

My dad looks at me and throws his arm around my neck. "I just realized that isn't very fair, is it?"

"It is a little sexist," I reply.

"I agree," Phillip says. "If it's okay, Dani, we'll celebrate your adulthood and your going to college as we celebrate Chase's birthday. And when it's Damon's and Haley's turns, I hope you will both be here to pass on the torch."

Emotions well up in me again. "I'd love that."

ON THE WAY to the country club, Jennifer is giving us instructions on how to properly smoke a cigar, so we don't get sick. Who knew she was such an expert?

"So, you're going to suck in air gently, which will fill your mouth with the cigar's smoke. What you don't want to do is fully inhale. You don't want it going down into your lungs. You want to relish the flavor and aroma of the smoke for a second and then blow it out."

"When did you learn how to smoke a cigar?" I ask her curiously. "Did my dad teach you?"

"I'm afraid not." She starts laughing. "Maybe once you turn twenty-one, I can tell you about the night Knox Daniels and Riley Johnson took me to Vegas."

"Epic story?" Chase asks.

"You could say that." She laughs again.

AT THE COUNTRY club, Damon is complaining about the whole thing.

"Are you telling me I can't have one?" he whines.

"Yes. It's a rite of passage," my dad says firmly. "We'll do it for your eighteenth birthday, too. Let Chase enjoy this."

I can tell Damon isn't happy about it, but at least he stops putting up a fuss.

While I was hoping to be Chase's partner, we do a scramble instead of keeping score the usual way, and we are constantly switching up partners, which makes our time on the course really fun.

It's good to spend time with our families like this again. Feeling fully a part of it all.

And I realize that it's not just my relationship with Chase that has suffered because of our breakup, but also my relationship with everyone. I've distanced myself from them emotionally, even when I was physically present. And as I slowly suck in smoke from my first cigar, I realize that needs to stop.

Today.

Birthday boy.

Chase

GOLF WAS FUN.

Seeing Dani prance around in a sexy little golf skirt, smoking a cigar, made it practically epic.

And although I don't know what our future holds romantically, knowing that we can be friends regardless makes me feel like my life is back in balance. Brighter. Sweeter. Happier.

After changing clothes in the locker room, I head toward the bar's big stone patio, where we're all meeting back up for appetizers before dinner.

Screeches of laughter catch my attention, causing me to turn in its direction.

I see my mom and Danny laughing hysterically over something Damon just did or said. I think about how close they are. How close they have been since they were kids. I know that Danny took my mom to prom, and I know that they kissed—and probably more. It's weird to think of your parents having lives before you knew them, but in this case, it's reassuring. If they managed to cross friendship lines at some point and still be friends today, there's got to be hope for Dani and me.

I'm standing there, watching their interaction, when I'm pinched on the back of my arm. I turn around to find Haley. She's pinched me numerous times today.

"I still owe you seven more," she says with a grin as she quickly pinches me again. "Make that six." She tosses her arm around my neck. "Happy birthday."

"Thank you."

"Golf was fun," she says.

"Yeah, it really was. We used to do stuff like this all the time, but we haven't as much since the babies were born."

"And it was fun, having Dani with us."

"It really was. Felt like old times."

"Don't screw that up, birthday boy, because here she comes," she says as she walks away.

And boy, does Dani ever make an entrance.

Her hair glistens in the sun as she walks down the path toward me, wearing a long, flowing skirt that hits about mid-calf in a deep rose-colored silk with a matching midriff top. Strappy heels on her feet make her closer to my height, and gold chains of varying lengths encircle her neck.

She pretty much always takes my breath away, but this is different. Because, for the first time in a long time, she's walking toward me, and I can't help but walk toward her, my arms outstretched.

"Birthday boy." She says the same words my sister just said to me but in a totally different context. The words roll off her tongue in a sexy tone as she steps into my arms and gives me a kiss on the cheek. "You've always cleaned up good."

I'm wearing club attire—navy dress slacks, blue-striped spread collar, and a rose-navy-and-emerald-green tie.

"Your dress matches my tie," I say, a grin on my face. "You plan that?"

"Just a lucky coincidence, it would appear," she says, tugging on it and pulling me closer to her. "Is it okay if I kiss you—like, really kiss you? Right here?"

I don't bother replying. I'd much rather show her the answer.

And I do, by sweeping my arms around her, pressing my lips against hers, and then deepening our kiss with my tongue.

Always had a crush.

Chase

AFTER WE HAVE cake and I open presents, Dani goes home to change. She's supposed to come back over to hang out later.

"Chase, I know it's your birthday," my mom says, "but since we're in a little lull in the celebration, we need to talk about last night."

She knows. How does Mom always know what happens?

She leads me into her office over the garage. I look down at the rug and realize that it looks familiar.

"Is this new?"

"Isn't it great? I loved the ones I installed at Tripp's lake house so much that I finally got one for myself."

And then I remember why it looks familiar. One just like this was on the floor of the honeymoon cottage Dani and I went to when we got caught in the rain. It was our first time, and I can picture her lying on the rug in front of the fireplace, looking up at me.

"So—" Mom says.

And since I know exactly what she's going to say, I start talking. Because I need to talk to someone about this.

Once I tell her most of what happened last night, I add, "But, Mom, please, you can't tell her dad. He'd *kill* me. I've heard the way he talks about boys she dates, and if he knew what happened on his brand-new pontoon boat, he'd literally kill me."

Mom's eyes are searching mine, looking confused. She blinks a few times, lets out an exhale, and then slowly says, "I *actually* brought you up here so we could talk about what happened when Ryder walked in on you and Lacey before the game. He's been telling all his friends about the boobs he saw. I had to have a chat with him about respecting boundaries."

Oh shit. She didn't know. "Um," I say, nervously rubbing my eyebrow.

"But it appears you have something else on your mind. Are you telling me that you and Dani slept together on the pontoon boat last night?"

"Yes. And I still don't know why. Well"—I chuckle—"I mean, I know *why*. I just don't know what it means."

"Chase, we've talked about this. You shouldn't be having sex with a girl unless you care about her. And with Dani of all people?"

"Mom." I give her my pathetic eyes. She's a sucker for them. "It's not that way. At least, it isn't for me. At all. It never has been."

"You've always had a crush on her, huh?"

"I have, but it's more than that. We haven't been close, you know, since everything. And she brought me pizza after the game, like when we had been friends. We went to the hot tub because it was nice out, but then people showed up, so we snuck out on the pontoon. She wanted to keep talking to me. And we haven't talked or *anything* since that summer."

"You were always best friends. I sort of assumed that maybe someday you would have sex. It wasn't the first time, was it? I never really believed the whole story surrounding the Great Ozarks Robe Fire."

"It wasn't." I bury my face in my hands. I can't believe I'm talking to my mom about this. But I need to talk to someone about it. "It happened the day it stormed. We almost got hit by lightning on our run. We were close to that honeymoon cottage at the back of the property. That's not why we went there. We were seeking shelter. But that's where it happened. It was both our first times. We were in love, for sure. We were going to tell everyone when we got back home that we had decided to date. I was even going to talk to her dad about it first. We planned to be in an official relationship by Homecoming, but then Hunter asked her on that first day of practice. And it's been a mess ever since."

"Until last night?"

"Yeah. We talked. Decided to be friends again. I didn't expect for it to happen. It just did. And it was—"

"Incredible?" Mom says.

I let out another sigh and nod. "I'm totally in love with her, and I have no idea what to do about it."

"And what about Lacey?"

"We're not in a committed relationship. I've been adamant about that. I tell her it's because I have to keep my focus on football, but really—"

"It's because she's not Dani."

"Basically, yes."

"Oh boy."

"Tell me about it."

"Hey," my dad says, interrupting us by knocking on the door as he steps into the office.

"I'm glad you're here, Phillip," Mom says to him. "I know I said that I wanted to wait, but now, after talking to Chase, I think we should."

"Okay," he says, moving toward her and squeezing her hand tightly.

She gets up, takes a box off one of her shelves, and then sets it in front of me. She pulls out what appears to be a journal of some kind. The cover is a rugged leather, but it's tied shut with pastel ribbons. She undoes the ribbons, and as she's flipping through the pages, I can see that there are a wide array of papers inside. Almost like scraps, but they coordinate in the sort of bohemian fashion my mother loves.

"Your dad bought me this journal when I was pregnant with you. I love all my children equally, Chase, but this day—your birthday—is special for other reasons. I know we've talked about them before. I know I've told you that you were meant for greatness your whole life.

"I have been saving this journal for you. I wanted to give it to you when you were expecting your first baby, but today, on your eighteenth birthday, I'd like you to read the last few pages. Because unlike the rest of the book, they aren't just about my pregnancy struggles; they showcase the way your dad and I have felt about you since the day you were born.

"I want to read you a passage and then let you read the ones that your dad and I wrote," she says, her eyes filling with tears, "when you have a few moments alone. And know that if you aren't ready to read them, that's okay, too. But I want you to have them now."

She pulls a few pieces out of the journal by untying the rib-bons, carefully ties them back up, puts the book away, and then reads to me.

"Phillip gave me this journal, so I could write to the baby, but that isn't really what I've done. The journal is written more for me than for him.

I wrote some things that probably aren't appropriate.

I wrote some things that are probably stupid.

I wrote some things that are probably silly.

But this journal represents my real journey. It's not a sugarcoated fluff piece.

And someday, I'll tell him that nothing in this journal prepared me for the way I feel right now.

Nothing.

No childbirth class.

No books read.

Nothing could have prepared me because there is nothing in the world that compares to the feeling of holding your baby for the first time."

She smiles at me and says, "After I wrote that, I decided I'd save it for when you were expecting your own child. Because I wanted you to know that, sometimes, life doesn't always go the way you planned it. And sometimes, tragedy can strike when you least expect it. But sometimes, it can be even more incredible than you ever imagined. You, Chase Michael Mackenzie, are more incredible than I ever imagined. And I am so incredibly proud of you. And just for the record, it has nothing to do with your ability to throw a football or look pretty in front of a camera. I'm proud of you because you are a good person. But—"

"But?" I say in astonishment.

"It's obvious that there's someone in your heart who—"

"Are you talking about Dani?"

"Yes," my mom says.

"I don't understand."

"I think what your mother is trying to say, son," Dad says, "is, not to let your head get in the way of your heart, or you just might miss out on something more incredible than you ever imagined."

I nod my head like I get it even though I don't. I know Dani and I would be incredible together. I just don't know how to get from where we were, to where we are now, to the future that we used to both dream about.

But I appreciate the sentiment.

Eight or eighteen.
Chase

"I HEARD YOU'RE in trouble," Dani says, startling me when I enter my room.

She's lying on her stomach, sideways across my bed, like she owns it. Her elbows are on the mattress, her chin nestled on her fist. Her knees bent and her feet up in the air. I could be eight or eighteen. It's like a moment wrapped in time.

"Not really," I fib, holding up the pages. "Mom gave me these. They are journal entries from the day I was born. She wants me to read them sometime."

"Nothing else is going on tonight, right?"

"Nope, and it's just you and me, if that's okay."

"It sounds perfect. Let's read them."

She sits up, pretzeling her legs, and I join her on the bed, matching her position, tucking my legs in, and facing her.

What I really want to do is kiss her. Not read some old letters.

I lean in and press my lips against hers. Her lips are soft and sweet, and the light floral scent of the perfume she puts on her neck envelops me.

We kiss for a bit, but before things start to heat up, she pushes back.

"Are you not dying to read them?" she asks, biting the corner of her lip with her teeth.

She has never had a lot of patience. Once she decides to do something, she's ready to roll. A characteristic she shares with her brother.

"I'm not sure reading them now is a good idea. Mom and I could have died, you know? They might not be that happy. Shouldn't I be happy on my birthday?"

The tooth slides off her lip, and she presses her lips against my cheek. "Do you want me to read them to you?"

And I feel lost in the moment. Emotions that I've tried to push back since that day come flying back. The closeness we shared. The tenderness. The vulnerability.

I nod gratefully. "Yeah, that would be nice."

"Okay," she says, squeezing my hand with one of hers and picking up a page in the other. "Here we go.

"*Dear Baby Mac,*" she says. "Aww, isn't that cute? *You were born three weeks early on September 7th, weighed in at six pounds five ounces, and were nineteen and a half inches long. You were early because you and Mommy got into a car accident, and it caused her to have something called a placental abruption. That's a bad thing because it meant she was bleeding and you were not getting all the oxygen you needed.*" She moves the paper away from her face. "That had to be really scary."

"I know. And I think it's going to get worse. I'm pretty sure, based on what I've overheard my parents say, that Mom, like, died. Or flatlined. And they had to bring her back."

"Can you imagine?" Dani says.

"If you were my wife and pregnant with our child?" I offer.

She tilts her head at me. "I know we've talked a bit about

being friends again. And it was probably stupid of us to sleep together last night—"

"That was not stupid," I say with a grin, but then I turn serious. "But I know what you mean. We first slept together and felt comfortable doing so because of our friendship."

"No." She laughs. "I think that was because we had almost died from the lightning and you looked so hot, dripping wet."

I can't help the wide smile that forms on my face.

She gives my shoulder a little shove. "Oh, you like hearing that you're hot, huh?"

"I would suspect anyone would like to hear that, but"—I point to my mouth—"this beaming grin is because I'm hearing it from you."

"That's sweet," she says, leaning the top of her head against my chest. I bend down and kiss it. "But I guess, if nothing else, sleeping together sort of broke the ice between us."

"I'll say," I tease.

She gives me a steamy kiss and then holds up the papers. "Let's get through this first, and then we'll see. Okay, where were we? Oh, yes. *When you were born, you were a little blue, and your Apgar score was low. But the nurses took care of you, and the next time they did the score, you were almost perfect. Your mom had a rougher time, and for a while, I thought we had lost her. It was the worst pain I'd ever experienced. Way worse than any of the bones I'd broken. Even the time I fell out of a tree and they had to screw my arm back together. But when you love someone the way I love your mom, you'd happily take physical pain over the emotional kind.*"

"That's how I feel about you," I blurt out.

I figure I'll get some crap about it, but she goes, "That goes both ways, Chase. I know we haven't been as close, but I can't imagine you not being in my life."

"But I really haven't been in your life," I counter.

"No, but when I look out my window, I see your room, and I

know you're there. College is cool, but I don't have that view. That connection."

I nod along with her. "I told you last night that I kept my curtains shut for two weeks. I couldn't bear to look at your empty room."

We stare into each other's eyes for a moment, but then she breaks our gaze and keeps reading.

"*She's in the ICU now. Stable but critical. They say the next twenty-four hours are crucial. And I'll admit, I'm scared. My parents are here—your grandparents. And Danny. Danny is my best friend, and he's never left my side through all of this. I hope, someday, you will have a friend like him.*" Dani looks up at me, tears in her eyes. "I'd like to think you got a friend like that in me."

"That is what I had."

"I want that back for us, Chase. Even if we don't end up together. I really need you in my life."

"And I need you," I reply, gently stroking her arm.

She shakes her head, appearing to rid herself of whatever thoughts she was having, and keeps going.

"*Everyone has been asking me what your name is. To be honest, I thought you were going to be a girl. We had agreed on a girl's name but not a boy's. But your mom's favorite was Chase, so I decided on Chase Michael Mackenzie. You have a grandpa and grandma in heaven. And it might sound crazy, but when I was crying in the waiting room, out of the corner of my eye, I thought I saw your grandpa rocking you. When I turned to see if I was just hallucinating, he was gone. But I'm pretty sure he was there. Helping us get through it. Wow. That's kind of cool.*"

"Or creepy," I tease.

"*So, I gave you his middle name—Michael. I have to admit, I always thought most babies were kinda ugly. But not you. You're perfect.*"

She reaches out and touches my face, her finger tracing across my cheekbone. "I can agree with that sentiment. I've always thought you had the most beautiful face."

"Me?" I say with a laugh.

"Yeah, even as a kid you were cute. And now that you're all grown-up, damn, Chase. And this morning, I was looking at your modeling portfolio. All those shirtless photos might have had me drooling."

I reach behind my back and pull my shirt up and over my head, taking it off.

"Hey," she says.

"What? You want to drool over me, I'd much prefer for it to happen in person. Although maybe no actual drooling. You do that when you sleep. It's kind of cute, but—"

She smacks my hard bicep. "Chase! I do not drool."

I kiss the top of her nose. "Oh, but you do."

"Stop flirting with me, or we're never going to get through this."

I pull her up onto my lap. "That's okay with me."

She wraps her arms around my neck and kisses me. A lot.

But when I slide my tongue in her mouth to deepen the kiss, she pulls back. "Not until we finish."

I grab her ass and leave my hands there. "You'd better read fast then."

She lets go of me, slides off my lap, and says, "Chase, this is your life. It's serious. Don't you find it interesting? The devastation your father must have felt when he thought he'd lost your mom? When he thought he'd lost you? This is the kind of love most girls dream about. And you're really lucky that your parents are still crazy about each other. And you."

I take a cleansing breath, trying to calm myself down. *What can I say? Dani gets me so worked up.*

"Plus," she adds, "giving you this today, on your birthday, is really pretty cool." She looks down again and starts reading. "*I've been holding you and feeding you until your mom is able to. And staring in wonder at your ten perfect fingers, ten perfect toes, and the cute little way you ball your fists up before you start crying. It's been killing your grandparents, but I won't let anyone else hold you until she has. She went through a lot to bring you into this world, and she deserves that honor.*

"And I've been telling you all about her. About how she's been writing in this journal. About how she couldn't wait to meet you. About how much she loves you.

"When your mom and I were young, we'd lie in a hammock and stare up at the stars. We'd talk about how infinitely big the universe was and how small we were in comparison. Your mom once told me that she felt small compared to how big our love felt. I didn't completely understand what she meant that day, but I certainly do now. The love I feel for the two of you is almost overwhelming, like the size of the universe." Dani looks up at me, tears in her eyes again. "I feel that way about you sometimes. That our love is too much for me right now."

"I disagree, but I get what you're saying. We have a lot of life left to live. What if you meet someone you love more? Like at college?" The words tumble out of my mouth, saying all the things I've been thinking and stressing over.

What if she meets someone else? What if she falls for someone who is not me? Like, really falls for them. Her dating guys who everyone clearly knew weren't for her is one thing. Her being with a guy we all like, who respects her and she loves, would be a whole other thing entirely. And I am not sure I could handle it.

"Heard a lot about that in rush. Some girls actually somehow researched the hottest frat guys on campus and then decided which sorority they most wanted in based on their relationship with said frat."

"Wow, that's a commitment." I laugh.

"Yeah, the kind that starts with a Miss and ends up with you having a different last name."

"Come on, Dani. It's the twenty-first century. Surely, girls aren't there just to get their Mrs. Degree."

"I think some might be hoping to achieve both," she says with a laugh. "Speaking of married couples—*Your mom has a special charm bracelet, and I sent my dad out to buy her a diamond star, so she'll always know we feel the same way about her. When she wakes up, we'll give it to her together.*

"I love you, Chase Michael Mackenzie, and I know your mommy can't wait to meet you. And as soon as she finds out you're a boy, she'll probably tell me she told me so. Sleep well, my precious baby boy. All my love, Daddy."

And I will admit, what my dad just said there really gets to me. I remember the days when I called him Daddy and not just Dad. And I know my mom still wears that bracelet every single day. I know I've spent my life wanting to get bigger, stronger, older, so I could be better, stronger, faster, but his words have me looking back. At the life my parents have given me. The love.

"Well, one down, one to go," Dani says, picking up another page. "This one is from your mom. *Dear Chase Michael Mackenzie. My perfect, sweet baby boy. We're still in the hospital. Your dad is taking a nap, and I've got your uncle Danny's football game on, but mostly, I'm watching you sleep in my arms. You're making the cutest little faces as you dream, and I can't wait until the day you smile at me for real. I wish my parents were here to see you, but I know for sure that they are watching over us."*

"I can't imagine having my first baby and not having our parents there, can you?" I say.

Dani shakes her head. "I really can't. Your mom and I talked a little bit in the Ozarks about when her parents died. How your dad was the one who got her through it all. I felt that way about you when my parents were getting a divorce. I knew if I could hold on to you, hold your hand, my world wouldn't completely crumble. And I don't think I've ever thanked you for that. Seriously, Chase, I don't know what I would have done."

"I'm glad I could help," I say sincerely.

"*There's something I want you to always remember. You and I could have had a very different outcome. We're both lucky to be alive. I'll be thankful for every single day I get to spend with you. And something else I know. You are destined for greatness. I don't know what you'll do or be, but I know it as surely as I feel my own heartbeat. And I'm going to do everything I can to prepare you for it. All my love, Mommy.*"

I look up at Dani. Her face is as emotional as mine.

She leans in and gives me a single sweet kiss. "I'm really glad you and your mom made it through all that, Chase."

I want to tell her that when she's in my arms, I'm really glad, too. And I am. But I also realize something else, too. "My mom read a little from the journal before she gave this to me. And she said she wanted me to know that, sometimes, life wouldn't always go the way I planned it. And sometimes, tragedy could strike when I least expected it. But sometimes, life could be even more incredible than I ever imagined."

She nods her head. "All the more reason why we need to stop acting like kids over what happened between us, right?"

"Right," I say, wrapping her in my arms and pulling her into a tight hug.

If I had known.

Devaney

I HOLD CHASE for a long time before I let go.

"I think about that night we got home from the Ozarks. When you took me parking in my new truck. I always wonder if I would have done anything differently that night if I had known."

"Known what?"

"That it was our last time."

"But it wasn't. And now, we're here. Together. In your bed. On your birthday. And although I've already given you your gift—"

"A football signed by the last Super Bowl quarterback, the literal GOAT. That was quite the gift, Dani. Seriously, I'll treasure it always."

"I know, and it just turns out that I'm in a giving mood tonight." I give him what I hope is a seductive grin.

And he must understand because he pounces on me and covers my face with kisses.

SUNDAY, SEPTEMBER 8TH

Friends with benefits.

Devaney

I SNUGGLE INTO Chase's neck and kiss it. Really, there's nothing better than waking up with him. My little bed at school is going to feel lonely.

He murmurs something into his pillow but then rolls over quickly on top of me, pinning me to his sheets.

"I'm so glad you came home for my birthday, Dani."

"What's on tap for today?"

He shrugs. "No real plans. I think the celebration is over."

"My dad mentioned maybe going out on his new boat."

He rolls off me with a dramatic thud. "The scene of the crime. Great. He probably knows what we did. He'll take me out, hit me over the head, say I fell into the water and drowned. That he tried his best to save me."

I laugh. "You're silly. My dad loves you. Like a son practically."

"What he and my dad said when we picked out the cigars was pretty cool, and the bag he and Jennifer gave me for traveling was really nice."

"It was. And it sounds like you'll be using it a lot. With all the university visits Damon wants to go on. Are you really considering going somewhere besides Nebraska?"

"Not as long as you're there," he says, pushing my hair off my face and kissing my forehead.

"So, why go through all of it?"

"It's part of the process, I guess. Damon likes the attention. And we'll be seeing a lot of the guys we've met at camps in the past. He's also sort of been questioning our choice. If, by chance, we decided to go somewhere else, would you ever consider transferring or a long-distance thing?"

"I don't think now is the time to talk about that, Chase. Let's just enjoy being friends."

"You mean, friends with benefits?"

"I guess, technically, that's what this is right now."

"While you're in college and I'm not?" he asks.

"You're busy. I'm busy."

"Friends with benefits it is then."

"I really liked the shirt Damon and Haley had made for your birthday," I say, changing the subject.

I don't want to ruin this weekend by trying to label it. We need to take this slow. Work our way back to being friends organically. It was easy, like putting on a worn-in pair of jeans, this weekend. I expect it will continue to feel the same when I'm back at school. We'll talk at night. Catch up. I'll see him at games. Come home as often as I can.

"They want me to wear it to school on Monday, so they can start taking orders. But it is really cool to see both our numbers together. My one. His eleven. We knew we were going to combine them, but then Haley started researching the history and meaning of the number one eleven."

"What does it mean?"

"Well, let's start with the numbers individually. In numerology, my number one represents motivation and independence. It also ties into success. Damon's number eleven is supposed to be a powerful number that has to do with life's purpose. Since Damon's goal is to play pro ball, he was pumped to hear that. Really, when we chose our numbers as kids, we never thought to consider all that stuff. Heck, I didn't really even know what numerology was until Haley told me that all numbers have meaning. Anyway, when you combine them, you get one eleven. And get this. It's the angel number."

"Oh my gosh, like your first dog, Angel. Like our dog, Angel the second."

"And the wing tattoos our parents have. It is also supposed to indicate the manifesting of one's own destiny. And there's something to do with prosperity in there, too."

"So, all in all, pretty cool."

"Yes," he says in an academic tone. "Because when you are at one with yourself, your thoughts can become your reality." He laughs. "Your brother *loved* that part."

"I expect they will sell out quickly."

"We hope so. Otherwise, Mom won't be able to get her car in the garage when it starts snowing, and she won't be happy about that."

"I suppose I'd better get home before anyone wakes up." I turn his wrist toward me, looking at the time on the new engraved watch his parents gave him yesterday. I give him a kiss. "I guess next time I see you, we'll be back at the scene of the crime."

Way too guilty.

Devaney

I SPEND THE morning with my family, having breakfast and

playing with my little sisters. I'm gathering up my stuff in the kitchen when Dad comes in and shows us his new tattoo.

"What do you think?" he says.

As soon as Jennifer sees it, she starts crying and muttering something about always wanting to fill up his arm. He kisses her, and they share a tender moment while Damon and I try not to make it awkward. Dad already has tall Roman numerals tattooed on the inside of his forearm with the dates of each of us kids' birthdays, but this is different. It's a big compass. Instead of the normal directional indications, where it would normally have an *E* or say *East*, it says Easton. Where West should be, it says Weston. I'm at the top of the compass, Jennifer is featured in the center of the design, and Damon is at the bottom.

I tell him it looks great and then head up to my room to finish packing my makeup.

Damon follows me.

"So, I'm south," he says. "I'm pretty sure it's because he thinks I'm the most likely to end up, you know, down there."

"Damon! You're such a pervert."

"What?" he says. "I was referring to Hell, not a girl's, you know, but I will admit, that is a funner thought. In fact, I like it. And I'm going to use that. Because I do love to go down south, if you catch my drift."

"You're a pig," I say, shaking my head at him.

"Oh, come on now, Dani. I'm sure *you* like it."

"That's none of your business," I say way too fast and sounding way too guilty.

"You do that with Chase? This weekend?"

"What?" I ask innocently.

He taps his foot and raises his eyebrows at me. "You two seem tight again. So, what is it? BFFs, friends with benefits, or love?"

"I don't know exactly," I answer honestly.

"As in you're going back to school and you haven't discussed what it means?"

"Like I said, it's none of your business. We're just happy to be talking again."

"Or *something*," he fires back.

"Don't make this all sexual."

"I don't have to. You already did."

"You know what I mean. Things are getting back to normal with Chase and me."

"Actually, no. They aren't. Normal would mean you were BFFs. Sure, when you were BFFs, you flirted some, but this weekend, the sexual energy rolling off the two of you could not be missed. We all noticed. Trust me. And while, on one hand, it makes me happy, on the other hand, I feel like we're all cruising along on the *Titanic*, waiting to hit the iceberg."

I throw my hands up in the air. "What do you want me to do about it, Damon? I don't have an answer."

"Which is clearly the problem. I want you to march back over there, figure out what you are, what your relationship is going to be between now and the next time you come home. When will that be, by the way?"

"October. For Homecoming. I have to pass the crown off."

Damon dramatically rolls his eyes and tosses his head back. "That's just fantastic. You're sleeping with Chase, and you will probably be crowning the *other* girl he's sleeping with? Nah. Doesn't sound like a recipe for disaster at all. Hope you can swim in ice-cold water, sis."

"First off, the former queen crowns the new king. The former king crowns the new queen. It's how it's always been."

"Regardless, you'll all be onstage together."

I take a moment to think about that. "I suppose you're right though. It might be a bit awkward."

"Especially if you haven't talked about it beforehand. Go."

"I'm going to say goodbye to him before I leave. But I already know the answer. Chase and I will talk at night. Stay caught up on each other's lives. I'll see you all at the football games. And I'll come home as often as I can. Christmas break will be here before we know it."

"You won't last that long in the water," he says, turning around and leaving my room.

Just talk to me.

Chase

I MAKE MY way down to the dock, looking forward to seeing Dani in a bikini and hoping to go up to her room to *help her pack* before she leaves. Although the thought of having sex in her room, under her dad's roof, freaks me out a little, I think I'll be able to manage.

When she comes out to the backyard though, she's wearing jean shorts and carrying a bag over her shoulder.

"Are you leaving?"

"Yeah, my dad wants me to get back to school before dark since I'm driving, and I have a sorority thing tonight that I almost forgot about."

"Oh," I say, disappointment probably written all over my face.

"Damon also told me that I need to talk to you about us before I leave. Do you have any expectations of me? For us? With everything that happened between us this weekend?"

"I was thinking about that after you left. And no. You're right. I'm here. You're there. Just talk to me sometimes, okay? At night, like we used to?"

"Okay," she says.

"I'm going to let you call me. I'd happily call you every night, but I know you're busy. And I don't want—"

"You don't want what?"

"For you to have to explain to your friends why you're talking to some high school guy," he says, nearly breaking my heart.

"I'll call you. I promise. And you're coming up for the game next weekend. So, you can come see my dorm and the sorority house and all that fun stuff."

Her dad waves at me as he comes out of the back door, tackle box in hand.

"Why don't I walk you to your car? I'm pretty sure the kind of goodbye kiss I want to give you shouldn't be witnessed by your dad just yet."

MONDAY, SEPTEMBER 9TH

Razzle-dazzle.

Chase

MOST EVERYONE HAS already left the locker room, but Damon, myself, and Pace—our star running back—stayed late to work on a few new plays.

I say goodbye to them and then stop in Coach's office.

"Liked what I was seeing out there, Mackenzie. You boys want to try that razzle-dazzle play during a game?"

"If a situation arises when you think it would work, sure."

"You know we haven't talked about your recruitment since the season started. There's sure lot of interest in you."

"I know. Damon and I are having dinner tonight with our parents to discuss which colleges we'll do official visits at. But I'm guessing it will be Oklahoma, Auburn, Ohio State, Georgia, and of course, Nebraska. In fact, we're going up to Lincoln this weekend. We've already had an unofficial visit, but since we'll be there for the game anyway, we'll consider it official from a recruitment standpoint."

"Stanford is really interested in you. You considered it at all? You'd be getting a hell of an education there."

"They already have a standout receiver, so it doesn't really work for us."

"Chase, I know that your and Damon's friendship is special, but you can go to different colleges and stay friends. You need to think of yourself. Which colleges produce top quarterbacks consistently."

"I'll keep that in mind, Coach. I'd better get home."

I head out to the parking lot, finding Lacey sitting on the tailgate of my truck, her car parked next to it.

"Hey, what's up?" I ask her.

I heard all about her cheer competition over lunch, and we're not supposed to get together tonight, so I'm not sure why she's here. Maybe cheer practice went late or something.

She smiles at me, pulls out her phone, and holds it up to my face. On it, there's a photo of Dani and me kissing at the country club before dinner on Saturday night. "This is what's up."

"Dani was wishing me a happy birthday."

"With her tongue?" she says, and I realize she's pissed. "And just what other parts did she use to do so?"

"I don't know what to say to you, Lacey. We're not in a relationship for a reason."

"And is *she* that reason?"

I don't reply, but I don't have to because she hops off the tailgate and starts pacing in front of me.

"I've never been able to figure it out. Why you date me but are never with other girls from our school even though you could be. I mean, I know you and Damon go out and hang out with girls. I'm sure you've made out with some of them, but I never got the impression you were sleeping with them. Have you been? Have I just been blind to it? Am I the only girl you're sleeping with, Chase? Or not?"

I swallow hard and try to control my temper, but it's hard to do when it's anything to do with Dani. "I don't sleep around, Lacey. And I'm *always* the wingman."

"You didn't answer my question. Am. I. The. Only. Girl. You

have slept with in the past week?"

"No, you're not."

"Which means you *are* sleeping with Dani."

I just stare at her, not sure what she expects me to say.

"What am I supposed to do about Homecoming, Chase? Are you going to ask me?"

"I was planning to, yes."

"God," she says. "I remember that day so clearly. How it was so cool when Hunter Lansford asked Dani to Homecoming. And so early. Like, no one asks that early. I knew he must have really liked her. But then you got in a fight with him. I thought it was because you were standing up for your friend, but you were jealous, weren't you?" I don't get a chance to reply because she keeps going. "No, that wouldn't be right. You were hooking up with that senior. Dance team captain. What was her name?" She snaps her fingers and points at me. "I know—Kelsey Jennings."

"Does it matter? That was, like, two years ago. And Homecoming isn't until mid-October this year. That's, like, five or six weeks away. No one will start asking until a few weeks before."

"That's because boys don't have to buy dresses." She pouts. "God, Chase. We're supposed to go together. Quarterback, cheer captain. I'll be up for queen."

"Somehow, I don't think you'll have trouble finding a date, if that's what you want."

She narrows her eyes at me. "Are you or are you not planning on asking me to Homecoming?"

"I *was* planning to," I say again.

"And now, you're not?" she smarts back.

I bury my face in my hands and rub my fingers up and down my forehead. "I need to go home, Lacey."

"Fine," she says. "We're through, okay?"

"Okay," I say and then get in my car.

I STAY UP late, waiting for Dani to call me but she doesn't. Just like she didn't last night. I want to call her. Or text her. Check on her and tell her what happened, but we agreed she would call me.

So, I wait.

THURSDAY, SEPTEMBER 12TH

Relationships are volatile.

Chase

LACEY'S BEEN FLITTING around school all day today with Pace, flirting with him.

Pace looks a little uncomfortable when they almost run into me in the hall between classes, but Lacey just giggles and wraps her hand around his bicep. A possessive move of hers I know all too well.

I'm sure I'll hear about it in the locker room. Damon, Pace, and I became fast friends on and off the field when he moved here last year.

He and Damon are both funny and good at playing off each other when they're joking around. They always make me laugh.

Right now though, I'm not laughing. And it has nothing to do with him.

I haven't heard from Dani since she left on Sunday. And it's starting to piss me off.

Especially when the girls in my physics class are going on about how cute it would be if Lacey and Pace dated since their names sort of rhyme and all that.

WE GET DONE with class early and are just sitting here, doing nothing. I ask the teacher, who happens to be our offensive line coach, if I can head to practice early. He agrees, so I grab my books, go to the locker room, and am the first one on the field.

I'm warning up when Pace joins me and is like, "Dude, what's up with you and Lacey?"

"Nothing."

"So, you broke up?"

"We were never in a relationship. We were just—dating."

"And are you *still* just dating?" he asks, starting to look frustrated with me.

"No, we aren't."

"Why is she hitting on me? To make you jealous?"

"I don't think so. She is the one who ended things. What, you don't like her?"

"I mean, Lacey's pretty and all, but she's not really my type. I kind of have my eye on someone here, and I've sort of been talking to a girl from South."

The town we live in is a suburb of Kansas City. It has an old historic downtown, but it's grown over the years, and it now has three high schools. The original school is called South, the second high school is North, and we go to the newest one, West.

"She's mad at me," I tell him. "Partially because I haven't asked her to Homecoming yet."

He sits on the grass and does a hurdler's stretch. "Dude, that's, like, two months away."

"Five weeks actually, but yeah. No one is asking anyone yet."

"That's because high school relationships are volatile, man. Can't ask too soon and be stuck with someone you don't like anymore." He switches legs and stretches out the other side. "The crazy thing is, I have also heard that Lacey has been inquiring, not so discreetly, about my size."

"Six foot, one eighty-five. All she has to do is read a game program. Although I think we all know you're really only five-eleven," I say with a laugh.

"Yeah, she wasn't talking about *that* size."

I start laughing. "Seriously?"

"Girls, right?" he says, standing up. "I swear, unless you're in love, the sex almost isn't worth the hassle sometimes."

What he says causes me to stop laughing. "Um, Lacey told me she loved me. Before our home opener. But then, on Monday, she saw a photo of me kissing Dani Diamond on my birthday."

"Ooh-wee," he says, slapping me on the back. "Damon's sister is, like, the ultimate hottie. She come back from college or something?"

"Yeah. She's been my best friend my whole life."

"Oh, so Lacey didn't understand that it was just a *friendly* birthday kiss?" he asks, picking up a football and tossing it to me.

"The kind with tongue," I say, and then I find myself spilling out details I've never really told any of my friends. I mean, Damon and Haley know, but that's about it. "Before you moved here, our families went on a summer vacation together. We hooked up. Actually, that makes it sound like just a hook-up. It was anything but that."

He squints his eyes at me. "You love her, don't you?"

"Yeah, but we're not together. We were supposed to be." I tell him about how we were going to start dating, how Lansford asked her to Homecoming early, our subsequent fight, and how we haven't been best friends since. "The day she left for college, we hugged. We talked on the phone some after that and expressed that we missed each other. Especially the best-friends part."

"Where does the tongue fit into those parts?" he asks with a smirk.

"You can't tell anyone this. If Damon hears—"

"I won't. Trust me. But I bet I can guess. She came back home for your birthday, and you slept with her?"

"Yeah."

"And now, it's all up in the air again?"

"Yep."

"And Lacey saw the photo of you kissing Dani and is trying to make you jealous with me. One of your best friends."

"That about sums it up," I say sadly.

"She's desperate, bro."

"The bitch of it all is that I like Lacey. I really do. She's a sweet girl. And I hate that I hurt her."

He spins the football on his finger and studies my face. "You planning to ask Dani to Homecoming?"

I laugh. "No."

"Do the right thing then. Ask the sweet girl."

"She thinks we'll be Homecoming king and queen. I think this is all part of some high school fantasy of hers."

"I would think it would be you, me, or Damon as king. Hey, you said you've been honest with Lacey about your feelings, so if you can't give her love but you care about her, at least let the girl have her dream. Do it up big. I'll help you brainstorm. Or at least watch some YouTube videos. What's your mom cooking tonight?"

"Fajitas, I think."

"Perfect. I'll come home with you after practice. We'll get Damon and Haley to help us."

I nod my head. "Yeah, you're right," I say because it's been four days and the girl who I do love still hasn't found the time to call me.

WE BRAINSTORM A little during practice and talk a bit about the logistics of asking her on the field. We stop in Coach's office.

"Coach," Damon says, "we want to get your permission on something."

"What's that, son?"

"Well," I say, "I'm going to ask Lacey to Homecoming sometime during the game on Friday. We haven't worked out all the details yet—"

"But we were sort of thinking, maybe right before the second half starts," Pace finishes.

"Sure. Why not? As long as she's going to say yes. We don't need Mackenzie crying under the bleachers if she says no."

"They've been dating since last year, Coach," Damon says.

"Except that she's been flirting with Pace here for most of this week because she saw a photo of Damon's sister kissing Chase on his birthday," Coach replies.

"Do you know everything, sir?" I ask.

"I sure do," he replies. "Now, get the hell out of my office."

AFTER PRACTICE, THE three of us go to my house. Dinner is a pretty quick meal because Madden has a football game. I tell Mom that we'll clean up, so they won't be late, and we sit around the kitchen table, still eating. Dani's name is mocking me just above my place mat, and irritated, I cover it up.

"So," Damon says to me, "you want it to be big. On the field. In front of everyone? Or do you, like, want to take her off to the side and ask in private?"

"In front of everyone," I say. "And there has to be roses involved."

"And probably a glitter sign," Pace says with a sigh. "Do you have any glitter?"

"I'm sure my sister does."

"Excellent," Pace says. "She needs to help us."

Damon shouts out, "Hay Girl, get down here! We need you."

Haley comes halfway down the stairs, phone in her hand.

What? she mouths.

"Get off the phone and come help us plan a homecoming proposal," Damon says.

"Oh!" she says excitedly and then tells whoever she's talking to that she'll call them back. She rushes over and takes a seat next to

Pace. "Who are you all asking?"

"Well, for right now, we just need a plan for Chase," Pace tells her. "I have a girl I like, but I'm not sure if she likes me."

"You're adorable, Pace," Haley says. "I don't know why she wouldn't. And what about you, Damon?"

"You know, I was just sitting here, thinking Chase might be on to something with this asking-early thing."

"Well, sure," Haley says. "Girls love it. They know if they are going to have a date, so they can plan. They can start shopping. All that stuff."

"And I get pick of the litter."

We hear scratching on the back door and see Angel and Winger on the deck, wanting in. They are panting, and I know, earlier, they were chasing each other in the backyard. But I thought Ryder was out there with them.

I stand up and go look out into the backyard. I'm actually surprised he didn't go to the game with my parents. Usually, we all go, but Madden sprained his wrist last week and has to sit out for a few games.

I open the door and let the pups in, giving them lots of love, and then look out to see where Ryder is. When I don't see him, I turn back and ask Haley if he was going somewhere.

"Not that I know of," she says. "I thought he was out with the dogs."

"I'm going to go check on him. Keep brainstorming."

I go out onto the deck and then down the stairs. I still don't see him, but I hear giggling coming from the tree house that's built into the play set and head that way. What I find is Ryder sitting in it—with a girl.

They are kissing, and he's got his hand up under her shirt.

I clear my throat.

The girl notices me first, blushes furiously, and quickly backs away from Ryder. I know he's in the eighth grade, and I know that

Damon and I were doing things like this back then, but it sort of freaks me out a little. Mostly because I never did talk to him after he walked in on Lacey and me last week.

"Um, I just wanted to tell you that I let the dogs in. They were at the door."

"Cool," Ryder says, seemingly not the least bit embarrassed.

"We're eating chips and queso and planning homecoming proposals. You two want to come in and help us?"

"No," Ryder says, but the girl goes, "Ohmigosh, yes!"

"Awesome," I say to her. "I'm Chase."

"Oh, I know who you are. I'm Sasha. I'm a cheerleader."

"Nice to meet you, Sasha."

She goes down the slide to exit the tree house. Ryder is still sitting in there, pouting.

"You suck," he whispers to me.

"I'm sorry, but I don't think you should be out here alone with that girl."

"You're one to talk," he sasses.

"Actually, I am. And if you don't do as I say, Mom's the one I'm going to be talking to."

He rolls his eyes and shakes his head. "Fine. Did I get you in trouble the other night? Is that why you're trying to ruin my life?"

I can't help but laugh as I watch the girl skip toward the stairs. "She's going to hear about romantic high school homecoming proposals. You have an eighth-grade formal coming up, don't you?"

"Yeah, so?"

"You going to ask her?"

He shrugs. "Depends on if she lets me put my hand up her shirt again."

"I really hope you're just joking about that."

Ryder grins at me. "I am. I actually really like her. And, yes, I hope she will be my girlfriend soon."

"Why haven't you asked her already?"

"It's new-ish."

When he gets out of the tree house, I rub my hand across his hair and tease him. "My little bro is growing up."

"Yeah, yeah," he says.

When we get back inside, the girl is already sitting next to Haley, talking excitedly.

"Sasha was thinking you should do a cheer, Chase," Haley says.

"A cheer?"

"Yeah, like one of those, *I've got spirit. I've got class. Boys want to touch my*—uh, maybe not."

The girl, Sasha, goes, "Actually, something more like this: *Say, hey, hey, my name is Chase. I am the greatest. And I'm looking for a homecoming date-est.*

So, hey. Hey, hey, Lacey. Yeah, yeah, hey, Lacey.

You're captain. And just gorgeous. And I think I need a little chorus.

And then, like, all the guys would start chanting with you, going:

Hey, hey, Lacey, Yeah, yeah, hey, Lacey.

He's got roses. And a suit. Now, all he needs. Is you.

Hey, hey, Lacey, Yeah, yeah, hey, Lacey.

What do you say? Hey, hey, Lacey?

"And then you'd pull out a sparkly glittered sign spelling out Homecoming with a question mark."

Pace looks at her in disbelief. "Did you literally just make that all up, like, just now?"

"Uh, yeah," she says, blushing again.

"Girl, that's the bomb. You're amazing."

"Thank you," she says.

"That was awesome," Haley says diplomatically. "We'll let Chase hear all our ideas, and then he can decide. Damon, you're up."

"Oh, yeah, mine is awesome. It's this." He holds out a sign that he's written: *Hey, HO. COme with me?* "Get it? The big letters spell out HOCO for homecoming."

Sasha shakes her head at him and says very seriously, "That's *not* a sign she could save to show her children. Let alone post on her social media, where her grandmother—or worse, her father—might see."

"True that," Ryder says, trying to sound cool.

It's hard not to burst out in laughter.

Damon grins at me and then slaps Ryder on the back. "What do you think he should do?"

"I'd do it right after the cheerleaders do their halftime performance. Go out onto the field, in your full uniform but with your helmet off, and just stand in front of her, smile at her, and hold up the sign. Oh, and I'd probably take flowers. Roses."

"Oh," Sasha says with a sigh, her hands clasped in front of her. "It's perfect."

"Hay Girl, you're up," Damon says.

"Okay, so I was thinking of using your name," Haley says. "Something like, *I'm up for the Chase.*"

"More like Chase-*ing* tail," Damon mutters, which earns him a smack on the arm from my sister.

"It's like an apology and a proposal, all in one," Haley counters. "I heard she saw the photo I took of you kissing Dani. I'm sorry about that. I showed a friend, and *that* was a mistake. She's also not my friend anymore, but whatever."

"I like it," I tell her. "Thanks, really. I love all your ideas."

"Oh, wait," Pace says. "We've saved the best for last."

"We have?" Haley and Damon say at the same time.

"We thought you couldn't come up with anything," Haley says.

"That's because I have been busy, working on my phone. Do

any of you know what's happening at the game on Friday night?"

"We're going to kick Brookville's ass?" Damon asks.

"It's Senior Night," Sasha and Haley say at the same time.

Sasha continues, "It's a big deal."

"That's this week!" Haley says, getting excited.

"The tradition gets flipped, right?" I asks.

"Yes," Haley says. "Instead of the cheerleaders and dance team lining up for your entrance onto the field, you line up for us, and we run out through the jaguar head and the streamer banner."

"Exactly," Pace says. "And the head cheerleader is *always* the first one through. That'd be Lacey, if you haven't been keeping up," he says, turning to Sasha and Ryder.

"And I'll be standing there, waiting for her. With a sign that says, *Lacey, I'm Chase-ing you. Homecoming?*" I look at my little brother. He doesn't know that Lacey told me she wanted roses. "And you're right, Ryder," I say, fist-bumping him. "I should have a bouquet of roses for her."

He gives me a grin and wraps his arm around the back of Sasha's chair. She leans close to him and whispers something in his ear that causes his smile to grow wider.

Hopefully, his smile is the only thing that's growing right now.

And it makes me wonder if Dad has had the whole sex talk with him yet. Surely, he has, but just in case, I should probably offer a little brotherly advice. Although, right now might not be the best time. I'd tell him to keep it in his pants because love is complicated and hurts way too much.

"Now, we just need a sign," Haley says.

"You got any glitter?" I ask her.

She rolls her eyes. "I'm a competitive cheerleader and a crafter. You really think I don't have glitter?"

FRIDAY, SEPTEMBER 13TH

I'm chasing you.

Chase

I CAN'T BELIEVE I'm waiting to ask a girl to Homecoming on the same field where, two years ago, my world fell apart when the girl I loved—*love*—got asked to Homecoming by someone else.

And I'm out here on Friday the freaking 13th, no less.

If only I could wipe that day from my memory.

It's probably for the best that I'm out here though. Ready to ask Lacey. To make the big gesture. Because I'm pretty sure that Dani has wiped me from *her* memory. She still hasn't called.

Lacey is beaming as she leads the team out through the streamers. She puts her hand up to wave to the cheering crowd but stops in her tracks when she sees me standing there, sign in hand.

I saunter over in her direction, ignoring the noise of the crowd, the football players, and the dance and cheer squads who have gathered in a half-circle around us, focusing only on her.

"Cute sign," she says. "That mean what I think it does?"

"That I want you to go to Homecoming with me? Uh, yep."

"The *chasing you* part is what I'm referring to."

I pull the roses out from behind the sign and hand them to her. "You're the captain. You'll probably be queen. And you're the first one to be asked. Yeah, I'd say I'm chasing you. I wouldn't want you to go with anyone else, Lacey. Will you go to Homecoming with me?"

"And what about Dani?"

"She's not here."

She grins at me, nods her head, drops the flowers to the ground, jumps into my arms, and kisses me.

I think that's a yes.

The crowd must, too, because it erupts in cheers.

MY PHONE RINGS as I'm getting ready to leave the locker room after another win.

I see Dani's number and answer.

"Saw your proposal," is the first thing out of her mouth.

No, Hello, how ya been, Chase? No excuses as to why I haven't heard from her all week.

"Interesting," I say.

"What's that supposed to mean?"

"It means, it's interesting that you see the proposal of me asking someone to Homecoming on social media, and you call me about it, yet you haven't had time to call me all week. I even broke down and texted you twice. It's hard to be BFFs with you when you don't have time to respond. Good to hear from you, Dani. But I gotta go."

And then I hang up.

LACEY IS WAITING for me by my truck.

She leaps into my arms and kisses me.

"That was amazing, Chase. Thank you. For asking me. For doing it up big. In front of everyone. On Senior Night. It was perfect. Really. Anyway, I just wanted to tell you that before you went home."

"You want to hang out tonight?" I ask her, totally breaking my usual routine.

"Like, at your house?"

"Actually, I thought maybe we could go out after the game. Celebrate. Any parties tonight?"

"Of course there are." She kisses me again. This time more passionately. "I don't know what has caused this change in you, Chase, but I like it."

"I was always planning to ask you, Lacey. And don't think this will be a habit or anything, but it's a special night, right?"

"Yeah, Chase, it is."

Always loved him.

Devaney

I'M STARING AT my phone, shocked that Chase just hung up on me. He's never done anything like that before.

I know I should have called him this week or responded to his texts, but I really have been busy. And tired.

Alyssa wanted me to go to a frat party with her tonight, but I just wanted to curl up in bed and finally call Chase. I knew he'd be home after his game, like always, and I figured we'd actually have time to talk. In fact, I was going to suggest that's what we do. Sort of make it a weekly thing. What I didn't expect was to have his homecoming proposal pop up first thing on my feed while I was waiting for him to get home.

Or how bad it would make me feel.

I had such an epiphany on his birthday. I realized so clearly that I'd been worrying too much about impressing people I didn't care that much about. And although I've been very careful about that during my short time here at college, only focusing on building relationships here with people I respect, I realize that I completely screwed things up with Chase.

Happy Friday the 13th, everyone. I think I'll just cry myself to sleep now.

But then my phone rings in my hand. It's Chase's mom.

"Hey," I say, quickly answering.

"Dani, hi. I know it's late, but I just got into town. And I was wondering, if you aren't at some totally cool party, would you want to do something with me?"

"Uh, sure. I actually just got home. It's been a long week."

"Oh, well, this can wait until tomorrow."

"No. What's up?"

"I really need to just show you, if that's okay. I haven't shared my idea with anyone else yet, and I wanted to run it by you first. I can pick you up outside your dorm in about five minutes."

"Okay, I'll be ready," I tell her.

I HOP IN the car when she pulls up. "What are you doing, coming up here this late?"

"I left after the end of the third quarter since the team was way ahead. I wanted to get here to try to figure some stuff out."

She drives us a few blocks from campus to an area filled with restaurants and shops. It's a busy area, but she seems to know exactly where she's going, and she parks in a reserved spot.

When we get out, I'm surprised to find a realtor waiting for us. Jadyn introduces me, and we're taken up over one of the restaurants to a new condo project.

The realtor starts talking, "Historical building. Wide-open loft-style condos. Two bedrooms each."

Inside each condo, we find really cool spaces. Exposed brick, lots of old wood, but modern furnishing and fixtures.

"It would be so cool to live somewhere like this," I say.

"I'm considering buying it," she says. "We come up for most

home games, and it would be really nice not to have to deal with hotel rooms for our families."

"But how would that work? This only has two bedrooms."

She laughs. "Well, I was thinking maybe you and Haley could eventually share one. Maybe one could be for Damon and Chase and a few more for when we visit. There are just five units, so I would have to buy them all. But I have a crazy idea that might work out better."

"Do you want to go see the other building now?" the realtor asks.

"Yes, please," Jadyn says.

"Just what are you up to?" I ask her as we walk across the street and then down half a block.

This area is actually just slightly closer to campus, if we're counting steps.

"It's a little rough," the realtor says, "but it's certainly got potential."

Now, we're standing in what looks like an old storage area. It's run-down, and there's possibly a hole in the roof based on some water on the floor.

"You want to buy this?" I ask.

"Yeah. Look at the bones of the place," she says, a big grin on her face. "Exposed brick, old wood floors, crown molding. If I renovated this building, everyone would have their own spaces, and it would be custom-designed just for us. Private, secure entry. Rooftop outdoor space. It would have wings that could be wide open or closed off. But basically, if you, Chase, Damon, and Haley wanted to live here, you could. And we'd have places to stay during football and volleyball weekends. Haley is already being recruited and given them a verbal commitment. I could see a big gathering area. Like our own sports bar. Full kitchen. Lots of couches and televisions."

"I've seen areas like that in big apartment complexes."

"Yes, sort of like that. Only private."

"And I could live here?"

"Well, that would be up to you. You all have to live on campus your freshman year. And you might want to live in the sorority house after that. So, it wouldn't be required. But I will tell you that your father, Phillip, and I shared a townhouse from my sophomore year on, and it was some of the best times in my life. You'd have to put up with us during home game weekends, but for the most part, you'd have the whole place to yourselves. I also think it would be a great investment."

"Could you put in an office?" I ask.

"Like for studying?"

"No, for Hierarchy."

"Oh, they decided to change the name. But, yes, that's a great idea. I heard the idea was conceived during the first trip to the Ozarks."

"Yeah, it was."

"Any chance you'll join us next year? We miss having you there."

"Maybe. The four of us talked about doing the company together. I know they started it this year—without me—but maybe someday, I'll be part of it again."

She turns to the realtor. "Can we see the rooftop space before we go?"

"Of course."

She takes us up there, and the view is pretty cool.

"This would be amazing."

"Exactly what I was thinking." She turns to the realtor and says, "We'll take it."

The realtor looks a little shocked. "Like, you want to make an offer now?"

"Yep." She spouts off a number, asks the realtor to get in touch with the owner, and tells her that we're going to get a late-night snack and to call her in the morning.

We go downstairs and across the street to a sports bar that is still serving food.

"I'm starving," Jadyn says. "But I just realized you were supposed to be in bed early. I can take you back."

"No, this is nice. And I'm kind of hungry, too." I let out a sad sigh.

"Do you want to talk about it, Dani?"

"Talk about what?"

"What's bothering you."

Tears fill my eyes. "When I was home last weekend, Chase and I, um, made up. And decided we were going to be friends again. I mean, it was so easy—surprisingly—to go back into our old roles. To joke. Laugh. Kiss. Have fun. We agreed to work on continuing that. Just being friends. We used to talk at night, before we went to sleep. Even if I had just seen him."

"Really?" Jadyn says. "Phillip and I used to do that, too. That's sweet."

"And we agreed that I would call him at night, when I had free time. He texted me a couple times, and I didn't respond. I should have. And I probably hurt him. Again. But I was waiting until tonight. I knew he'd be home after his game. And I didn't go with my friend to a frat party, so I would have the room to myself and I could do nothing but talk to him. Almost like I was there with him, having pizza. I was even going to suggest we make it a regular thing. Like maybe not worry about talking during the week. With classes, studying, the sorority—pledge meetings and all the activities and mixers—and getting used to it all, it's been a lot. I mean, it's fun—don't get me wrong—but it's been busy. Really busy. And then, while I was waiting to call him"—I stop and take another deep breath—"I saw the video. Of how he asked Lacey to Homecoming."

"You know, she broke up with him this week."

My eyes get big. "She did?"

"Yeah. Haley had taken a picture of you and Chase kissing on his birthday. She stupidly shared it with a friend, who passed it around. Eventually to Lacey."

"Wow."

"It all makes so much more sense now."

"What does?"

"Why Chase asked her today. So early. In such a big way."

"Why do you think that was?"

"Dani, really? You didn't call him all week."

"Oh. I guess that's why he hung up on me."

"He hung up on you?"

"Yeah. I called tonight. Stupidly, the first thing I said was that I saw the video of the proposal. He assumed that was the only reason I'd called. Said it was hard to be BFFs with me when I didn't have time to respond. He said it was good to hear from me but that he had to go and hung up. He probably hates me again."

"He doesn't hate you, Dani."

"I still love him," I say, breaking down. "And we were all so close that summer. Me, Damon, Haley, Chase. And they are all still close. Without me. And last weekend, I even felt like that was back. I just ruined everything."

"Dani, I'd be willing to bet that you didn't."

"You really think, after all this, Chase and I could possibly still have a chance of being together?"

"I think you need to figure out what *being together* means to you. I mean, I understand you are busy, but you couldn't find a *single* moment in six whole days to even send a text?"

"I didn't want anyone to know I was talking to him."

"Why?"

"Because he's still in high school. I don't think the girls in my sorority are like that, but I don't know them well enough yet to know. So, I was trying to wait until I had time alone. And that has been difficult to come by."

"I'm not judging you in any way, but that sounds like a lot of excuses."

I nod my head in agreement.

"At some point, you need to stop making them. It's really too bad you can't do a play-by-play, you know, of that day. Chase watches a lot of game film. Too bad no one recorded the whole thing."

"And you think that would help—to watch it?"

"If you talked through your decision-making each step of the way. How you felt. Maybe." She sighs. "He's coming up for the game tomorrow. Everyone is. Just so you know."

"I did know that. But then when he hung up on me, I sort of forgot."

"I guess you can talk to him tomorrow then."

She closes out our tab and then takes me home.

SATURDAY, SEPTEMBER 14TH

Like that day.

Devaney

SINCE ALL THE sororities on campus are dry, there aren't tailgates at the house, but everyone seems to come here—many hungover from the night before—for brunch and to get ready together before they go off to tailgate.

One of the things I needed to talk to Chase about last night was if he actually would have time to see me since they are here on an official recruiting visit. An official visit equals a packed schedule, but I think since they have been here unofficially before, their schedule might not be quite as full as it would normally be.

And after last night, I suppose the chance of Chase even wanting to see my face, let alone my dorm room, is slim to none.

"Ohmigawd, Dani," my sorority sister Lauren says to me, "your friend Chase is so adorable! He's totally hot, but he seems sweet. Nice. Why can't I ever date a really nice guy?"

Another sorority sister, Amber, says, "Because really nice guys don't usually look like that. Your brother Damon, now, he could charm your pants off." She laughs. "Almost did mine."

"What?" I say.

"Oh, I didn't do anything." She and Lauren start giggling. "Okay, so fine, I kissed him. Whatever."

"When?" I ask. "How did you meet them? Are they outside?" I get up and rush over to the window, looking out into the crowded area.

"No," Amber says. "They came by to see you, but we didn't know you were here, so they left."

"And what was Chase doing while you kissed my brother?" I ask her.

Lauren raises her hand. "He was talking to me. Did you know he's a five-star recruit? A quarterback. And he might come here next year?"

"Might?" I say, my heart dropping into my stomach.

"Well, your brother said *might.* Chase said they were, but your brother said they have to visit more schools before they come to a final decision. And the fact that they are going to the same school together and are BFFs is just, well, friendships like that are so rare."

Amber narrows her eyes. "Oh no. They aren't together, are they? Chase and your brother?"

"Chase and my brother?" I want to laugh in her face. "My brother was just kissing you."

"I know," Amber says. "But they're good-looking. Going to the same school."

"And almost too perfect to be true," Lauren goes on. "Also, Chase models. Did you know that?"

"Yes, I did," I say flatly.

"Anyway! I recognized him! Thought I knew him, but when I couldn't figure out why, Damon was like, *Probably seen one of his ads.* And then I was like, OMG. I ran up to my room and got the ad I cut out with Chase in it. He was with a group of five people, and they were all dressed up for a preppy fall day at college. It's hanging on my bulletin board! So, I made him sign it for me, and we took a picture with me holding it." She grabs her phone. "You have to see it."

I study the photo. Chase is smiling. But he doesn't look all that happy. Probably because Damon dragged him here, kicking and screaming.

"Any idea where they are now?" I ask.

"I'd probably do a bed check." Amber laughs.

"Actually, they were looking for you, Dani," Lauren says. "They said they texted you, but you didn't reply."

Shit.

I run downstairs to the dining room, where I think I left my phone, and see it lit up with texts.

I call Chase, and I'm nearly breathless when he answers.

"Heard you're looking for me."

"Yeah, you weren't at your dorm. Or your house. Met some of your sisters though." He's speaking to me in that tone. The mad tone. The *I really don't want to be talking to you* tone.

I hate that tone.

"Heard that, too. Where are you?"

"Um, about three houses down. You know Damon. He's talking to everyone. Wants to get a feel for college life."

"By feel, does that mean my sorority sister's lips?"

"Ha. Exactly what he means. He cracks me up." And finally, he sounds a little more normal.

"And what about you? Are you kissing anyone?"

"You offering?" he says in a cocky tone. One that sounds more like my brother than Chase.

And that worries me more than him being mad at me.

"I, uh …"

"We'll head that way, I guess," he tells me. "Meet us out front, okay?"

"Okay."

The second I hang up, Amber and Lauren are like, "Are they coming back?"

"Yeah," I say.

"Good, because we want to get their numbers," Lauren says.

Over my dead body.

But I can't really say that. Instead, I go with, "You'd date a younger guy?"

"When he looks like that? Yes. Also, he's already eighteen. I'm eighteen, too. Aren't you?"

"Yeah."

"Your brother is a little younger." Amber shrugs. "But who cares?"

"They're still in high school," I push, wanting to understand if they really would date them.

"So what? They'll be here next year," Lauren says, "and I'll already have first dibs on our team's future quarterback." She grabs my shoulder. "Don't move. I'll be right back."

When I get a text from Damon, I do move, going outside to meet him.

I expect to see Chase.

What I don't expect is to see Lacey draped all over him.

I'm barely out the door when I hear a couple of the girls, who are people-watching from the rocking chairs on the porch, point and go, "Oh, look at those two cuties."

"One of them is with a girl," one says.

"They're hot, regardless," the other counters.

I ignore them and make my way down the grand steps, onto the sidewalk, and to the fence.

I am a college girl. A sorority girl. I am strong, smart, and worldly. I will not let the fact that Lacey is here ruin what should have been a really fun day. I am going to forget last night's stupid video and the fact that Chase hung up on me and greet him like I always would. No, scratch that. I'm going to treat him like what he is—my friend with benefits.

I open the fence, let them in, give my brother a hug, and then give Chase a kiss right on the lips.

"What are you doing?" he whispers.

"Greeting my best friend."

Because it's one thing to have a friends-with-benefits relationship with two girls at the same time; it's another thing completely to hang out with them together.

I mean, what did he expect? For me to act like nothing had happened between us because she's here?

I let go of Chase and then say, "Hey, Lacey! How are you? I didn't know you were coming."

"Well," she says, "Chase asked me to Homecoming last night at the game, and then we hung out, and before he dropped me off, he asked me to come up here today. Which is so cool. I've always wanted to come here. You all talk so highly of the place."

So, he asked her last night. After he hung up on me.

He's trying to make me jealous.

Or they're dating now. Officially.

But I doubt it because I know that would have been all over her feed.

"Chase told me you're thinking of going to Auburn. Are you going to rush?"

"Uh, yeah," she says, seemingly getting over the shock of me kissing Chase on the lips in front of her.

But the thing is, Lacey is a nice girl.

And so am I.

Especially today.

"Awesome. Come on. I'll show you all around."

I act like the belle of the ball—actually, it's not an act. I feel happy to be here. Happy for them to meet my sisters. Especially Chase since we talked in-depth about why I chose this house.

When Lacey goes to use the restroom and Damon is off, flirting somewhere, Chase leans against the corner of the wall and just stares at me.

"You look happy," he says. "In your element."

"I love it here. I really do, Chase. What do you think of all the girls?"

"I understand what you told me about. How they all seem like individuals with varying interests. I like them." He pauses and then cups the side of my face in his palm. "I'm sorry I got mad last night. It was a crazy week. Lacey broke up with me."

"Yeah, your mom told me."

"I was out on the field, asking her. But all I could think about was you," he says, his voice cracking. "It was like that day. And you hadn't bothered to call me all week."

"I'm so sorry. It's just that when we talk, it's always been just us. When I talk to you, I want it to be special. Private. I skipped going to a frat party with my roommate last night, so I could stay home and call you. I was even going to suggest that should be *our* time. Instead of trying to talk during our busy weeks, we—I don't know—maybe, eat pizza together. But then I saw the video. And I was hurt."

"I like your idea," he says, his face brightening. "It's a date."

I smile at him. "Really?"

"On one condition."

"What's that?"

"That you kiss me again before Lacey comes back out."

"Because friends kiss?"

Chase nods in return.

The kiss I give him isn't steamy. It doesn't get me heated up. Instead, it soothes me. And seems to make everything right with the world again.

When our lips part, he says, "Actually, two conditions. If either of us can't make the call, we let the other person know in advance, okay?"

"Okay," I agree.

AFTER THEY TAKE off, one of the girls from the rockers says, "So,

Dani, who were those guys?"

"My brother, Damon; our best friend, Chase; and another friend, Lacey. The boys are here on a football recruitment trip."

"You should introduce me to that Chase guy later," she says.

"He's a high school senior," I explain. Because this girl is older, like twenty-one.

"He sure doesn't look like one. And who cares? He's fine."

I tilt my head at her. "You would date a younger guy?"

"One who looked like that? Definitely. Don't tell me you haven't noticed your not-so-little brother's best friend is hot."

I can't help but laugh. "Oh, I've noticed."

"Boys at my high school didn't look like that. Is he legal?"

"As a matter of fact, he turned eighteen just last week." And what a birthday it was. But I'm interested to hear her thoughts on this. "He's actually not just my brother's best friend. He's mine."

"Oh, the plot thickens."

"So, you really wouldn't care that he's so much younger than you?" I ask.

"Who would care about that?"

"You don't think people would give me crap about it?"

"About what?"

"About the fact that he's still in high school?"

"Is that why you're not together? The age thing? Are you that much older?"

"Five months. But I've always been a year older in school."

"Oh, I get it," she says. "You were one of those girls."

"One of what girls?"

"Well, if I had to guess, in high school, you prided yourself on the fact that you dated older guys. I went through that phase when I was a junior. When I thought only college guys were good enough for me. I thought high school boys—or the ones at my high school anyway—were too immature. But then I came to college and realized age doesn't matter so much as the person. I've dated older guys who are more immature than younger ones. I got a mature vibe from him."

"And my brother?"

"Not as mature, but smart. And he's definitely a charmer."

I roll my eyes. "You're right about that," I say.

"Hey, Dani."

"Yeah?"

"If you do decide the age difference is a problem for you, then give him my number."

WHEN I STOP by the box at the half, Lacey isn't there, but neither is Jadyn, so they probably went somewhere together. And I don't mind that at all.

After greeting my dad, Jennifer, and covering my little sisters' faces with kisses, I saunter over to Chase. "One of the older girls in my sorority wants me to give you her number."

"What for?"

"Because she thinks you're hot and an old soul. She's twenty-one."

"Interesting," he says.

"As in you are interested?"

"I said it's interesting. That she'd be in college and interested in someone still in high school."

"She says that doesn't matter as much in college. The age thing."

"I'm excited to get to college then."

"So you can date older women?"

"Yes, one who happens to be just a mere five months older than me. And for the first time in our lives, maybe it wouldn't be an issue."

"It was definitely not an issue on your birthday," I flirt.

"True."

"And, it's not an issue here."

"Does that translate to us?" he asks.

"Are you saying you think we should renegotiate the terms of our friendship already?"

He smirks at me and raises an eyebrow. "Depends on if you want to give that girl my number."

"Well, considering you have a date for Homecoming and recruitment visits and I have a lot of sorority stuff coming up—"

"We should probably be friends."

"With benefits," I say, pulling him into the bathroom, locking the door, and kissing him.

FRIDAY, OCTOBER 18TH

Started without me.

Devaney

CHASE AND I only managed to do our video chat on two out of the four Friday nights since we'd last seen each other. And even though our parents came up for a couple of football games, Chase wasn't able to attend. We've managed to text a bit off and on. Just enough.

All I know is that I am excited to be home and to spend the weekend with him, but when I get to the house and see the yard decorated with homecoming signs, I realize that I probably won't actually get to spend that much time with him.

Tonight is his game. Tomorrow night, he has the dance. And on Sunday, I have to fly back early.

Even though my family knew what time I would be here, no one is at my house, so I go over to the Mackenzies' and find Jadyn with piles of shirts spread across the kitchen table.

"Help!" she says, giving me a hug in greeting.

"What is all this?"

"This is a whole lot of One Eleven shirts. The kids started with just one option, but they've added more designs. I have to get these organized. I'm really proud of them for starting this company and for it to be doing well already, but with the boys playing and Haley cheering, I've gotten stuck delivering them. I have a bunch of people stopping by this afternoon to pick them up before the game. Thought I'd put them all on a table in the garage. Want to help me?"

"Sure," I say, looking around the room with a smile. "You know, sometimes, I feel more at home here than I do in my own house."

"Why's that, Dani?"

"Maybe because it's next door. Maybe it was always a reprieve from the rules at my house. Maybe it's because I relax every time I walk in the front door. Or maybe it's the cookies," I say, walking over to the snack bar and getting one out from under a domed lid. After I take a bite, I grin. "Actually, it's definitely the cookies."

"Or maybe," she offers, "it's because Chase lives here."

"That, too. How was your first semester of college? Was it a big adjustment for you?"

"Well, my parents had passed away in April of my senior year, so for me, college was a needed change of scenery. A new adventure to sink my teeth into. Something to take my mind off missing them. Being at home, all those memories were both comforting and painful. And because of it, let's just say that I embraced college life fully."

"How did you turn out so normal? If something like that had happened to my parents—"

"After my parents died, I worried that I had taken them for granted. I know things have been a little strained with your mom the past few years. How are things now? Since her big revelation."

"Good, honestly. Her and Van came up for one of the games. They took me out for dinner after. It was nice. But I sort of keep waiting for her to tell me she was just kidding."

"I think your relationship will continue to grow. You always have been a daddy's girl though. I was, too. I loved sports."

"And my mom couldn't throw a spiral pass to save her ass."

"My mom took me dress shopping for my eighth-grade grad-uation. Wanted me in something pink and blinged out."

"And you got a daughter who loves bling."

"Yes, I did—two of them. Seems Emers is going to follow in Haley's footsteps on that," she says with a laugh. "And I've learned to like a little bling myself. Although Haley hasn't talked the boys into doing any of these with bling." She holds up one of the shirts on the table.

I take it from her and study it. "This is really cool. I like the font and how the One Eleven is placed inside a circle. It's so simple, but perfect. Who designed it?"

"Haley. She's got a natural talent for this. Has been studying how to make graphics and doing research on everything from athletic to designer brands. And it's really cool for all of us to be able to support both boys in one shirt. Pick one out to wear tonight. There are three designs to choose from. A football-jersey style with their combined numbers, a Shock and Awe design, and the One Eleven logo you're holding," she says. "I'll be right back. I need to run out to the car."

I hold the shirt in my hand, and instead of seeing the cool logo design, my mind is playing back a memory from our summer at the lake.

"Speaking of college," Damon said, "where are we all going?"

"Are we all going to college together?" Haley asked.

"I hope so," Damon replied. "It's going to suck if Chase and I don't get to play college ball together."

"Mom wants me to go to college on one of the coasts," I said. "Has she said anything about that to you?"

"No. She knows better than to try and manipulate me like that," he said.

"What do you mean?"

"You know Mom," he said with a sigh. "I love her and all, but

she has different life priorities. She wants you to go to a school on the coast so that you won't end up stuck, living next door to your best friends. So that you will expand your world." He said the last three words in a voice that sounded freakishly like Mom's.

"And you don't think expanding our worlds is a good thing?"

"Sure it is, but we can travel and meet people lots of different ways. Chase and I met a ton of cool guys playing seven-on-seven ball this summer. We traveled to four states to play and saw the sights. We go to California often. We've made friends there. We have a private jet basically at our disposal, for goodness' sake. But then, I don't have to land a man in college."

"Damon," Haley chastised, "neither do we. We'll be there to get an education, so we can get good jobs so that we don't need a man. Of course, that doesn't mean we don't want one. It just means we'll be able to support ourselves financially either way."

I raised the dark beer sitting in front of me in the air. "Hear, hear."

I noticed that Chase had been pretty quiet during this conversation so far. He opened his mouth to speak but then picked up his still-full beer.

He set it back down without taking a drink and said to me, "The question wasn't where your mom wants you to go to college, Dani. It's, where do you want to go? You'll be the first of us."

"As a kid, I always imagined myself going to Nebraska."

"Me, too," Haley said.

"Me three," Damon added.

"And where do you think you'll commit?" I asked Chase since he didn't say, Me four.

"A lot of schools have been watching both of us since we were in middle school," Damon said in response. "Nebraska is just one of them. And even though it's where we want to go, we have to think of what's going to be best for us. Where do we have the best chance of playing, of starting, of winning, of getting drafted?"

"You have one more year before the schools can officially recruit *you, right?" Haley asked.*

"Yeah, start of our junior year. How did you know that?" Damon asked her.

"They were talking about it on my elite volleyball team," she replied. "A lot of the girls I play with are older. And the camps they go to are sponsored by colleges as a way to recruit before they can actually be recruited. I've never told anyone this, but I think I might like to do that. Play college volleyball."

"You have a killer serve. That's for sure," Damon said. "Oh shit. Actually, you could be part of my and Chase's brand."

"Your brand?" both Haley and I asked.

"Yeah, I know you both think we sit around, playing video games all the time, but we are actually making plans for our future. Take our brand, for instance. Chase is going to major in business and eventually get his law degree."

"So you can be your own agent?" I asked him. Why did I not know that?

"It will be nice to understand the legal side of that, of course, but we'll need it for our business. We'll be doing contracts with other athletes," Chase explained.

"And I'm going to major in marketing and sports management, so I'll understand the other side of it."

"What is your brand going to do?" I asked.

"Oh, it will be an athletic line. Sportswear. Football first, every other sport to follow," Damon said.

"Should we tell them the name of it?" Chase asked Damon.

Damon fist-bumped him and said to Haley and me, "Only if you promise not to tell anyone. We don't want someone to steal it before we get the chance."

"We promise," Haley and I said.

"It's called Hierarchy. Our logo is going to have a crown on the bottom and our name on the top. And, of course, in the crown, there will be diamonds."

"Run faster. Jump higher. Ball harder," Chase said. "That's our *slogan. Or sales pitch thingy."*

"I love it!" Haley said. "And I want in. I'm going to major in design. I'm just not sure if I'll go architectural or interior, like my mom, or into clothing and fashion."

"Wouldn't that be amazing?" Damon said. "We could all work together."

"What about you?" Haley asked me.

"I'm going to be a sportscaster," I said out loud. It's the first time I've told this to anyone other than Chase. But it feels right.

"Which would be sweet," my brother said. "You could get us even more contacts and could wear our stuff on TV. Just so we all agree, we'd love to go to the same college together, but if it doesn't work out to be what's best for us, we'll still end up working together." He started to pick up his glass, like he was going to toast to it, but seemed to think better of it and held out his pinkie instead. "Pinkie swear."

"Pinkie swear," we all said, hooking our fingers together.

"As long as I'm top dog in the hierarchy," I said with a laugh. "I am the oldest."

My brother tilted his head, and for once in his life, he didn't have a comeback for me. "Deal," he said.

I smile at the memory but realize that they've started without me. Which makes me sad.

Haley comes through the garage door the next time it opens, not her mom. She's dressed in her game-day uniform, and there are glittery red strands woven through her braid.

"You look adorable!" I screech, tossing my arms around her and giving her a hug. Because of volleyball and cheer competitions, she hasn't been up to a single game, so I haven't seen her since Chase's birthday weekend.

"Thanks," she says. "What do you think of the shirts?"

"They are amazing. You're really talented, Hay."

"We were supposed to work on them together," she says softly.

"I know. We pinkie swore, but you haven't asked me for help. I'd love to though."

"Good," she says with a grin. "You can start by wearing one to the game tonight. Which is your favorite?"

"This one," I tell her, picking up the One Eleven jersey.

"That's my personal favorite, too."

"How many shirts have you sold?"

"We're on our third printing, and we're only halfway through the season. Damon handles the brand's social media. We all brainstormed on designs. It's been a fun project."

"I bet."

She squints her eyes at me. "Are you serious about us working together?"

"Absolutely. Now, tell me all about Homecoming while we sort through these. Do you have a date, or are you going with friends?"

"Date," she says with a smile before pulling a long chain out from her shirt. It's got a guy's class ring dangling from the end of it. "Boyfriend actually, as of today. And you'll never guess who."

"Who?"

"Pace Williams! He's been coming to my volleyball games all year, and he would talk to me a lot, but I kind of thought it was a *being nice to my friend's little sister* sort of deal. I was so surprised when he asked me to Homecoming. And he did it in the cutest way. He decorated a volleyball and tossed it to me at practice. I figured Chase and Damon would have a fit about it. But I guess Pace told them he liked me, and they sort of approved of it before he ever asked me to hang out. We had our first date on September the eighteenth after one of my games, and today, on our one-month anniversary, he asked me to be his girlfriend."

"That's so cool. I like Pace. He's really nice."

"And so cute, right?"

"He is very cute. I'm happy for you."

"I'm happy for me, too. Homecoming is going to be a blast, and I love my dress. But I feel so bad for Chase."

"Why?"

"Lacey has the chicken pox!"

"The chicken pox?"

"Yeah, she got it from her little brother. She doesn't really have very many pox, but she's been running a fever for a couple days, and she's contagious."

"So, she can't even go to the dance?"

"Nope. No parade. No cheering at the game. No dance. And she's up for Homecoming Queen."

"Oh, that's awful," I think, actually feeling really bad for her. "What's Chase going to do?"

"He hasn't said for sure. A group of us are supposed to go in a limo together. Me and Pace, Chase and Lacey, Damon and his date, Bella, and a couple other guys on the team and their dates. We got a party limo, and we're going to the Plaza to take photos by all the pretty fountains, then dinner, and the dance."

"I'll be at the dance," I say.

"That's right! You have to crown the next king. I'm really sorry," she says, a blush spreading across her face. "I totally forgot about that. I didn't even know you would be here this weekend. But I'm so glad you are. You should come with us! Like, for dinner and stuff."

"Oh, no. That would be weird. I'm only going to the dance. I have to be there a half hour before the coronation, and then I'll leave right after. I had my homecoming dances; it's your turn now."

She holds her hands together and happily spins around in a circle. "Yes, it is."

I hear noise coming from upstairs, and a few moments later, Emersyn and Winger come down the steps.

"Me and Winger take nap," she says, patting the dog, "so we

can see Chase play football!"

"Does Winger get to go to the game?" I tease.

"No," Haley says, "but she's obsessed with that dog. I swear, they are best friends."

Haley picks up Emersyn and says, "Come on. Let's go tell Mommy you're awake."

"And I'd better go see where my family is," I tell Haley.

"Oh, I saw them pulling in the driveway when I got home."

"Awesome. I'll head that way."

And I'm about to—until Chase comes walking through the front door.

"Hey!" he says, his face brightening. He rushes toward me, picks me up, and swings me around. "You're just the girl I was going to see."

"You were?"

"Yeah, I figured you were home. I was going to drop my backpack in my room and then go to your house. But since you're already here"—he gives me a wicked grin—"why don't you help me with that?"

Needless to say, I follow him up the stairs.

When we get into his room, he sets his backpack down and pulls me into his arms. I expect him to kiss me right away, but he just hugs me.

"You okay?" I ask him. "Nervous about tonight?"

"It's been a stressful week," he says, still holding me tight.

I don't say anything else, just nuzzle my nose into his neck and try to transfer my positive energy to him through my tight embrace.

Finally, he lets out a deep sigh, lets go of me, and pulls me onto the bed with him.

"Lacey has the chicken pox," he says.

"Yeah, Haley told me. That sucks. I feel bad for her."

"You do?" he asks, studying me closely.

"Of course I do, Chase. It would suck to be up for queen, to miss the parade, the game, the dance, the crowning, the after-parties."

"I sent her flowers this morning to cheer her up, and I wish there was more I could do. But Pace's dad—he's a pediatrician—strongly advised me against it. Her case is mild, but she's very contagious. And I can't risk missing a game."

"Still, that was really sweet, Chase."

He nods his head.

"Has all that been a distraction from your preparation?"

"Fortunately, our opponent doesn't have a very good record, but yeah, it's been a distraction. She's freaking out, and then there's all the usual festivities. It's just a lot."

"I can imagine. And I talked to Haley. It's so cool she's dating Pace. And that you are all going together."

"You know, you could come to dinner with us, if you wanted. Since we all have to be there anyway."

"Haley offered the same thing, but—oh my gosh, Chase, remember my freshman homecoming, when you got me chicken and set up dinner in the garage?"

He laughs. "I thought I was so suave."

"You were actually. It was sweet."

"You want to do that again? Keep me all to yourself?"

"I'm sure you want to go in the limo with your friends."

"I was thinking of bailing. Don't want to be the third wheel, you know."

"Yeah, but it's not just about your date. It's about the memories you'll make with your friends. With your sister."

"If you really feel that way, you're going to come with me. We never did get to go to Homecoming together. I'm assuming somewhere in that closet of yours, you have a fabulous dress you could wear."

I laugh.

"What?" he says.

"I was told to wear something simple but pretty for the crowning, but I do actually have a gorgeous dress that I've never worn. My mom made me get it when we were shopping this summer because it looked so nice on me. I thought it was silly, but"—I grin, warming up to the thought. The thought of going to the dance with Chase. It's like I'm getting the most incredible do-over ever—"I'm glad now."

"It's settled then." He glances at his watch. "Kiss me. One more time. Tell me I'm going to have a great game."

I do as he asked. Kiss him deeply and then gently slide my hand down his throwing arm. "You're going to have one of your best games ever. That's what I think. Let's see, your best ever game was last year, just over four hundred yards passing. Four twenty-six, right?"

"Yeah," he says, looking at me in amazement. "I'm surprised you know that."

"I know all your stats, Chase. I also predict, tonight, you will have something like four sixty."

"All right, well, what do I get if I do?"

"Hmm. Fame and glory, I would suspect," I tell him, running my finger down his chest. "But I could probably throw in a couple of pizzas after the game." I press my lips against his ear. "And me. In the tent."

He kisses the side of my face. "I like the sound of that. Okay, so I have to get some food and then head to school."

"And I need to go see my family. Good luck, tonight, Chase."

Something to remember.

Chase

I ONCE READ that sports is ninety percent mental and ten percent physical, but even though most people agree with that sentiment, the large majority of sports practices revolves around physical as opposed to mental abilities. Damon and I are really lucky that his dad was an elite athlete because even when we were kids who didn't really comprehend the importance, he was teaching us mental toughness and having us reading books about a positive mind-set.

Imagine an athlete who needs to drop a long putt, hit a buzzer-ending three-point shot or game-winning free throw, make a two-point conversion after triple overtime. And although we try to avoid those situations by playing solidly all game, many times, it happens to a player—that single moment where it feels like the whole game is riding on your shoulders. That it's up to you whether your team wins or loses. And those moments can be quite daunting, mentally. If you get the correct result and win, you're the hero. If you don't, people say you choked. It isn't due to lack of skill when that happens; overinvestment and fear of failure are often the cause.

Isn't that weird—that fear of failing can make you do the very thing you fear?

For the last few years, I've been working my mental "muscles"—confidence, intensity, motivation—as a part of my daily practice. By using mental strategies—such as controlled breathing, imagery, and positive self-talk, combined with goal-setting and routine development—an athlete can maintain the optimal physical and mental states for being successful.

We've all seen it happen. A quarterback throws a couple inter-ceptions or takes a few sacks, and all of a sudden, the whole team starts playing poorly and making mistakes. Failure snowballs into those embarrassingly lopsided losses.

As a quarterback, who is the leader of the offense on the field, it's my job to control the huddle and the mental management of the team. How we rebound from a missed opportunity does affect all of us. I've never lacked motivation. I have a large amount of internal drive. Not pressure, but I just like to succeed. And in football, each play is a chance to do so. A series of small successes can lead to really big success.

The team we are playing tonight has one of the worst records in our district, and games like these often bite athletes in the butt because they assume they will win, that it will be easy. So, instead of focusing on the current game, they look forward to the big opponent they might face the following week. And we've all seen that happen, too. The unranked team with nothing to lose, playing out of their minds and knocking off one of the best teams in the nation.

And you always wonder, *How does that happen?* And the an-swer to that is that their heads weren't in the game.

It's a personal and team goal to have another undefeated season, winning the state championship. I never have personal goals for myself regarding yardage gained or number of passes thrown, but tonight, I will admit, Dani has made me think twice about that. And although I definitely want her in the tent in my room tonight after the game, it would go against all my mental training to focus solely on the goal she set for me.

But, I might have to give it a shot tonight. Our offensive plan already revolves around us airing it out. Showcasing our passing and receiving ability against a team with a weak secondary.

So, when the offense comes off the field mid-third quarter, ahead by three touchdowns, I know Coach is probably going to put my backup in soon. So, for fun, I ask how many passing yards I've had tonight. The answer is four hundred and eighteen.

"Mackenzie," Coach says, "you want one more set of downs?"

Honestly, I know from a possible injury standpoint, it's smart to get taken out of the game when we are winning big, but it's something I've always hated.

I'd like to be out there playing the whole time, so I answer, "Yeah. What would you think of trying that play we were working on?"

"Ah hell, why not? Give this homecoming crowd something to remember."

Our opponent gets a field goal and then kicks off to us. The offensive unit goes out to the twenty-yard line. Instead of lining up under center, Pace—our running back—takes what is called the wildcat formation, meaning the ball is snapped directly to him. Technically, whoever takes the snap, regardless of their position, becomes the "quarterback" for the play, and usually, the wildcat is done so that there's no need for a handoff. The running back can get snapped the ball and immediately take off running. In this case though, Pace takes two steps back and throws the ball to me laterally, meaning I'm still behind the line of scrimmage.

In the meantime, Damon is doing what he loves the most, shrugging off his defender and flying down the field as fast as he can, which, in this case, isn't as hard as it should be because his defender is sticking closer to the line in anticipation of the run.

I launch the ball down the field, and Damon catches it in stride and runs into the end zone for the score.

And the crowd goes nuts.

Coach slaps me on the back and says, "Son, I gotta tell you, I was expecting a fun little pass and score here. What I wasn't expecting was for you to throw the ball from the sixteen to somewhere near the opposing team's ten-yard line. Well over seventy yards in the air. We're going to have to do some digging, but that's got to be some kind of record."

AFTER THE GAME, the parking lot, which is usually practically empty by now, seems to be in full-on celebration mode. The team comes out of the locker room to cheers, and everyone is talking about *the play*, *the throw*, and *the catch*. It's exciting, but there's only one person I want to see right now.

And she's sitting in my truck.

Of course she would know the code to unlock the doors. It's her birthdate.

The driver's door is open, her long legs are dangling off the side of the seat, and she's got a big smile on her face.

After getting a bunch of high fives, signing a few autographs for kids, and hugging my family, I finally make my way there. She jumps out of the truck and straight into my arms and kisses me.

"Overachiever," she says with a grin.

"So much for mental preparation. You might have to give me a goal for all my games."

"The family wants to go out for pizza to celebrate. You okay with that?" she asks.

"Are *you* okay with that?"

"I think it will be fun. And after a game like that, you guys deserve it."

"As long as there will be some tent time after the celebration."

She runs her fingers through my hair and says, "I think that is a given."

WE END UP at a local sports bar. Their kitchen typically closes at ten, but on Friday nights after a home game, they make an exception, taking orders until everyone is served.

"Hell of a game, boys," Pace's dad says. A thought that is echoed by our families. "I have a feeling that play of yours is going to get some national recognition. The video the school posted online already has a ton of hits and was liked by two of the big sports networks."

Damon and Pace are pumped about this.

The fun thing about this sports bar and why Damon comes here after every game and always wants me to is because the place is full of people who were just at the game. He works the crowd, knowing and talking to everyone from old guys to little kids. My mom says that his dad was the same way, and it's something I've struggled with. I want to be accessible to fans, especially as my career progresses, but while Damon gets hyped up, talking to so many people and feeding off their energy, I find too much of it drains me.

When Emersyn starts to get cranky around midnight, I feel her. I'm tired and ready to go home, too. Jennifer boxes up the leftovers, so Damon, who probably didn't eat a bite, can have some later, and then we all head out.

Dani rides home with me, and I can't help but glance over at her. She's got on a short, almost-cheerleading-style skirt with one of our new One Eleven jerseys tucked into it. On her feet are a pair of black cowboy boots with a brightly colored embroidered design that matches our team colors.

"I have a love-hate relationship with my truck," I tell her.

"Why?"

I look at her expectantly.

"Oh. Yeah," she says. "We christened it the first day you got it. Out by the lake."

"That's where the love part comes in."

"And the hate?" she asks softly.

"Getting in it and remembering that moment when we were no longer friends."

"Do you remember the music that was playing that night?"

"Uh, something country?" I reply.

"Yep. Did you know that I can't listen to it anymore?" she

says as we pull into my driveway.

"Like, *any* country songs?" I ask incredulously.

"That's correct. They all make me sad."

"You took out a whole genre of music because of me?"

To this, I am shocked. She seemed to get over it all way faster than I did.

She nods her head. "You weren't the only one who was hurting, Chase."

I've replayed that day over in my head so many times, trying to recall everything that was said, wondering if I should have done something differently, but all I can remember is the crushing hurt.

She undoes her seat belt and leans toward me. "Regardless of what happened between us, I've always loved you, Chase." She gives me a kiss and gets out of the car, saying, "I'll sneak over later."

Teach you a cheer.

Devaney

WE GET HOME the same time as everyone else, so I walk in through the garage door with Dad, Jennifer, and Damon. Angel barks at us and rushes up, her tail wagging furiously, happy to see us.

She's followed by Weston and Easton, who both yell, "Mama!"

"What are they doing up?" Jennifer says to the babysitter, who just shrugs.

"They both went down at eight thirty, as usual, but Weston woke up an hour ago. I tried keeping her quiet, but then Easton woke up, too."

Easton is carrying her blanket and doesn't look thrilled to be awake. Jennifer picks her up and snuggles her into her chest.

Weston pouts. "I no go to football game."

She goes zooming out into the family room and runs back with a set of pom-poms. She usually gets to go to Damon's game. But since they knew they'd probably be going out afterward tonight, they got a babysitter, and Weston is clearly not happy about it.

Jennifer, who always has a smile on her face, suddenly looks exhausted.

"Hey, Westie," I say. "Why don't you come in my room? I'll teach you a cheer, read you a story, and put you to bed. How does that sound?"

She waves her little pom-poms and goes, "Yay!!!"

"Thank you," my dad says to me. He turns to Jennifer. "Why don't you go get ready for bed yourself, maybe run a warm bath, and I'll tuck Easton in?"

"That sounds wonderful," she says, letting the babysitter out the front door.

"And you, little miss," Damon says, grabbing Weston and picking her up, "look like you need a piggyback ride upstairs."

"Piggy! Piggy!" she yells and shakes her pom-poms in Damon's face as he makes his way upstairs.

I follow them, laughing, and thinking that it's good to be home.

Can't risk that.

Chase

I TELL MY family good night and go up to my room. I change clothes, lie on my bed, and then close my eyes.

I hear my phone buzzing from inside my duffel bag. I let out a heavy sigh. I haven't checked my phone since before the game and wasn't planning to until tomorrow morning, but I get up and grab it in case it's Dani.

What I find are a lot of texts and direct message notifications, some of them from the coaches hoping to recruit me and quite a few from journalists about the game and specifically the play tonight. But the one that just came through is from Lacey.

Lacey: *I'm home sick. Missing out on one of the biggest moments of my high school career, and now, I find out that you're taking Dani Diamond to the dance?*

I don't bother replying. This deserves a call.

"Hey," I say when she answers.

"Chase, really?" she says, her voice sounding like she's been crying.

"Where in the world did you hear that?" I ask her.

"Does it matter?" she snaps back.

"I guess not."

"So, you aren't exactly denying it?"

"As you know, last year's queen comes back to crown this year's king."

"Yep," she says.

I'm starting to get one-word answers, which is never good.

"I was thinking of bailing on the whole thing since you

weren't going to be there. I thought I would surprise you, bring you dinner and your corsage, and only go to the dance for the court part."

"You were going to do that?" she asks, sounding a little brighter.

"Yeah, Lacey. I know it has to suck, missing everything."

"It does. That's really sweet, Chase."

"Well, when I asked Pace's dad—he's a pediatrician—if I could be around you since I already had the chicken pox, he said no, that I could get it again. And I just can't risk that. I've already been searching my body every day, looking for spots."

"I think you're good. I didn't see you the few days I was probably most contagious. We were too busy getting the float ready for the parade. I'm praying none of the girls on the squad get it."

"Anyway, I was telling Dani I was thinking of not going, and she said that it wasn't just about the date part; it's about the memories I'll make with my friends. And my sister. I told her if she really felt that way, she needed to come, too. Like, in the limo with us." I'm telling the truth—that's exactly what I said. But I also know that I'm downplaying it because I do kind of see it as a date. This whole friends-with-benefits thing, which is supposed to make things easier for us, is actually surprisingly complicated.

"So, you're just all going together?"

"Yeah."

"Everyone is going to think it's a date."

"You know I don't care what everyone thinks, Lacey."

I can practically hear her rolling her eyes. "I know." She lets out a pathetic-sounding sigh and then says, "Congrats on a great game, Chase. I'll talk to you later."

Snuggle up.

Devaney

THE CHEER-TEACHING, STORY-READING, putting-Weston-to-sleep process takes much longer than I expected, and it's nearly one thirty before I'm finally ready to go over to Chase's.

I run back in my room, change into something cute but comfy, and wash my face.

I grab my phone and check it, expecting to see a message from him, wondering where I am. There isn't one, but I head over there anyway.

When I sneak into his room, I find him fast asleep. The tent is up in the corner, and although I definitely want to be with him in that way, it's not all I want. So, I slip under the covers and snuggle up next to him. He rolls over, wraps me in his arms, puts his lips on my shoulder, and murmurs my name before going back to sleep.

You're here now.

Chase

I WAKE UP sometime in the middle of the night, tangled up with Dani. And it's the absolute best feeling. I move her hair and sprinkle kisses across her neck and shoulder.

She responds by rolling over and kissing me. "You were crashed when I got here. I'd said I'd put Weston to bed, and I hadn't expected it to take so long. I'm sorry."

"You're here now," I say, sliding my hand down between her thighs. "That's all that matters."

And in the scheme of my life, it really is.

SATURDAY, OCTOBER 19TH

Incredibly sweet.

Devaney

I SNUCK BACK home early this morning, and it was a good thing that I did, because in what seemed like five minutes—but was really a couple of hours—later, my little sisters come barreling in my room.

"Dani, Dani!" Weston yells. "Pancakes!"

Easton crawls up into bed with me while I hear Weston screaming down the hall.

"Day-Day! Pancakes!"

"I sleepy," Easton says to me.

"I feel ya, girl," I say to her, pulling her under the blankets with me.

She puts her thumb in her mouth and closes her eyes.

But sleep is not to be had.

"No sleep!" Weston screams when she comes back into my room. She gets on the bed and starts jumping. "No sleep! No sleep! Mama makes pancakes because Dani home from college! We eat! We eat pancakes. With smiley faces! And blueberries!"

I squint my eyes open. "Maybe you should lie down with Easton and me. You look tired," I say, hoping I can convince her while at the same time knowing it will do no good. Once she puts her mind to something, there's no changing it.

Damon walks down the hall. His hair is sticking up, he's shirtless, and he doesn't look too thrilled about being up either, but he sees the girls on my bed, gets a naughty gleam in his eyes, and takes off running toward us.

"Better watch out!" I tell Weston, who screeches with delight when Damon flies onto the bed and gently tackles and then tickles her.

"What's all this noise about?" he asks as Weston giggles.

Easton peeks her head up and says, "I tired."

"We're all tired," Damon says, ruffling her hair. "But I bet you're hungry."

She nods her head in agreement.

Damon then says, "Westie, do you know what's for breakfast?"

She gives him a playful swat and says, "You're silly. I just told you."

"I was asleep," he says.

She rolls her eyes and starts screaming again, "Pancakes! Bacon! And blueberries!"

"What if I'm not hungry?" he asks, snatching her off the bed and carrying her upside down.

"Ahh!" she yells. "You're always hungry."

He looks at me and grins. "Guess it's time to go eat."

"SO, YOU'RE GOING in the limo with everyone?" Jennifer asks me at breakfast.

"Uh, how did you know that?"

"Everyone knows that."

"Well, maybe. Chase asked if I wanted to go, and it sounds like fun, but I wanted to ask Damon and Haley if they were cool with it."

"Of course we're cool with it," Damon says, shoving another

bite of pancakes dripping with maple syrup in his mouth. "It will be fun."

"I just don't want anyone to think it's, like, a date, you know. Chase feels bad for Lacey getting the chicken pox."

"Yeah, that sucks," Damon says. "But Chase was trying to back out, and if you go, he'll go. And he needs to go. It's our senior year! The limo is half the fun."

"I told him that. Plus, I know Haley is so excited. What do you think about her and Pace together?"

"It's pretty new. But I fully approve because Pace knows Chase and I will kick his ass if he messes with her."

"Haley was impressed that he asked you both if you were okay with him asking her to Homecoming."

"That was pretty cool. I thought it was a little odd that he had developed a sudden interest in the girls' volleyball team and always wanted to hang out at Chase's house. Our little Hay Girl is growing up, isn't she?"

"Yeah, she is," Jennifer says as she reaches down to sneak a piece of pancake to Angel. Although it's probably not necessary. She's smart enough to sit under the high chair, where there tends to be plenty of scraps flying around. Not to mention, it delights Easton when Angel sits and wags her tail, causing her to toss her pieces on purpose. "I got to go dress shopping with her and Jadyn, and although she always looks cute and fashionable, with full hair and makeup, she's going to look much older."

"And of course, she is probably thrilled about that." I laugh. "I always wanted to look older and more sophisticated when I was her age."

"So did I," Jennifer says, shaking her head and laughing. "Now, I wish I could look younger!"

Her phone rings, and she jumps up and screeches. "Oh my gosh! They're here! My babies are finally here!"

"Who's here?" I ask as she runs out the door.

Damon drops his fork and follows her. "Her cars!"

"WELL, I GUESS it's official," I say, seeing Jennifer's exotic cars all lined up with some form of *Diamond* personalized plates on the back. "You're a Diamond."

"And almost all my babies are here with me."

Jennifer has kept the name Jennifer Edwards since she and Dad got married, but now with two kids, she's changing it to Diamond. She hasn't decided if she will for her acting career, but it doesn't matter that much right now. When she was pregnant with Easton, she stopped taking on new roles and took a hiatus from work.

"Good timing, too," Jennifer says. "I think I might be pregnant again."

Dad's eyes get huge. "Are you serious? Is that why you've been so tired?"

She grins and nods. "I'm a little late, so we'll have to see."

"That's more exciting than the cars," Dad says to her. He's got Easton on his hip while holding Weston's hand.

Damon is moving around the cars. We've seen them before out in LA, but I know he's dying to drive them all.

"I think I'm going to drive a different one for each day of the week," Damon says to me. "Let's see. Maserati Monday, Ferrari Friday—no, that won't work. Maybe we go alphabetically. Bentley Monday. No, that sounds dumb. McLaren Monday, Bentley Tuesday—no, shoot, it's too hard to decide. Maybe Sunday could be like a free day."

"You could drive Chase's truck," I tease.

"Speaking of Chase," Chase says, sneaking up behind us, wrapping his arms around my waist, and pulling my back against his chest. He leans down and kisses the side of my neck. And it surprises me, especially considering Jennifer and my dad are out here. "Haley just left to go to the spa with some of her friends, said to tell you she wished you could go but there were no more appointments."

"That's okay. I got a pedicure earlier this week and can paint my own nails."

Damon is now sitting in one of the cars while Jennifer stands next to the door, spouting off a million facts about it.

"Why don't I come up to your room and watch you get ready?" he suggests. "Or you can get ready in mine?"

I END UP back in Chase's room, lying across his bed while he shows me the suit he's going to wear tonight.

"Is it hard to believe that just a year ago, you were getting crowned queen?" Chase asks me.

"You didn't watch," I say sadly, remembering how he was going to escort me after my date ditched me.

"I couldn't," he says quickly, hurt flashing across his face. "I knew you won and all. Homecoming is a tough time for me, honestly."

"Me, too. I don't have a very good track record."

Chase smiles. "You're right; you don't. Last year, that Baker guy ditched you. Junior year, Hunter asked you but then got back together with Taylor. Sophomore year, you went with a group of girls, your limo broke down, and you were stuck on the freeway for, like, two hours, waiting for a tow truck. Maybe we shouldn't have asked you to come with us."

"I did have one good year. Freshman."

"You were supposed to go with Dalton."

He hangs his suit back up and then sits on the bed next to me. I lay my head in his lap and stare up at him.

"You told me you'd take me to the Eiffel Tower. Hard to compete with that," I say as he gently strokes my hair back off my face.

"And instead, you ended up with fried chicken in the garage.

The decor was a little cringeworthy. I was lame."

I shake my head and say seriously, "No, Chase, there was nothing lame about it. What you did for me was incredibly sweet. You made me feel special. Like a princess. It's not about the decor; it's about what we shared."

"I guess it was your first time, wasn't it?" He winks at me, teasing.

"For fried chicken and champagne, yes. Someday, maybe we—"

"Could do it again?" he says, finishing my sentence.

"Yeah, although I guess the whole point is that it's to celebrate something special."

"And we haven't had a moment like that since ..." He stops and looks up at the ceiling, trying to remember.

"That summer," I say softly.

I figured he'd look upset when I said it, but he doesn't.

He bends down and kisses my forehead. "It's been too long. We need to change that."

I smile up at him. "Yeah, we do."

So many memories.

Chase

WHEN HALEY GOT home from her spa appointment, Dani went to get ready with her. And I started making plans. While I want Dani to come in the limo with us, it feels awkward or weird maybe to have the exact same plan, just inserting a different girl into it.

Because Dani isn't just some girl.

I think about what we talked about earlier. About how other

than winning queen last year, none of her homecomings ever really worked out the way she'd hoped.

This year, I want to make it special.

My plans with Lacey were to go in the limo, take photos around the Plaza, have a nice dinner, and then go to the dance.

I go over to my desk, find the folder that has all the photos in it from the birthday confetti toss, and sift through them to find the one I'm looking for.

I think about the pretend homecoming in our garage.

And I know I'm going to need some help.

I run downstairs and call out, "Hey, Mom!"

I'M DRESSED IN a suit and ready to go when Damon, Pace, and the other guys going with us—Jax, Luis, and Reed—arrive.

Pace glances at his watch. "So, the girls are supposed to be here at four?"

"You know they will all be late," Damon says. "Jennifer said to plan on pictures at around four thirty."

"It's crazy what girls do to get ready for these things," Jax says. He's a big guy of Samoan descent, who I am fortunate to have guarding my blind side when I'm on the field. "I woke up late, worked out, got a haircut, and talked to my uncle about my tattoo. I'm ready to get it now, but my mom says I have to wait until I turn eighteen in January."

"Did you finally decide on a design?" Pace asks with a grin.

It's a running joke that Jax will never get a tattoo because he can't make a decision to save his life. Pace, on the other hand, already has three of them.

"Yep. This is *the one*," Jax says.

He pulls out his phone and shows us a really cool Polynesian design. He's been showing us *the one* for about two years now—of which none have been the same. I can see why his mom wants him to wait.

And that's when it hits me. I like our One Eleven logo, but I have always felt it is a little too simple. That it is missing something. And now I know exactly what it needs—angel wings wrapped around the current logo. After Homecoming, I'll have Haley draw something up. But for now, I need to focus on the present.

"So, wanted to update you guys," I say. "You all know Lacey is sick, so I invited Dani to come with us. She has to be at the dance to crown this year's king. But we're going to do things a little differently than planned."

I tell them the rest of it and get their agreement and understanding.

"And I've got a backpack with a vodka-filled water bottle," Damon says.

"Just don't get my sister drunk," I tell him.

He rolls his eyes at me. "He's been my best friend my entire life, and he still doubts me. Trust me, no one is going to do anything that might get us kicked off the team. In fact, if you prefer we have a few shots now and leave it here, I'm cool with that."

"Honestly, that's probably smart," Luis, our team kicker, says. "The last thing any of us wants to have to deal with is a drunk date."

"Word," Reed, our cornerback, says in agreement.

"Let's go wait in the basement. Watch a game or *something*," Damon suggests with a grin.

I look at my backpack sitting by the door and know there's something in it that could get me into trouble, but tonight, for once, I'm willing to take the risk.

I'm going through a mental checklist, making sure I've thought of everything before following the guys, when Dani practically floats down the staircase, taking my breath away.

She's in a creamy-colored gown that has spaghetti straps,

highlighting tan shoulders. Her long waves are tousled like she could have been outside, riding bikes in the breeze with me just a few seconds before. I stare in wonder, so many memories of growing up with her by my side flashing through my brain.

She notices me and goes, "Chase, you scared me. I didn't see you sitting there. Where is everyone?"

"The guys are all here. Just went downstairs."

"Why aren't you with them?"

I shake my head and smile. "I was making sure I had everything ready for tonight. But I think I was meant to be here. To see you walk down those stairs. Just now. You look stunning."

She continues walking in my direction. "Stand up," she says. "What are you wearing?"

"Well, I changed things up a little."

"Why? I liked your suit."

"The navy suit and paisley tie matched Lacey's pink dress," I admit.

"Ah, good point. So, you decided to go with just a black T-shirt instead?" Her hand slides across my forearm and then up to my bicep. "I love you in black."

"I hardly ever wear it."

"I know. And it practically devastates my heart every time you do."

"Really?"

"Yep. And I can count on one hand the number of times I've seen you in it. Once was when we were young and you wore black for Halloween."

"I was a vampire."

"And that summer, when we went to dinner, you wore all black—tee, shorts, and loafers. Then again on the golf course for your birthday. That's it."

"I guess I need to add more of it to my wardrobe, huh?"

"You do. Although, that day I brought you the cupcake, you

were in nothing but a pair of white linen shorts. Those'll do, too."

I lean down and give her a kiss. "Just so you know," I say, grabbing my suit jacket and pulling it on, "I'm still wearing a suit, but it's black, and I thought maybe the tee would be okay. I wore a look like this in a shoot I did, so I thought—"

"You'd look incredibly hot?" she says with a grin.

"I was thinking, dressed appropriately, but that will do, too," I say, repeating her earlier words.

A few more kisses later, the doorbell rings, and all hell breaks loose.

Okay, not actually hell, but we've got six couples and, due to remarriages, fifteen sets of parents, some of who brought their other kids.

Fortunately, Jennifer and my mom took charge by hiring a professional photographer, so only one person is taking pictures, but still, all the parents are standing behind her, trying to get early proof of this rite of passage.

We're lined up in groups and individually in three locations—on the dock overlooking the lake, which someone installed a balloon arch on in our school colors; in the lawn in front of a tall bed of flowers; and standing up on the deck.

Thirty minutes later, the limo arrives, allowing us to finally get on our way.

As we're walking to the limo, I stop my sister.

"You changed," she says, finally having a chance to look at me.

"Yeah, I changed a lot about tonight, too. Pace can fill you in, but that's not what I wanted to talk to you about."

"Is there drama?" she asks, her face brightening at the thought.

"No. I just wanted to tell you how nice you look, Hay. My little sister is all grown-up. Your dress is pretty, and I don't know how long it took to get your hair in those braids and then twisted back into the bun thing, but it's beautiful. You're beautiful."

She launches herself into my arms. "Chase, you're going to

make me cry."

"Don't do that. We wouldn't want the fake lashes falling half off. You'd look like you had a spider crawling up your face."

She scrunches up her nose, punches my arm, and then laughs.

"You're doing something special for Dani, aren't you?"

"I didn't want it just to be what I planned with Lacey, you know?"

"Yeah, and I think that's a good thing. I love you."

"I love you, too, sis. Have fun tonight. But, like, not too much fun."

Back in Time.

Devaney

WE TAKE A lot of pictures, and by the time we're done, I feel like I never want to smile again.

But when the limo arrives and we all load up, Chase pulls me onto his lap and kisses me.

And I wonder if it's weird for his friends. Especially Jax's date, who, like Haley, is on the cheer squad and friends with Lacey.

But no one seems to think anything of it. They act like it's normal for me to sit on Chase Mackenzie's lap and kiss him. That it's normal for us to be together.

And I guess, in a way, it is.

Everyone, except for Pace, has played sports with Chase and my brother for years. They were friends in grade school. And back then, we were inseparable.

And really, at this point, I don't care. I don't care that I'm basically filling in for Lacey. Although I am glad Chase decided to wear something different, especially after learning she picked the other suit out.

We listen to the music loud, dance around, crack jokes, and have a lot of fun on the ride.

WHEN WE ARRIVE at our destination, we get dropped off near a fountain, so we can take more pictures. These are much more fun though. Lots of selfies, kissing, and the kind of goofing around no one did in front of our families.

When it's time to walk over to the restaurant, Chase takes my hand. "So, I hope it's okay, but we aren't joining them for dinner."

"Why not?"

He hands me a stack of photos. "Well, first, I want to re-create these. They were in the hundred and eighty from my birthday."

I look at the photos of Chase and me at various ages in front of the fountains here at the Plaza.

"Want to know why my mom was obsessed with taking pics of us down here?"

"Yeah."

He pulls two other photos out of his coat pocket. Both are of his parents. One when they were probably in middle school and the other from their wedding day, re-creating the same pose.

"You know, everyone says you look like your mom, even me, but you look a lot like your dad in this picture, Chase," I say, pointing to the wedding one. "Exact same body type, broad shoulders, lean torso. Same face shape. Same goofy grin when he was teasing her, like you do me."

"My mom said she told him if he didn't stop making bunny ears behind her, she was going to push him in the fountain."

"I can picture her doing that," I say with a laugh.

"But she didn't," Chase counters.

"And he put bunny ears on her while she was in her wedding

dress. Are you telling me you're going to do that to me?"

"Basically. My parents will get a kick out of it."

We spend a little time taking a few more photos, and then he leads me back to the limo, which just pulled into a parking spot near where we were.

"Are we going somewhere else?" I ask him, wondering what he has planned and where we might be going.

"You could say that," he says with a smirk. "Like back in time."

And when he opens the door and I step in, I'm shocked.

So shocked and happy that tears instantly burst from my eyes.

The inside of the party limo has been decorated with streamers and signs. A little table is set under the disco ball in the middle of the limo, a bucket of fried chicken sitting on top of it.

I launch myself into his arms, crying.

"Please tell me those are happy tears," he says.

"I can't believe you did this for me again." I look into his eyes. "Why did you do this?" I ask, but all I'm thinking is that I'm pretty sure I just fell completely in love with him all over again.

"Because we have something to celebrate. A do-over—sort of. We are finally going to a dance together."

He kisses me and then moves to pull out the chair for me. I smile and take a seat.

"I was just going to say, it's too bad there's no bubbly, but I just noticed this bucket of ice on the floor next to the table with a bottle in it." I lean down and read the label, laughing. "Sparkling apple juice, just like back then."

"Let's have some before we eat," Chase says.

I notice that the bottle has already been opened, and there's a special lid on it to keep the bubbles in. "Why is it open already?"

He doesn't say anything, just grins, pours us each a glass, and then raises his plastic flute into the air.

I do the same.

"To second chances," he says.

"I will definitely drink to that even if it is only apple—" I take a sip. Stop. Look over at him.

He winks at me, puts his index finger up to his lips, and goes, "Shh."

Now, I realize why the bottle was open. He replaced the sparkling cider with real champagne. I take another drink, letting the bubbles tickle my nose. I'm not much of a drinker, especially compared to a lot of the girls at school, who get so drunk at parties and then are hungover the next day. After chatting with a few, I realized that most of the repeat offenders had super-strict rules regarding alcohol in high school, and now that they have no parental supervision, they are just on one long binge. We were allowed to have a beer or a glass of wine at home. So, I guess it doesn't have the same appeal to me. A cheer party when I was a freshman in high school was the only time I've ever gotten sick from drinking. And honestly, that was one time too many. At the lake on vacation, I did drink a little too much wine and was definitely tipsy, but still.

After a few sips, Chase refills our little plastic flutes. While he does that, I take his plate and pile it high with chicken, mashed potatoes, gravy, and corn, adding some coleslaw on the side.

"Same for you?" he asks me.

"Hmm. Definitely same assortment. Possibly a slightly smaller portion."

We eat our chicken, surrounded by the homemade decor, and then clear the table of our dirty plates.

"Should we get rid of what we didn't eat?" I ask him.

"Heck no. Ten bucks says, everyone will come back and chow down on it."

"But they are having dinner."

"A fancy dinner. Lots of perfectly prepared and delicious food but tiny portions."

"True," I say, but then I forget all about it when he pulls me onto his lap.

We kiss until everyone gets back to the limo.

I'M IN HEAVEN at the dance, flitting around and talking to everyone, telling them how amazing college is, and dancing with Chase. The dancing with Chase is the best part of all because I feel like I've been redeemed in a way. That I'm finally here with the right person. The cheerleader and the quarterback, who just happens to be my hot best friend. Seriously, I feel like I could write an entire book about this very moment. The music, the way Chase holds me, the fun we have line-dancing to some of our favorite country songs, jumping up and down and grinding during the electronic ones, and slow dancing to others. It's exhilarating. And it doesn't hurt that when we walked in, Chase told me I had to put on my crown. Which, technically, I am supposed to wear— at least until the next queen is announced later tonight.

And when Chase twirls me around, my dress flaring out and a crown on my head, I literally have a fairy-tale moment.

With the boy I love.

I never want this night to end.

And I'm not going to let it. I'm going to spend every second of it in his arms—until I have to go back to school.

AT NINE THIRTY, as planned, we make our way backstage. The senior court members, including my brother and Chase, are directed to one side, while the underclassmen and I are sent to the other.

The night has been amazing, and I feel like I'm living in a dream.

A school administrator gives us a quick rundown of what will happen next—which is not super complicated. When they call your name, you go onstage.

She sets the new king and queen crowns on a little table next to me. "You may have to crown both," she tells me. "Last year's king couldn't come, and it looks like our backup hasn't shown."

She scurries away, envelopes in hand, and makes her way up onto the stage, where she starts announcing the Homecoming Court by grade, starting with the freshman.

"Lookin' good, Dani Diamond," a voice says from behind me.

I turn around to find Hunter Lansford giving me a wolfish grin.

"What are you doing here?"

"I guess Douglas couldn't make it. They asked me to step in. I thought it was kind of lame, but now, I'm glad I did."

"Great," I mutter.

Hunter gives me the chin raise. "So, you're a college girl now. You dating anyone?"

"I'm here with Chase."

"Mackenzie?" He laughs. "He still have a boner for you? Although I know you're lying. I was at the game when he asked Lacey. It was Senior Night, and my sister is on the dance team. Don't worry, Dani." He suggestively slides his hand across my shoulder. "I can pretend to be your date if you need one."

"Don't touch me," I say, quickly moving away from him.

"Why is it one of the prettiest girls in town never has a date for the ball? Want me to be your prince? Find your shoe? Of course, I'd want some kind of a special reward to give it back."

The sophomores are being called up now.

"I'm here with Chase. And I literally have no idea what I ever saw in you."

He throws his arm around my shoulders and leans in close to my face. "Shall I kiss you and remind you?"

"I said, don't touch me." I forcefully remove his hand from my shoulder. "And if you do it again, I'll be the one punching you in the face this time. Are we clear?"

He shrugs. "You must not be getting any in college. Or from Mackenzie. Probably because you're a bitch."

I react by kneeing him in the crotch.

"Ugh," he says, buckling and falling to the floor dramatically.

The junior girls behind me start clapping.

And I can't help but smile.

I'm thinking about how I stood here last year. Worried about not having an escort. A tradition that they have stopped, thankfully.

I remember freaking out about it—how it would look if I didn't have a date. How I begged Chase to walk me out onstage. How even though he thought I should have the confidence to walk out there myself, he showed up.

"Because I'm your brother's best friend," he said, "I'm giving you the option. Walk out by yourself or on my arm."

"In other words, what's it gonna be—the shame of being alone or the shame of being with a younger guy?"

"Wow. Okay. So, helpful hint—neither one is supposed to be shameful. You still don't get it," he said, "and maybe you never will."

My name is called. I grab both crowns, leave Hunter—who is still whimpering—in the dust, and walk proudly out onto the stage by myself.

I take my place next to the junior court as Pace is announced as the first king nominee, followed by my brother, and then Chase. They line up opposite me as the senior girls are announced.

I look over at Chase, who smiles and then winks at me, causing me to melt.

"And this year's Homecoming King is … Damon Diamond!"

I take the crown and happily walk across the stage, put it on my brother's head, and give him a big hug. Damon's beaming, and I'm so happy for him.

"And this year's Homecoming Queen is … Lacey Turnbull."

Hunter, who has made it up onto the stage, snatches the queen's tiara out of my hands, but once he realizes Lacey isn't here, he looks dumbfounded about what he should do. Chase takes a step forward and meets Hunter in the middle of the stage. Hunter narrows his eyes at Chase in what appears to be some kind of testosterone-filled challenge.

But Chase simply takes the crown from him, and then he goes to the mic and says, "Lacey is home sick with the chicken pox, but I know she will be thrilled to be your queen. I'll see to it that she gets this."

Hunter snickers at me.

But I don't really care what he thinks.

Love worth fighting for.

Chase

"HEY," I SAY, joining Dani back at our table once all of the festivities are over.

"Hey," she says breathlessly as I take her into my arms.

I know she's been happy tonight, high almost. In her element. And I've been right there with her, feeling like I've been given a long-overdue gift. That we finally got to this point.

But I feel a little guilty. Because even though this was my dream—to be at Homecoming with Dani and dance with her all night—she's already had her year as queen.

And this should have been Lacey's year.

"Let's get a few more dances in," Dani says, "before Damon wants to go party."

"I can't," I say.

"Why not?"

I hold up the crown. "I need to take this to Lacey."

"It was really nice you accepted it for her, Chase. But you aren't saying that you want to take it to her now, like tonight, are you?"

"Yeah, I am. This was supposed to be her moment. I should be out there, dancing with her right now. I'm sure you can understand since you've been there already. Since you got to feel that way last year."

"Are you serious?" she asks incredulously. "There's no reason you can't take it to her tomorrow."

"It needs to be tonight. And it won't take long."

"I can't believe you're doing this to me," she says, which causes me to flinch.

What she should have done was offered to go with me or said she'd be here when I got back.

"Dani, as much as I have dreamed of you being my date for every single homecoming, you ended up saying yes to Hunter. You could have apologized. You could have asked me. But you didn't. And you're not my date tonight either. Tonight, we're just two people tossed together by circumstances beyond our control."

"But you got me chicken and champagne."

"Yeah, because I felt like I was being given a second chance. But standing up there, I realized that if we're ever going to be together as more than friends, it shouldn't be due to circumstance. It shouldn't be because I happen to be there. And it shouldn't be because it's the path of least resistance. I want the kind of love worth fighting for, Dani, and I wish with all my heart that this were us for real. But I have to stop wishing my life away. I'm cool with the whole friends thing. I'm even cool with the whole friends-with-benefits thing, But if you ever want to be more than a broken promise, you're going to have to let me know. In the meantime, I'm sorry, but I've gotta go."

I LEAVE THE dance, wondering what I just did.

If I ruined my chance of ever getting what I want. Of being with her fully.

I don't know what the answer is, but I am compelled to do what's right.

Our limo driver is out front, and I know Damon isn't planning to leave for another half hour or so. He wants to fully enjoy his reign as king before going to the after-parties.

So, I hop in the limo, get driven to Lacey's house, and then send the driver back to the dance.

I can walk home from here.

I know I can't risk getting chicken pox, so I carefully place her crown, sash, and bouquet of roses in front of her door, and then I step out into her yard and call her.

"Chase," she says when she answers.

"I'm out front. Can you come to the door?"

"Uh, I look horrible."

"You're the queen, Lacey. Come put on your crown."

"My friends videoed my name being called. Thanks for accepting it for me. I'm really surprised you are bringing it to me tonight since you were there with Dani and all."

"You were my date," I say as she opens the door, wearing a pair of flannel pajamas.

She sets her phone down, and I hang up. Her mom joins her, putting the sash over her head, adding the crown, and then giving her the roses.

Even from out in the yard, I can see that she's crying.

"I know we can't dance together," I say to her, "but there's no reason we can't dance together—separately."

I play a song on my phone, turning the music up loud.

I bow to her from the front yard and then pretend to put one arm around her waist and the other up for a waltz.

"You're crazy," she says, but she mimics me, coming out onto her porch and slowly swaying with me to the music. Her eyes are closed, but there's a smile across her face.

And I know that I did the right thing.

When the song ends, Lacey opens her eyes and looks across the lawn at me. "Thank you for doing this, Chase. It means a lot to me."

"Get well soon," I tell her. "You know I need you out there on the sidelines, cheering for me."

She laughs. "Don't think I didn't see a video of *the play*. You do just fine without me, Chase. Always."

I WALK HOME, go up to my room, take off my shiny shoes and suit, change into some sweats, and then go out back and sit on the dock.

I end up lying back and staring up at the stars, remembering the night in the Ozarks when Dani and I laid in the back of a pickup and did the same. She made some comment about me flirting with girls at the resort. Which I had—in an attempt to make her jealous.

"I'm not going to beg, Dani. A guy can only take so much of having his heart stomped on before he just gives up."

She whipped her head in my direction and sucked in a breath. "I've stomped on your heart?"

"Maybe you are like my mom. Everyone said she was clueless, too."

"But she told me she wasn't! She told me how they used to stare up at the stars and think about how infinitely big the universe was and how small they felt in comparison. She said that's why it took them so long to get together. Because she felt small in comparison to how big their love felt."

"Is that how you feel?" I asked her, desperate to know the answer. Any answer that would give me hope that someday—

"I understand why she felt that way. When you're young, like our age, it does feel that way, you know," she said, sounding confused.

And maybe she was.

"And I completely disagree. Sitting here with you, under the stars, makes me feel like anything and everything is possible."

And then she kissed me.

Tonight felt like that kind of night. The kind of night when I could envision our future.

Until I decided to take Lacey her crown.

Was I wrong to do that?

The dock sways, and I open my eyes, surprised to see Dani coming toward me. She's still in her dress, like she just got home.

"Funny you're out here," she says.

"Why's that?"

"On the drive home, I was thinking about the Ozarks. About the stars. I wanted to come out here to look at them. Remember what it felt like to fall in love with you."

"Are you mad at me?" I ask as she sits down next to me.

"I felt like that tonight," she says, not answering my question. "Like I was falling in love with you again. It sounds weird. Because I love you. I've always loved you. As my friend, my confidant, but it's much deeper than just best-friend love, Chase. It always has been. And I just—"

I know what she's about to say. And I don't want to hear it. I don't want to rock the boat—or in this case, the dock.

"I get it, Dani. You're in college. I'm here. Someday, the timing will be right for us."

She pulls her knees up to her chest, wraps her arms around her legs, like she's hugging them, and rests her chin on her knees. "Do you really think so?"

"I know so."

"I know so, too," she says. "Thank you for tonight. I know I got a little pissy when you left, but taking Lacey her crown and stuff was sweet of you." She lets out a little chuckle. "Do I need to worry about getting the chicken pox, sitting by you?"

"No. I put the stuff outside her door but then stood out in the lawn."

She reaches out and wraps her fingers around my hand and lies flat on her back. "Can we just lie here together and stare up at the stars?"

"Of course we can," I tell her, quickly lying back.

"Good, because someone once told me that doing this makes them feel like anything and everything is possible."

I turn my head toward her. She moves closer to me, her lips as close as they can be without touching mine.

I reach up and gently stroke her face as I say, "Someday, it will be forever, Dani, but we don't have to start forever today."

SUNDAY, OCTOBER 20TH

Separate ways.

Devaney

EVENTUALLY, CHASE AND I went up to his room together. No one was expecting me home with all the after-parties.

I loved being in his arms, in his bed. With him intimately.

And although last night was the night of my dreams, something seemed to shift in Chase. I don't want to say it felt like he'd given up on us because that isn't quite right. Maybe it was just that he didn't send off the same intense emotional vibes I usually feel when I'm with him.

It was more like he is now resigned to the fact that we'll be going our separate ways for a while. At least until next fall when he comes to school with me.

And I suppose that's the grown-up thing to do.

WEDNESDAY, NOVEMBER 20TH

Catching up.

Chase

TONIGHT, WE WON the state semifinals, and in a couple of weeks, we'll be playing for the championship. As typical, Damon wants to go out to celebrate, but I feel like I need to do something else.

Plus, it's not really hard to feign exhaustion. The five weeks since the homecoming dance have been a football-filled blur. School, practice, and homework all week, game on Friday night, followed by a flight to one of our top five colleges for an official recruitment visit. Home on Sunday night and then repeat.

About two weeks into it all, I messaged Dani and told her that I was sorry I got mad at her for not texting me when she got back to school after my birthday. That with the recruiting visits and school and everything, I finally understood what she'd meant when she said there just wasn't time. She replied, told me thanks, and said that she looked forward to us catching up at Thanksgiving.

And I know what that means. Just like on my birthday and for Homecoming, *catching up* has taken on a whole new meaning. At first, I wasn't sure about the whole friends-with-benefits thing, and maybe I've grown up a little or something, but I'm okay with it now—for a while. I understand it's a timing thing, not that we don't want to be together eventually.

All I know is that I can't wait for her to get home on Tuesday. To tell her the good news. That after visiting beautiful campuses, meeting a lot of great guys and gorgeous coeds, looking hard at programs, and weighing all our options, Damon and I have come to a final decision. We will be signing our Letter of Intent with Nebraska, as planned.

Meaning we'll be there together. I can picture it now. She'll be thrilled to learn our choice, but then I'll kiss her and tell her the best part of all. That when she goes back to school after Christmas break, I'll be going with her. She'll jump into my arms, wrap her legs around my waist, and kiss me. And we both know what that will lead to.

When I applied to my top schools this fall, the thought of being there a full semester without Damon really bummed me out. But now, I think it will be kind of nice for Dani and me to have a semester to ourselves.

The renovation on the building Mom bought will be finished later this winter, and even though we'll be living in separate dorms, once the project is complete, we'll have a private place to hang out. To be together with no distractions.

A love nest, if you will.

It's been a long two years since that day Hunter asked her to Homecoming, but I know we've both grown up a lot since then and that the trials we've gone through will only make our relationship stronger in the end.

And I know, my end—my destiny—is to be with her.

And in less than two months, it's finally going to be our reality.

My phone buzzes, letting me know that my delivery has arrived. I go downstairs, answer the door, collect my pizza, and then take it back into my room.

I eat it in the tent that's become a permanent fixture in my room and dream of our future together.

THURSDAY, NOVEMBER 21ST

Thought you should know.

Chase

I'M IN THE basement, watching a college football game on the big screen with my dad.

At halftime, I run upstairs to make a quick smoothie—mixing protein powder with almond butter, cocoa, bananas, and cashew milk. But instead of putting in the normal amount of milk, I add just a little to keep the texture thick. This is one of my favorite combinations, so rich and decadent that I can eat it with a spoon, like ice cream. I take a few cold bites and decide to run up and grab a sweatshirt.

When I walk past Haley's room, I find her and Damon with their heads together. Their voices are hushed, but they seem to be discussing something very passionately.

So much so that they don't even notice me when I walk into the room.

I tap my sister on the shoulder.

She screams and jumps up.

Even Damon sucks in his breath. "Dude, you can't sneak up on us like that," he says, his hand to his chest.

"What are you two conspiring about?" I ask them.

"Uh, nothing," my sister says unconvincingly. "Just talking

about school."

"Okay, what about me at school then? I heard you say my name."

They share a glance, and Damon tilts his head back and forth like he's weighing options in his head. He ends up giving her a slight head nod.

Haley takes a deep breath. "We were actually discussing whether or not we should tell you about something that we believe you will find upsetting now *before* it happens or if we should just let you find out, uh—"

"Organically," Damon says.

"Organically?" I ask.

"Yes, like, on your own," Haley repeats.

"And it's something that will upset me?"

"Yes, but this, um, *event* isn't going to happen until next week. And we were arguing about what to do. Basically," Haley explains.

"So, do you want to know?" Damon asks, cutting to the chase.

"Are we talking *upset me*, like Winger is sick? Or Grandpa has cancer kind of thing?"

"Oh no!" Haley says. "It's nothing like that."

"Oh, for goodness' sake," Damon says. "You're freaking him out worse than just telling him. So, the deal is that my sister is bringing a friend home for Thanksgiving."

"Oh," I say. "Like, one of her sorority sisters? That's cool. Why would you think that would upset me?"

"Because this is a *guy* friend," Haley clarifies.

I study their faces. Haley is giving me the kind of smile reserved for when she feels bad for someone. Damon is looking at me like he's worried I might punch him in the face.

"Wait. Like a guy *friend*. Or a *boy*friend?" I ask.

"More like a boyfriend." Haley replies.

"And?!"

Before, they were all talk-talk, and now that I actually want to know more details, they've suddenly gone mute.

"And that's it," Haley says. "We just thought you should know."

"How did you find out about it?" I ask them.

"I overheard Mom and Jennifer talking about it."

"I see," I say softly even though I'm practically seeing red. "Well, thanks for the update."

I storm out of the room, grab my stupid sweatshirt, and stomp down the stairs, looking for my mom. I know she already put Emersyn to bed, and I should be quiet, but I can't help it. I'm pissed.

I find her downstairs on the couch with Dad.

I march in front of the television, towering over both of them.

"I understand you'll be setting an *extra place* for Thanksgiving dinner," I bellow.

Mom licks her lip and then bites it, like she's trying to think of what to say. She knows she's busted.

How could she do this to me?

"Haley overheard you talking to Jennifer. Were you not going to tell me?!" I say, my voice rising more.

"Tell him what?" my dad asks her.

It's pretty obvious that I'm upset.

"Dani is bringing a friend home with her," my mom replies.

"Oh, well, what's wrong with that? We always welcome—"

"This isn't *just* a friend, Dad. It's not her roommate. She's bringing home her *new boyfriend*, and Mom didn't tell me."

"Oh," my dad says, his forehead creasing.

"So, Mom, what do you have to say for yourself?" I sass.

She makes a little hmmph sound and gives me a closed-lip smile, like she's trying to hold her temper. "It just so happens, Chase, that this is *my* house, and *I* can invite anyone for dinner that *I* want *without* asking for your opinion or approval."

"I don't care. It's my house, too, and I don't want her here. Dis-invite her."

"Chase, don't be ridiculous," Mom says. "She's your friend. She's my goddaughter."

"Fine then, *she* can come. Her boyfriend can't."

"Chase, look, I was going to tell you. I actually came down here to talk to your father about how we should handle this delicate situation. It's usually a pretty big deal to bring a guy home to the family. It tends to indicate a, um, certain level of serious-ness—"

And that's when I lose it. "He's *not* coming to our house. If he does, I'll leave. You can spend Thanksgiving without me. Sorry, Mom, but you're going to have to choose."

"Chase," my dad says.

"No, Dad," I yell. "There's nothing to say because we already know how it's going to go. He'll ruin Thanksgiving for all of us because he's a dick, and we'll have to deal with it."

"So, you've met him?" Mom asks, looking confused.

I throw my hands up in the air because I don't understand why they are being so freaking dense about this. "I *don't have to meet him* to know that. That's the *only* kind of guy she dates."

"She dated you," Mom fires back.

"No, Mom. Actually, she never has."

"Well, regardless, Chase, they're coming."

"All right then. Fine. But don't say I didn't warn you."

"About what?" she asks.

"Oh, I don't know, Mom. Like, if I end up punching him in the face. That kind of thing."

I hear my little sister start crying.

"Dammit," Mom says, storming off.

My dad gets up off the couch in a flash.

I figure I'm in trouble for yelling at my mom, but I need her to understand. I need my dad to understand.

He goes to the fridge, grabs two beers, pops off the caps with an opener, and then hands one to me.

Which means he's not going to ground me.

I take the beer, let out a massive sigh, and plop down onto the sectional couch, exhausted. I set the bottle on the table, and then I close my eyes, cover my face with my hands, and rub across my forehead.

I need to calm down. My blood pressure feels like it's through the roof. I might have a fever. And my heart feels like it is about to beat out of my chest. Maybe I'm coming down with something—like a heart attack.

Actually though, maybe I *could* come down with something. Like the chicken pox Lacey had during Homecoming. We'd have to, like, quarantine the house. We couldn't have *anyone* over.

"Have you ever wanted to just punch a guy in the face because—" I start to say.

"He's dating your girl?" my dad asks in response, taking a seat next to me.

"Sort of. Except she's not your girl."

"But you want her to be?"

"Maybe I used to want that. I don't even know anymore."

"The move from best friends to a couple is tricky, Chase. And to answer your question, I wanted to punch every *single* guy your mother ever dated in the face."

"You did?" *Maybe I'm not going crazy.*

"Yeah. She was my best friend. And with that came some, uh, territorial feelings. And the shit of it is, when they dumped her, guess whose shoulder she always came to cry on?"

"Yours," I say with a nod, totally understanding.

"Yep. And I would always tell her that if she'd date the right guy—*hint, that guy was me*—this wouldn't happen. But she never got the hint. And if she couldn't see it, I didn't think I could risk it. Is that how you feel about Dani?"

"She doesn't complain to me about them anymore at least."

"Chase, I know you think because I'm old that I won't understand, but I do. If I had to take a wild guess, I'd say you slept together in the Ozarks. That you thought you'd be together forever, and when you got back, she got asked to Homecoming by Hunter. And it devastated you."

I swallow hard, close my eyes at the flash of pain I feel, and nod my head. "We actually got, um, *close* again when she was back for my birthday and possibly on homecoming weekend, too. And I just assumed when she came home for Thanksgiving that—"

"You'd be *close* again?"

I nod. Grab the beer and take a sip. "Instead, she's bringing a guy. To *my house*. For dinner. And I don't think I can handle it." I wave my hand in the air. "Just forget it. Really. I'll deal with it. I'll apologize to Mom for my outburst. And I'll be nice to him. Can we talk about something else?"

"Sure. What do you want to talk about?" Dad asks.

"I'm not going to Nebraska."

"But you and Damon just finished your visits. I thought you'd made a decision."

"Please don't tell anyone. But I can't do it. Not anymore. It was just some stupid promise."

My dad's eyes go wide with surprise. "You've wanted to play there since you were a kid. You and Damon both have."

"I know, but honestly, we have a ton of better options."

"Isn't it a little rash to change your mind because Dani is bringing a guy home for Thanksgiving?"

"It's not rash actually. More like it's been a long time coming. That first summer in the Ozarks, we decided that we'd all go to college together—not just me and Dani, but Damon and Haley, too. That we'd run our business together from there. It's not just the guy. *It's everything.* Dani hasn't done a single thing that she promised. And I'm not convinced that she ever will."

My dad takes a sip of beer and leans back in his chair, like he has nothing to say. But I know he thinks before he speaks. And that when he finally says something, it's well thought out.

So, I sit here silently. I know I sort of just dropped a bomb on him, and he probably needs to process.

"Chase, you know that your mother and I will fully support whatever your decision is regarding your college choice. But I would caution you not to give up your dream because of a girl."

"What do you mean? Don't choose not to go to Nebraska just because she's there? They want me up there in January, Dad, so I can play spring ball. If I do that, I know I'll win the starting job. Which means I'll be up there for a *full semester* of just me and her. Damon doesn't have enough credits to graduate midterm."

"Like I said, it's *your* dream. And you need to remember that."

"Actually," I say pathetically, "it was *our* dream."

"Chase, yes, your mother and I—"

"No, Dad, I don't mean you and Mom. I mean, it was our dream. Me and Dani's."

"Oh."

"She even put it on that stupid cupcake." I take out my phone and show him a picture of the cupcake she made me in the Ozarks and explain what each decoration meant. Although I don't tell him that an actual photo of it has been hanging in my locker all season, driving me through until I could get to college and be with her all the time.

"Do you want my advice, son?" Dad asks, a conspiratorial grin on his face.

"Desperately."

"This weekend, I want you to be her friend. Her *very* best friend. Like you used to be. When the guy comes, be nice to him. Be *especially* nice to him. Act like it doesn't bother you, no matter how much it does."

"I don't know if I can do that. And why would I want to?"

"If you have to ask that question, Chase, then it really isn't *your* dream," Dad says harshly.

I sit quietly and contemplate that. Dad doesn't say anything further. He just gets up and goes upstairs.

And I don't know if what he said helped or just confused me more.

Because I don't think I can be *just* her friend when I want to be her forever.

TUESDAY, NOVEMBER 26TH

Total frat.

Chase

I'M UNPACKING MY bag when I hear a car door slam next door. I look out my window and see that Dani has just arrived home.

I run down the stairs, fly out the back door, and haul ass from our backyard to theirs. The dogs follow me, running, barking, and wanting to play, but I don't have time for that. I go into the garage through the side door and then into the house via the laundry room.

I take a deep breath to slow my heart rate and step into the kitchen.

Danny and Jennifer are greeting Dani and the guy by the front door.

Dani looks as beautiful as always, but my eyes go to the competition.

The guy—the boyfriend—is dressed in total frat. Khakis, button-down, bow tie, blazer. If I had to guess, it's all Brooks Brothers or J. Crew. I never really cared about brands all that much, other than sports apparel, but since I've been modeling, I've learned a surprising amount about them. And I know bow ties are very cool on the right person. A few of my favorite pro QBs wear them often, and I think they look very *dapper*, I guess you'd say, in them. This guy looks like he's trying too hard. I size him up some more as he tells them about how he's in a fraternity.

Shocker.

How he's majoring in accounting.

Insert eye roll.

But then Dani wraps her arm around his and says proudly, "Eddie is a scratch golfer, Dad."

And I realize that's more how I'd peg him. Like the guy in that old movie, *Caddyshack*—golfing all day, drinking and picking up women all night.

I wouldn't say he's good-looking, but he seems to have the charm factor going on because something he says causes Jennifer to giggle.

"We all love to golf," Danny says to the guy.

"Really? I would have bet that your kids were born with a football in their hands," he says, reaching down and picking up one off the floor, seemingly to prove his point.

It's the dog's toy, but whatever.

"I was raised with a club in mine. My family is really close."

"Eddie's family owns the country club in his hometown," Dani says.

I like a good country club as much as anyone, and I love to golf, but it's time to make my presence known.

I walk into the room, causing Dani's eyes to go wide with shock.

Eddie sees me and immediately comes to shake my hand. "You must be Damon. Nice to meet you," he says, looking up at me. "You're bigger than I thought."

Dani looks like she wants to correct him, but instead, she's just staring at me. And I know why. I'm wearing all black. *On purpose.*

"That's because I'm not Damon." I look from Dani to him. "We don't really look related, do we?"

He studies me, confused, but now, he's quickly trying to figure out my threat level.

I decide to help him out. "Nice to meet you. I'm Chase."

"Chase," Jennifer says, coming to give me a hug.

What can I say? She loves me.

Jennifer and I are like kindred spirits, except she says what she thinks in a way I never could. I mean, not to be gross, but Damon's stepmom is pretty hot, and I never really mind it.

"You're back!"

"Where were you?" Eddie asks. "At college?"

"Oh, no. He's a high school senior, like Damon. But he was off, modeling again," Jennifer says, patting my chest.

Big strapping boy that I am.

I smile and wave toward the only girl I have eyes for in any room. "Hey, Dani. Welcome home. How's college?" I let out a laugh and look at Eddie. "You brought home a guy, so it *must* be good."

I'm worried her dad can see right through my charade and is going to call me on it, but he just says, "Why don't we all go sit down?"

Which is like music to my ears.

"So, Eddie," I ask the guy, "if you are so close to your family, that must mean Dani is really special—to take you away from them on such an important family holiday."

Eddie goes, "Oh, no," and I can't help but break out in a smile and glance at Dani.

See, he doesn't really care that much about you.

"I went home last weekend for my great-grandmother's eighty-seventh birthday, and we celebrated Thanksgiving early since everyone was in town."

I guess that's reasonable.

Damon rolls in the side door just as we're all shuffling into the family room. And Damon isn't exactly quiet about anything he does.

"Dude," he says to me, not even noticing anyone else in the room, "you just missed Sally Ann's boobs falling out of her—"

His dad clears his throat.

"Oh shit," Damon says, seeing the train wreck behind me. But as is his style, he can roll with anything. He picks his sister up and gives her a bear hug—something he never does. And then he turns toward the threat. "And you must be the new boy toy."

"Damon," Jennifer says while his dad chuckles.

Danny works his way into the kitchen and grabs some beers.

And starts passing them out.

"Oh, none for me," I say to him. "I actually just stopped by to drop something off in Dani's room. She forgot it last time she was over." *I'm such a liar.*

This gets both her and frat boy's attention. For different reasons, obviously. I take something out of my pocket and toss it to Dani, who is now sitting on the couch. She catches it easily. One of the things I've always loved about her is her excellent eye-hand coordination.

I turn to Damon and say, "You ready?"

Damon drops his duffel on the floor. "Yeah."

"Where are you going?" his dad asks. "Your sister just got home."

"Figured I'd let you interrogate the new guy on your own, Dad. Chase and I have some business to attend to."

"What business?" Dani asks. She's got a smirk on her face, like she thinks it has to do with girls.

"One Eleven," I say, watching her lips turn down.

"We have some new designs to go over with Hay Girl," Damon adds. He flashes his watch and says, "Won't be more than an hour. We can have all sorts of fun family bonding when I get back." He runs his hand across his stomach. "And hopefully dinner."

"We're having dinner at the Mackenzies' house tonight," Jennifer tells him. "It's their annual Taco Tuesday Thanksgiving kickoff celebration."

"Oh sweet, that's right. I'm starved," Damon says. "Well, that's where we'll be. I guess we'll see you all there." He turns around and shakes the guy's hand and goes, "So nice to meet you."

Kind of hurts.

Devaney

I SIT IN my spot and don't dare open my hand to see what Chase tossed to me. But I can feel it.

And I know what it is. A penny.

He wants to know what I'm thinking. Why I brought a guy home with me. And why we aren't going to spend the holiday weekend in his bed.

But his timing was a little *too* perfect.

And also, they are having a company meeting without me. And that still kind of hurts.

Make her jealous.

Chase

LACEY CALLS ME as I'm getting ready for bed. "I heard you have an unexpected guest."

"What do you mean?"

"Dani brought home a guy from college."

"How do you know that?"

"Um, your little sister is on my squad."

"Oh yeah. And, yes, she did."

"Can I come over?" she asks.

"Like, now?"

"Yes, Chase."

"Well, I was just going to bed."

"Perfect," she says and then hangs up.

A few minutes later, she's in my room.

She walks straight over to the window facing Dani's room and pulls the curtains open.

"What are you doing?" I ask her as she struts toward me.

"Believe it or not," she says, grabbing the hem of my shirt and pushing it up over my chest, "I'm helping you."

"By taking off my shirt?" I say with a chuckle.

"By taking off your shirt in front of your window."

I freeze. "I don't understand."

Once the shirt is tossed on the floor, she slides her hands up my chest and then around my neck, where she leaves them. I glance over at the window and can see that Dani is in her room. What I'm worried about is whether or not she's alone.

"Haley seemed off today," Lacey says. "It's my job as captain to notice stuff like that, so I had her stay for a few minutes after practice and asked what was wrong. I figured it had something to do with Pace, so I wasn't exactly expecting it when she started rambling about you and Dani and Thanksgiving and some guy. It actually took me a few minutes to figure out what was going on, but in the end, I said what I always say to my girls and asked if there was anything I could do to help. She flippantly responded with, *Not unless you can make Dani crazy jealous.* Then she said she had to get home for the train wreck."

"The train wreck?"

"She said the guy would be coming to your house for dinner tonight. She said you got into a fight with your mom. Didn't want the guy to be allowed in your house."

"Yeah, I did," I say with a sigh. "But my dad told me to embrace it. Said I should befriend the guy."

"I just talked to Haley."

"What did she say?"

"That the guy is nice."

"Yeah, he is. It would be easier if he wasn't."

"And I'm here to make Dani jealous."

"But why?"

"You brought me my crown. You danced in the yard with me. I know you don't love me, and honestly, I don't know that I ever really saw us together long-term either. But you have become one of my best friends. You've always given me solid advice when it comes to school, cheer, and life. And I'm going to pay you back for that."

"What makes you think she'll even notice you here?"

"Because your sister is slightly devious. And the guy is staying in the guest suite over your garage."

"He's what?"

She runs her hand down my bare chest, and I will admit, it feels nice. "Your sister arranged that somehow. But the real question is, does Dani know that we aren't sleeping together anymore?"

"We haven't talked about it."

"Maybe you should have," she says.

"I didn't want to bring anyone else into the equation—"

"Which could be why *she* just did."

I should have.

Devaney

To MY HORROR, after dinner, Eddie was shown to his room by my dad—the guest suite above the Mackenzies' garage. Which means he and Chase will literally be sleeping under the same roof. Which is so messed up that I can barely process it. Dad passed it off as a normal thing, mentioning something about how, with the new babies, we're short a guest room and that he'd be a lot more comfortable there than on the couch. Which he definitely will be, but that's not the point.

And what the heck was Chase doing at my house the second we arrived? And why did he have to be wearing all black?

And I don't know where or what he was modeling, but they must have cut his hair for it. While it used to be longer on the top and was pushed up and back, today, the top was shorter, layered, and swept to the side. Probably some new trend.

And I like it.

I pull the penny out of my pocket.

And I feel bad.

I should have told him about Eddie.

I should have told him how it just sort of happened.

Us dating.

Him coming home with me.

I pick up my phone to call Chase when there's a change in the light behind me, causing me to turn in the direction of his window.

Maybe he's signaling for me. Wants me to come over—

But then I see, that's not the case.

Lacey is in his room.

I watch as she takes off his shirt.

And I feel like I'm going to throw up.

Bit of a charmer.

Chase

LACEY SPINS ME so that my back is to the window. "You need to stop looking over there. For this to work, you need to at least pretend to be into me."

"What did Haley tell you about Eddie?" I say as I pick up my shirt and put it back on.

"Um, he's a sophomore. Cute. And a bit of a charmer."

"Like, she thought he might be sort of a ladies' man?"

"She didn't use those words, but I could see for myself, if you want."

"I appreciate you coming over here. I really do. And I want to make her jealous—I do—but this just feels wrong."

Lacey tilts her head at me and smiles. "And now, in retrospect, I suppose it could backfire. Push her closer to him."

"And I don't want that. But—"

"I like where you're going with this," Damon says from just outside my door.

"Me, too," Haley says. "If Eddie flirted with Lacey …"

Lacey and I break out in laughter.

I lean in, give her a kiss on the cheek, and say, "Let's get out of here."

"I thought you'd never ask," she says flirtatiously as we leave my room.

Out in the hall, I tell my sister and Damon, "You guys are

terrible."

"Let's go watch a movie or something," Haley offers.

"I probably need to get home," Lacey says.

So, I walk her out to her car.

They don't.

Devaney

I EXPECT FOR the lights to go off. For them to jump into bed together.

But they don't.

And I am surprised when Chase puts his shirt back on.

And when they leave his room.

And when I see him walk her to her car.

And when they *don't* kiss goodbye.

WEDNESDAY, NOVEMBER 27TH

More erratic.

Chase

"IT'S UNSEASONABLY WARM today," Damon's dad says when all of us are at breakfast. "How about we go golf?"

"Oh, sir," Eddie says, "you don't have to do that because of me."

"Well, we're a slightly competitive family," Damon says, "and I happen to be a scratch golfer, too."

"What were you planning on doing today before?" Dani asks.

"Bowling," Jennifer says. "But it's nice out, and we probably won't get many more days like this."

"Especially for us who are farther up north," Eddie agrees.

"SO, WHY'D YOU join a fraternity?" Jennifer asks Eddie later, when we're out on the course.

After Lacey left, I nixed Damon and Haley's whole scheme of trying to make Dani jealous. I shouldn't have to resort to bullshit like that to get her to love me. And I won't.

"The camaraderie, honestly," he says. "I play a lot of golf but was a three-sport athlete in high school. I have always liked being part of a team, so a frat felt right. I have made a ton of friends, and we have a very competitive intramural league that I take part in."

He stops talking long enough to sink a fifteen-yard putt into the hole for one under par. And I have to admit, I kind of like the guy. Even though it's pretty obvious he's being asked a million questions, he doesn't even blink over a single one, giving what seems to be an honest answer for each.

"Plus, you know, I wanted to meet girls. And girls flock to the house, as we're known for our parties. And we do mixers and socials with the sororities. That's actually how I met Dani."

This causes my ears to perk up.

And it must do the same to Jennifer, too, because she goes, "Oh, Dani, tell us about how you met."

Traitor.

We're playing some kind of scramble. My dad's idea. Probably because he knew a head-to-head competition between us wouldn't end well.

Right now, my foursome consists of me, Jennifer, Dani, and Eddie. But we're switching up again at the end of this hole, so everyone is standing around, watching us.

I'm waiting for Dani to say something. Anything. To tell me what this guy did that made her want to be with him.

"It was a Halloween party," she says.

"But it was early," he adds. "We tend to celebrate Halloween for a couple of weeks since dressing up is so fun. It was a Tuesday night—October 22nd, to be exact."

Dani went back to school after Homecoming on the 20th. *Was she mad at me because I took Lacey her crown?* But that couldn't be. We ended up back together that night. Stargazing and then going up to my room. My bed.

"It was a match party. You draw the costume you have to wear from a hat, and then at the party, you have to find your match. Like Cinderella and Prince Charming, or Salt and Pepper, that sort of thing. She was dressed as an angel," he says. "I was the devil. We had a lot of fun. The next day, I sent her flowers."

"Flowers, huh?" I say, my heart literally dropping like my ball just did as I overshot my putt, sending it down the incline and off the green.

"I know," Eddie says, "not your typical frat move. My brothers gave me a hard time about that, but when I asked her to lunch, she said yes."

Eddie comes over and pats my shoulder. "I used to have the same problem. I'd see a hill and think I needed more speed. My normally smooth motion became a jab, which only made it more erratic. The ball would either go over the back of the green, like yours just did, or stop ten feet short."

"And what did you do?" I ask him, but I'm really not talking about my putt. I want to know what happened at lunch. How he went from the devil to getting invited home for a holiday.

"My grandfather gave me some good advice. He told me to widen my stance and take a longer but not harder stroke. Give it a try."

I compare the hole to my and Dani's relationship. Is that why things aren't going where I want them to? I think back to Homecoming. I did something completely romantic for her with our private chicken dinner. And then we had a good time at the dance. I could tell she was having the time of her life. I was, too, but I felt guilty. Bad for Lacey. And I think part of me worried that Dani was enjoying it a little too much. Like some of the things she said and did seemed more about redoing the past. And I couldn't help but wonder if she hadn't really grown up as much as I'd thought she had.

Did I tell her about taking the crown to Lacey to see how she would react?

Maybe.

Because what she said and what I hoped she would say were pretty far apart. She should have told me it was a sweet gesture. She should have offered to go with me or at least ride together, just a quick stop. A feel good, doing the right thing moment before we headed on to the after-parties together.

Instead, she got mad.

Have I been playing our relationship like I have this golf game—erratically, not following through? Should I have pushed for a relationship instead of this stupid friends-with-benefits thing we have?

Or used to have.

And it makes me wonder if she told him. About me.

After three more missed putts, I give up, picking my ball up, and move on, wondering if it's what I need to do in life.

Pick up my ball and move on.

Without her.

THURSDAY, NOVEMBER 28TH

past the madness.

Chase

WE'RE ALL STUFFED from a wonderful Thanksgiving Day meal with our families, including our grandparents; Dad's sister, my aunt Ashley; and her husband, my uncle Cooper. The cool thing about this year is that Damon's mom and her husband, Van, joined us. Which meant that he and Dani didn't have to split time between the two. And everyone has been getting along really well.

Once the food is all cleared and put away, we'll rest for a bit and then go outside for our annual game of flag football. It always starts around four to give everyone time to do their own dinner, but a ton of my parents' friends join in. I know Marcus and Madison will be here along with Nick and Macy, Joey and Chelsea, Katie and Neil, and all their kids.

But for now, most of us are still sitting at the table, chatting. Including Eddie, who is fitting into the family seamlessly.

And he loves it.

"I don't think we told you about how my brothers and I serenaded her the other night," Eddie says to Mimi. "When I gave her my pin."

Mom's head whips in Dani's direction. "You're pinned?"

"What's pinned?" Haley asks.

"It's a precursor to getting engaged," Jadyn replies.

Eddie's eyes get big. "Uh, it's my understanding that—to use an old-fashioned term—it means we're going steady. Like, she's my girl."

I am going to lose my shit.

I feel like I can't breathe.

I have to get out of here.

"Uh, I, um, I just realized I need to go do something." I suddenly get up from the table, banging into it with my knees and causing the whole thing to vibrate.

"That's right, Chase," my dad says. "I'll come in the garage and help you."

I drop to the ground the second I get into the garage. It's that or fall.

"Knockout punch," my dad says.

"Yeah."

"Have you ever heard the saying, *Love is friendship gone mad*?"

"I haven't," I say. "Who said it?"

"A Roman philosopher named Seneca said it a very long time ago. I first became acquainted with it because when we were engaged, your mother had a little case of cold feet. Actually, it was a big case. She went down to Lincoln and partied with Nick and a bunch of the guys, which was no big deal. What was a big deal was, they went to a bar that we frequented. The guy who owned it used to, um, date your mom."

"Oh, wow. Is that why she went there?"

"No, but as people sometimes do, she spilled her guts to said bartender, who was getting a doctorate in philosophy, about these wedding-disaster dreams she had been having. Basically, he told her to stop freaking out."

"Do you think it's true? That love is friendship gone mad?"

"In our case, yes. And possibly in yours. You have the friendship with Dani, and you have the chemistry, but you just have to

237

get past the madness."

"I'm not sure I can."

ONCE I'VE HAD a few moments to regroup, Dad suggests we go back inside. "Maybe you shouldn't play flag football today, Chase. I don't want you getting hurt. Not with the championship game next week."

"I'm not sitting out, Dad. I'll be there shortly."

DANI CORNERS ME the second I step back in from the garage.

"Are you serious? We've been here since Tuesday afternoon, and Eddie is still getting asked a million questions. Can't you just leave the poor guy alone?"

"Hey, you bring a guy home for the holiday, and everyone assumes it's a pretty serious thing," I say with a shrug. "And, apparently, it is. You know, since you're practically engaged."

"I was surprised by it, Chase. We'd only gone out a few times, and they weren't really dates. They were more us just hanging out. It was fun. I mean, he's awesome."

"I think we're going to be best friends by the time he leaves here. We all love him. I can see why you do, too," I say.

"Chase, it's not like that. It just sort of—happened."

"What do you mean?"

"I literally don't know what I was thinking, bringing him home with me. I'm sorry, okay? As I said, it just sort of happened. We got matched up at the party, he sent me flowers, and we hung out a few times. Then he was telling me that he wasn't going home for Thanksgiving, and I was like, *You could come home with me.* I meant it as a friend thing, but then he was at the sorority house, and his fraternity was serenading me. And then he gave me his fraternity pin. My sisters were so excited. And it is a really cool tradition. And I couldn't say no. Everyone was watching."

I cross my arms across my chest and let out a sigh. "Are you freaking kidding me right now?"

"What?"

"I mean, I don't get you. Growing up, all I ever heard out of your sassy little mouth was no. *No, we can't climb that high because it's too dangerous. No, you can't eat more cookies; you'll get sick. No, you can't play with my Barbies because you'll ruin their hair. No. No. No.* And now, it's like you forgot how to say the word. Is that what you want your life to be? A series of events you have no control over, so you just end up with someone who asked you a question publicly? And are you so blind that you can't see history repeating itself? Does it not sound like the *exact* same situation as the day Hunter asked you to Homecoming? When you just *couldn't say no.* And now, more than two years later, you *still* haven't learned your lesson? Call me sometime, you know, when you decide to grow the fuck up."

She gets a pissed look on her face and drags me into the laundry room, shutting the door.

"When I grow up? Really?" she says, getting in my face. "I know you never invite Lacey over for holidays because I've been to all of them. And now, suddenly, here she is? I know you're just trying to make me jealous."

"She's here because Haley invited her, not me. So, actually, I'm not." I take a step toward her, causing her to back up against the washing machine.

"Yeah, you are." She takes ahold of my shirt, grabbing it in her fist and pulling me closer.

Causing our faces to almost touch.

The second she looks down at my mouth, I know exactly what she's thinking. And I don't hesitate. I pick her up, set her on top of the washing machine, stand between her legs, and kiss her.

I half-expect her to slap me across the face, but instead, she grabs the back of my neck, bringing me closer. She forces her tongue into my mouth, and I accept it, greedily sucking on it. I slide my hands down her backside as she moves herself to the end of the machine, her thighs wrapping around my waist.

Her hands are running roughly through my hair, and I pull my lips away from her mouth before sucking my way down her sweet-smelling neck. She lets out a little moan and moves her face downward, meeting mine, so I will kiss her again.

Her hands glide down my chest, settling on my waist and then undoing my belt.

And I'm definitely ready for it.

But then I think, *What the fuck am I doing?*

"This is bullshit, Devaney," I tell her, pulling away. "I can't do this. Way to cheat on your boyfriend. Real classy."

I don't like you.

Devaney

I SIT THERE for a second, my anger growing. I run home and then up to my room, grab two items, and go back next door.

I stand in front of Chase, who is in a circle outside with Eddie, Damon, Lacey, and Haley, all laughing, having a ball, waiting to choose sides for the game.

I walk around them and tap Chase on the back, motioning for him to come with me. When he doesn't, I basically take his hand and mad-march him over behind the tree house.

He leans up against it, like he doesn't have a care in the world. "What do you want now, Dani?"

I hold out my fist.

He scrunches his nose and rolls his eyes at me, but finally, he does what I want—holds his palm up.

"Here's the answer to your stupid penny," I whisper madly. He opens his hand, and I drop the penny and the *dream* ring into it. "Because this friendship is over."

"Shocker," he sasses.

"I don't get it," I tell him. "Why are you being such a dick about this?"

"I'm not. At all. I've been really nice to Eddie."

I let out a frustrated sigh. "To me, not him."

"Well, that's probably because, right now, I don't like you very much. How could you bring a boyfriend into my house and not have the decency to tell me? What? You thought it would be fun to just surprise me?"

"So, is that how friends with benefits works for you? I'm not allowed to date anyone else even though you are?"

"You really don't get it, do you?" he says, and then he walks away.

With my ring in his hand.

FRIDAY, NOVEMBER 29TH

Want you to be happy.

Devaney

ON FRIDAY, THE Mackenzie and Diamond families along with our grandparents and, of course, Eddie fly up to Lincoln for the game.

By the end of the first quarter, I'm ready to leave. I feel like I'm suffocating. I just want to go back to my little dorm and cry.

Eddie stays in the box until the first touchdown and then wants to go sit with his frat brothers. And probably get a drink. Honestly, I wouldn't blame him. This break has been a roller coaster of feelings, and I'm not off the ride yet.

I give everyone hugs and kisses, especially my little sisters. I hold them tight, feeling like I might never see them again.

I hug Haley and Damon last, and then Chase grabs my hand and pulls me outside. He looks as bad as I feel, and I know the emotional toll that's been this weekend is affecting him, too.

"I need to say something before you go," he says.

I don't reply, just give him a curt nod, knowing if I speak, I'll probably fall to pieces.

I expect him to yell at me, so I'm surprised when he pulls my *dream* ring out of his pocket, slides it on my finger, and says, "Just because we're not together doesn't mean that our dreams can't still come true. I love you, Dani, and at this point, I just want you to be happy. If Eddie is that guy, so be it."

His gaze meets mine, emotions moving in waves across his face.

"I just don't understand why you've been such a jerk about it though. Especially when you're still sleeping with Lacey."

He grabs my chin, so I have to look him in the eye.

"Because I'm not, Dani. I haven't slept with anyone *but you* since my birthday. You know how your dad talks about the perfect pass, that moment when everything goes right, how the second the ball leaves your fingertips, you know it's going to reach its intended destination? And when you throw those kinds of passes, you know they are rare. Because no matter how hard you try to throw it perfectly every time you let go of the ball, there are other factors involved—getting rushed, having to scramble, broken plays. And even though, in those situations, you can usually successfully connect with a receiver, it doesn't feel the same. I could successfully connect with other girls, Dani, but I'm smart enough to know it wouldn't feel the same. *You* are my perfect pass." He stops, lets out a ragged breath, and then says, "Or at least, you were."

Tears fill my eyes as I slide my hand over his heart.

He kisses my forehead tenderly, says, "Bye, Dani," and goes back into the suite.

What I have to do.

Chase

IT'S A FRIDAY night. After a game.

We're back home from Nebraska, not my game, but still.

I look at the tent, still sitting in the corner of my room, sadly waiting for the weekend that never came.

I grab my phone.

Order pizza.

Eat it in the tent alone.

And I know what I have to do.

TUESDAY, DECEMBER 3RD

Can't do it.

Chase

ON SATURDAY, WE'LL be competing for the state championship. I should be focused on the game, but really, something has been weighing heavily on my mind.

I talked to my dad about it before Thanksgiving, and I did what he'd suggested—thought about it and did not make a rash decision.

Because it was a big decision.

One I made last Friday night in the tent.

The one that I need to tell Damon about.

WHEN I GET over to their house, I find his dad at the kitchen island, eating a snack.

"Hey, Uncle Danny," I say. "Damon upstairs?"

"He just ran to the store to pick up something for Jennifer. Should be right back."

"Cool," I say.

"You want some cinnamon apples?" he asks me.

Normally, I would say yes. I love those things, but right now, I'm feeling a little nauseous.

"Ah, no, thanks. I just ate."

245

"Ready for the big game this weekend?"

"Yeah, and how about you? I heard you are going to be in the booth for some upcoming bowl games. You ready for that?"

"I hope so," he says. "I'm thinking about taking Damon with me to a few. Thought it might be fun for him to see behind the scenes—"

I frown and interrupt him, "With all due respect, sir, you should take Dani. You know what she wants to do for a living, right?"

"She's never really said. Just that she wanted to major in journalism."

"She wants to be a sideline reporter. For football. It's her dream."

Danny narrows his eyes and looks torn between being confused and touched. "Really? That would be incredible. She certainly knows the game well enough."

"Yeah, she does. She wants to apply for an internship at a sports network this summer, but she sort of didn't want to tell you."

"But why not? I could help her."

"I think maybe she wants to do it on her own. I think it's kind of like when she went through rush. She initially thought she would cut the one she was a legacy to because she didn't want to get in because of that. She wanted them to like her, not feel compelled to take her because of family."

"She's a lot like me, isn't she?" her dad says. "Wants to forge her own path."

I nod. "She's your biggest fan. And she has always wanted you to be proud of her."

We hear the garage door open, and I add, "Please don't tell her I told you."

"I won't. And, Chase, thank you. I will ask her."

DAMON COMES IN the house and puts the food away, and then I follow him downstairs. He used to have a game room upstairs, but with the addition of his little sisters, that room got made into a nursery, and the game room got relocated to the home theater. Which is better anyway because no one's little ears can hear us cursing when we get blown up.

He starts the game, but I quickly pause it and turn to him.

"I can't do it," I finally say the words out loud to him. "I can't go to Nebraska anymore. I'm sorry. I totally understand if you still want to go."

"Because of my sister?" he asks.

"Because of me. I just can't be there with her. I need to be able to focus on playing. On getting to the pros, going high in the draft. I can't do that there. Where she is. I love her. And I just"— my voice cracks—"can't."

"It's like you've been drunk on love or something," he says with a little chuckle, trying to lighten the mood.

"I probably have been. But it's not good for me. It has to stop. I'm over her—well, I'm working on getting over her."

"You're going cold-turkey sober?" he says with a smile.

"Why don't you ever have girl drama?" I ask with a laugh.

"Because, me, I'm less of a *binge drinker* and more of a *day* drinker. You sure you aren't just, like, hungover? You know, the day after is always the worst, but then it gets better. It *will* get better."

"I considered it before Thanksgiving, solidified my decision after we came home from the game the day after Thanksgiving, and have continued to think about it since. I'm firm on this. And I am *never* drinking again."

This causes Damon to laugh out loud. "Dude, you're going to become—what's that word—a tittillater."

"I think you mean *teetotaler*. Someone who abstains from alcohol."

"Hmm. I think I like the tittie one better. As a matter of fact, when we were on our recruitment visits, I ranked all the schools in some very important categories. One of which was boobs."

"Boobs?"

"Yep, how pretty the girls were. I mean, if all else is equal, it's a good tiebreaker, for sure."

"You don't have to do this, you know. I haven't wanted to tell you because I know it's your dream. To follow in your dad's footsteps."

"Chase, we're in this together. Where you go, I do, too. We've be planning this since—"

"We were eight," I finish as relief washes over me. "So, what else did you rank them on?"

"Game-day experience. Coaching staff. Number of top-ranked draft picks. Facilities. Campus. The town around campus. The weather. And last but not least, the tacos."

"Tacos?"

"I mean, yeah. It's my favorite food. I can't go somewhere that doesn't have a really excellent Mexican restaurant. Did you think during our meal on our own at each school that it was just a coincidence we ate Mexican food?"

"I don't think I realized that."

"Did you have a favorite one?"

"I don't remember, honestly."

"Did *you* rank the schools?" Damon asks me, his head tilted at me, looking puzzled.

"No." I laugh. "I just went along for the ride."

"Dude, it's like we've switched brains or something."

"I knew the word teetotaler," I tell him.

"Good point. Plus, if we'd switched brains, I'd know all the dirty things you've thought about my sister. So, it's probably a good thing we didn't."

"I'll drink to that," I say, holding up my Gatorade.

"Hold that thought." He gets up and runs upstairs then comes back down with a notebook and hands it to me. "Here, take this. Let me know what you decide. But can we put it on the back burner until after Saturday? We need to finish our last high school season with another state championship."

"Now that I know we'll still go to college together and I can stop freaking out about it, yeah, actually, I can."

WHEN I GET back to my house, I find Lacey waiting for me in my room.

"Hey, I was just over at Damon's. Why didn't you tell me you were here?"

"I think I'm a little bit in shock." She waves a folded-up piece of paper toward me and says flatly, "I got in. I'm going to Auburn."

I pull her up off the chair and hug her. "Lacey! That's amazing! I'm so proud of you! Were your parents excited?"

"Yeah, they were. I honestly still can't believe it. I keep thinking someone will call me and be like, *Yeah, we meant that other Lacey.*"

"It's really cool you already know where you're going."

"What do you mean? Nebraska is all I've ever heard about from you since we've been friends."

"Yeah, well, I'm thinking it might not be the right fit for me anymore."

"Wait. What are you saying?"

"I'm considering my options."

She grins. "Well, you visited Auburn, right? Come there with me."

"Lacey, I wouldn't want you to think—"

"That it meant something? Don't worry; I'd have no expectations."

"Well, the thing is, I wouldn't be going with you exactly. I'll be graduating in December and starting college in January, so I can play spring ball."

"Chase! It's December. How long have you known about this? Like, you're accepted and basically enrolled in college? You planned this?"

"Yes, I had to plan for all options."

"When were you going to tell me? And what about prom?"

"I won't be here."

She lets out a huge sigh. "Oh, Chase, you infuriate me. I really don't know why I put up with it."

"Honestly, Lacey, you shouldn't. You deserve better. Someone who really loves you. I hope you go to Auburn and find him."

"We're over, officially now, aren't we? I mean, we sort of already have been, basically since your birthday, but ..." She studies my face. "Did you change your mind because Dani brought that guy home for Thanksgiving?"

"I'd say, that's definitely part of it."

"Well, if you're not going to Nebraska and you decide to go to Auburn, let me know. Especially if you'll already know the ropes when I get there in the fall."

"Did you have tacos there? Like, when you visited?"

"Actually, yes! They have this great Mexican restaurant a few blocks from campus. I went back twice in one weekend!"

And I can't help but smile.

Mr. Too-Nice-For-You Guy.

Devaney

"WELL, CONGRATULATIONS," MY brother says when I answer his

call. "You finally broke him. And probably me in the process."

"What's that supposed to mean?"

"Your little Thanksgiving stunt. Bringing that poor guy home. I bet he had no clue what he was getting sucked into."

"I liked him."

"Yeah, I liked him, too. We *all* liked him. But that's not the point. The point is, you were using him. At least Chase has been honest with Lacey about what's up. You paraded Eddie around like he was the greatest thing since cell phones. We all felt sorry for him. And what's worse is that you made out with Chase in the laundry room and probably would have had sex with him had he let you. *Sex*, Dani. *With Chase. In the laundry room.* While your boyfriend was two rooms over, talking to Papa!"

"I, um, did Chase tell you about that?"

"He didn't have to. I could tell by the way things went down. You really think no one notices the chemistry between you and Chase? Or the anger or whatever you both happen to be feeling at the moment? Fortunately, the nice guy, Eddie, didn't seem to, but still, it's just wrong."

"You all wanted me to be with a nice guy."

"Except that you don't love him. Or did I misinterpret the way you looked at Chase? I understand you were all hyped up at Homecoming, feeling like a big shot, and you were pissed when he took the crown to Lacey, but if the tables were turned and you had been sick the night you won, wouldn't you have wanted your date to do that for you? Simply out of respect? All the girls—and I mean, every. Single. One—was swooning about it at school. How sweet it was of him. But you got pissed and then decided to get even. Enter Mr. Too-Nice-For-You Guy."

"You're not being fair to me, Damon. Chase and I had an agreement. Friends with benefits. No commitment. And he was still dating Lacey, so why is that okay for him but not for me?"

"It's different because you know he loves *you*. And so does

Lacey for that matter. But you brought this guy home to flaunt him in Chase's face."

"I actually didn't. I gotta go, Damon."

"No, you're going to listen to me. I didn't say anything to you about this at Thanksgiving. Chase was nice to the guy. I was nice to the guy. Everyone was nice to the guy. But I'm done being quiet now because you just screwed with *my* future. The state championship game is this weekend, and eleven days later, we are going to sign our National Letters of Intent. Which is a legal commitment to spend our first year at that college. Our plan was to go to Nebraska."

"And you should sign with them regardless of what my relationship with Chase is."

"Yeah, well, guess what, Dani. Those plans got changed. Chase says he can't do it. He can't go there. Which means neither am I. And it really sucks because it's what we've *both* dreamed about since we were kids."

"Wait, you're not committing to Nebraska? But what happened—"

"*You* happened. Your plan to make Chase jealous or piss him off or whatever your little deal was has become a *big* deal. I hope you're happy, Devaney."

"I don't—"

"I know, sis. And *that's* the problem."

"Damon."

"What?"

"I broke up with Eddie right after the game on Friday."

"Why?"

"Because if I really cared about him, I wouldn't have kissed Chase in the laundry room. He took it well. Told me it was a bummer. That he loved my family and to tell you and Chase that if you ever want to hang out, are considering joining a frat next year, or just need a place to party, to let him know. He seemed fairly unfazed by the whole thing."

"Why in the world haven't you told Chase?"

"Because."

"Because why?"

"I don't want to hurt him again. And I need to figure some things out."

"Well, I hope to hell that you can do that fast. There isn't much time."

WHEN HE ENDS the call, I do something that I started during rush week but never finished. I watch the video of that day.

All of it.

From start to finish.

Then, I watch it again.

And I realize something important.

Something that makes all the difference in the world.

FRIDAY, DECEMBER 6TH

Sometime is now.

Chase

AFTER DINNER WITH my family, I excuse myself to go to my room. I want to watch some game film of the opponent we'll face tomorrow in the state championship game.

I barely get the video started when Dani walks in.

"What are you doing here?" I ask, shocked.

She stands up straight and tall, looking serious. "I want to explain why I did what I did that day on the field with Hunter because it got all mixed up."

"It's in the past, Dani. It doesn't matter anymore."

"So are your games, but you still watch film of them, right?" she counters.

"Uh, yeah, I guess, but that's so I can learn."

"Exactly. And that's why you and I are going to watch the video of that day together. I want to explain to you what I was thinking and why I said what I did."

"The last thing I want to do is relive that day," I say.

"You have to. That's exactly how it is when you have a bad game. You don't want to watch the proof of your suckage, but you do. And you, Chase, are an athlete, not just a quarterback. You've played soccer, tried hockey, you golf, play baseball, wakeboard, water ski, run track, and"—she smirks—"have even been known to play some sand volleyball."

I sigh and roll my eyes at her, clearly remembering our conversation when she was cockblocking me that summer. "Do you have a point?"

"I do," she says, and she's smiling.

Why is she smiling?

"When you're out there with the ball in your hand and your offensive line gives you time to make the play, there's nothing to affect you; you perform at your peak. Differently than you would if you had to, say, scramble or you got a bad snap. I mean, who wouldn't panic a little when a big lineman or a defensive end has one goal, which is to put you on the ground and make it sting a little?"

"And?"

"And when those things happen, you forget your perfect passing motion, you become the shortstop and throw it sidearm, you throw off your back foot. Sometimes, you're so busy looking for a receiver that you don't see that you're open for the run. So, what do you do to get better, Chase?"

"Practice?"

"No, you *watch film* to figure out why you missed the wide-open guy downfield. You watch film to see why you threw an interception. And all I'm asking is for you to allow me to show you a different kind of film. One that didn't just affect some game, but our lives. I know we've done our best to hide it from everyone. I know we've been cordial and spent time together with our families. I know that all those times, I put on a smile for everyone while my heart felt like it was breaking over and over again. *We* lost the big game, Chase, because I fumbled the ball at the end. Although watching the film did me some good because I realized just like in all games and relationships, it's never *one play* that causes a loss. It's a team effort. It's a bunch of little mistakes.

And I thought if I gave you a play-by-play of what I did, told you exactly what I was thinking at the time, what I was feeling, then maybe it might help us become friends again. For real this time."

"Fine. I'll watch it sometime," I say noncommittally.

She grabs my hand and grins at me way too much, like she used to, and for a moment, I can pretend that things between us are normal.

"Sometime is now," she says, leading me over to her house and down to their movie room, where it becomes very obvious she knew I'd agree to this.

Sometimes, I think I'd agree to anything she asked me.

But that day.

On the field.

When push came to shove, when she should have taken my hand and walked away with me, when we should have shown everyone.

It's funny how life—just like a game—becomes a series of decisions, a series of consequences that follow those decisions, and how they push you down a path. For better or worse.

My life after that summer hasn't been that bad. I've made incredible strides in my game. I've excelled in school. I have some really awesome friends and am blessed with a close, supportive family. So far, the only loss I've experienced is when we had to put my beloved dog to sleep. She'd slept under my crib when I was a baby and in my room with me for every one of my first thirteen years. Her loss devastated me. For months, even after Dani's dad surprised us with a new puppy—our dog, Winger—I'd still want to call out to Angel or reach down from my chair to pat her head or give her some Cheetos.

With Dani, it was different. I lost her from my life, yet I didn't. It was more like if Angel had told me she wanted to go live with another family, but I still had to see her, still felt the same way about her even though I was so hurt by her decision and even though all I wanted was for her to come back to me.

And here I am, stupidly agreeing to another one of Dani's plans. The plans she never seems to follow through on.

My mom says that the trouble with trouble is that it always starts out as fun. She talks about how she and Dani's dad used to get into trouble as kids, and I finally get why. He and his daughter share that same magnetism, that same smile. And while Damon also seems to have gotten a similar gene, I can reason with him. He'll listen when I caution him. Devaney is a wild card—always has been. She rarely takes my advice, and sometimes, I wonder why she ever even asks for it.

And over in my room, I stupidly assumed she was making it up as she went, but when we arrive in the movie room, she grins at me, waving her hand toward a bottle of tequila and two shot glasses on the bar. The theater-style popcorn machine is full of freshly popped corn.

And I can't decide if I should be mad at myself for allowing her to rope me into this or flattered that she went to the effort.

"I thought we might need this," she says, pointing at the tequila. "To get through it. Together." Her sentences are short and choppy. Coming out as she thinks them.

"I'm not drinking," I say incredulously. "Tomorrow is the state championship." I glance at my watch.

She takes my wrist in her hand, looking at the watch. "Your birthday gift. I'm sorry I slept with you on your birthday."

"Yeah, whatever, and pretty soon, you'll be back at school. What's it got to do with anything anyway?" I react defensively, as if a lineman were getting ready to tackle me.

Dani pushes a tub into the popcorn machine, fills it up, adds melted butter, tops it with M&M's, and hands it to me.

Why does she have to be the only girl who knows this? When I took Lacey to the movies, why could I never bring myself to order my favorite combination? Because it wasn't *our* combination.

Don't ever fall in love with your best friend, people. When it goes bad, the repercussions are far and wide.

Dani doesn't reply to my comment. She takes the popcorn over and sets it down on a table in between our two favorite seats—third row back, middle of the row—then she comes back and pours us each a shot.

I try not to notice the sway of her hips as she walks toward me. The fact that her head is held high, her back straight. That she seems confident tonight.

I've relived the scene from the field so many times that I even dream about it. And every time, I get to that one pivotal moment where I reach my hand out and tell her to come with me.

She doesn't.

And I wake up.

I had a tough time my freshman year, trying to win the re-spect of the upperclassmen, and not only did I lose her that day, but I also lost everything I'd worked for in that department. It didn't help that, despite his suspension, Hunter Lansford made constant comments about her in the locker room. It took every ounce of my self-control not to punch him in the face daily.

But then again, it wasn't his fault Dani had chosen him over me. And when we won the state championship again that year, he tried to play all nice, like he hadn't tormented me all season even though he and Dani never ended up going to Homecoming together.

All that destruction in my life because some idiot had been trying to make his ex-girlfriend jealous.

Every night, when I stare over at Dani's window, I think about how if he had not asked her that day, things might have been different for us. But I know they probably wouldn't have been. Devaney seems to have bad taste in guys. And I wonder what that says about me. Because for a brief, wondrous time, she chose me.

The second I think it, all the emotions and feelings come rushing back. The ones I constantly suppress. Even our friends-with-benefits time couldn't cure it.

"This is a bad idea," I say, shaking my head.

But I still take the glass.

She pauses, and I think she's going to change her mind, but instead, she grabs the bottle, turns down the lights, and moves us to our seats.

"There's a drinking game that goes with this."

My eyes get huge. "You played a drinking game with your friends while watching this?" I'm so offended that I'm ready to throw this tequila in her face. Instead, I take a drink.

"No, Chase, I didn't. But I have watched it a few times by myself. And for the record, you just drank without me. Without a toast first."

I take in a breath, trying to control my erratic heartbeat.

She takes her seat, motions for me to do the same, and then holds up her glass.

"To us," she says, causing me to roll my eyes. Because there is no us. No matter how hard I've tried. "So, the game goes like this—every time you want to cringe over something someone says, you drink. It doesn't have to be the whole shot, and it probably *shouldn't* be. I tried that with vodka—didn't go well. Probably will never drink it again in my life. Thus, we've moved on to tequila. So, just a sip or a gulp sometimes seems to work best." She pauses and looks into my eyes. "And the most important part, when either one of us wants a drink, before we actually take the drink, we have to pause the video and tell the other person what we were thinking at the time and what we wish we had said or done differently. Deal?"

She grins at me again. I clink the glass against hers. She takes a sip. I down the shot.

She pours me another and presses play.

I hit the remote, stopping it. "Do you really think we can just push rewind?"

"Yes," she says.

"I don't know, Dani. Sometimes, I think we can, but I just feel like regardless of what's happened between us this year—becoming sort of friends again, sleeping together—we've had some really amazing moments, but no matter how great they are, they have felt kind of—"

"Hollow," she says.

"Exactly. I feel like you weren't ready."

"I think, Chase, that maybe *we* weren't ready."

"What do you mean? I was in love with you. I was ready," I say, considering downing shot number two.

"I mean, we, as a couple."

"There's a difference?" I scoff.

"I think so. And I know you think this is crazy, but I think if you're brave enough to watch this with me—and I mean, the whole thing—it will make a big difference." She hands me the remote. "Up to you."

"Fine, on one condition. That you talk me through all of it. Tell me what's happening the whole time." I start to feel like I might cry. "And hold my hand. Through all of it."

She doesn't reply, just squeezes my hand.

I press play, and our football field appears in practically life-sized form on the massive movie screen in front of me.

"Okay, here," Dani says, "you can see that I'm on the sideline with my squad. We just finished our workout, and we are now stretching and catching up." She takes the remote from me. "I think I need to control this, or we'll miss something and have to rewind. Anyway, I knew that I should have been listening to what they were saying, but my eyes were on you. Can you see that? The love in them? I was looking at you, Chase. You can't see yourself right now in the video, but I remember it so vividly. You were wearing the red jersey that reminded the team not to hit you, and you had been working with Damon on his favorite route. Do you remember?"

"Yeah. We were doing the fly route. And actually, it's both me and Damon's favorite play."

"Because he loves running fast and you love throwing long."

"Exactly."

"I was also studying your form—and I'm not talking about your sexy body. I could tell that you'd been to camp. Your throwing motion looked better, as did your wrist follow-through."

"It's really cool how you notice all that," I tell her. "I know you want to be a reporter, but you'd probably make a good coach, too."

She takes a deep breath. "Okay, here we go."

"How was your summer vacation, Dani?" her squadmate Brandy asks on the screen. *"Family trips kind of suck. Especially with no phones. Seriously, I don't know how you survived."*

"Actually, it was pretty amazing. We had a lot of fun, doing family activity things together."

"Sounds kind of lame," her friend Shaylie says.

"It sounds better than my summer," one of the sophomore girls pipes in. *"We didn't go anywhere. Had a staycation, which basically consisted of arguing over what pizza toppings and movie we wanted to watch on our family fun night."*

"If I have to hear about your family fun night again," Brandy says in a voice that says she's over it.

"Was there anyone cute there?" Megan inquires. *"A hot surfer maybe?"*

"We went to the Ozarks." Dani laughs, shaking her head. *"It's a lake."*

She hits pause again. "So, what comes next is what I thought was my opportunity to ease them into the idea of you and me being in a relationship. Like we'd talked about."

"Actually, I have something to tell you guys. Chase and I got sort of close this summer."

"Close?" Shaylie scrunches up her nose.

"Yeah." Dani smiles—beams really—and it makes my heart happy for a moment. *"I'm not exactly sure how it happened. We've been friends for so long—"* she starts before being interrupted.

"Wait. It?" Megan stares at her blankly. *"You're not saying that you hooked up with Chase, are you?"*

"I wouldn't call it hooking up—" Dani insists.

"Oh my God, you did!" Megan gasps, covering her mouth. *"Was it hot?"*

"Well…" Dani smiles at her, but when her cheeks flush, my stomach drops.

I eye the shot glass and let out a deep breath as I squeeze her hand. She hits pause.

"You blushed there. Were you embarrassed?"

"I was embarrassed because it had come out wrong or she had taken it wrong. I didn't want her to think we were just a hook-up. In fact, this was the point where I decided that easing into it wasn't going to work. I was going to tell her we were dating. That we were in love."

"Really?" My heart feels like it's going to beat out of my chest. "But I thought—"

"I know you did, Chase. That's why we're watching this. So you can know. I tried to tell you after, but you were so upset that you wouldn't really listen."

I pick up the glass and take just a sip. "Okay, keep going."

"Uh, it totally was," Megan says, shaking her head. *"Wow. Who knew getting stuck in the Ozarks would end up being so much fun? I thought you'd go there and die of boredom."*

"No, actually, my trip was, well, in one word, amazing."

"Okay," Megan says slowly, her eyes narrowed. *"But wait. You don't have, like, feelings for Chase, do you?"* And she's looking at Dani like the answer should be no. And it makes me understand a little of the pressure she felt.

"We got close this summer," Dani reiterates.

"Yeah, we heard. But come on. I mean, a summer fling is one thing. And don't get me wrong, Chase is cute. He's a great quarterback. But he's your little. Brother's. Best. Friend. Besides, I thought you were talking to Hunter. Although how were we to know? No phones and all. Anyway, look!" Megan says, pointing to Hunter, who is now on camera, walking toward Dani.

Brandy jumps up off the turf and smiles in Hunter's direction. Almost like she expected him.

"Diamond," Hunter says to Dani, giving her the kind of cocky smirk that makes me want to go punch the screen. *"Come here."*

"Uh ..." she says.

"Go," Megan urges, pushing her shoulder.

"Why would I want to talk to him?"

"Because he's the hottest senior," she says.

"Who blew me off," Dani mutters as she pulls herself up off the ground and marches over toward Hunter.

"What were you thinking here?" I dare to ask because what I thought—that she was happy about him asking—isn't showing on her face.

She looks pissed at him.

"Honestly, I wanted to punch that smug smile off his stupid face. I couldn't imagine what he would have to say to me. He was supposed to call me every day. And he had, like, once. In three weeks? And now, he wanted to talk to me?"

"That's the take-no-shit Dani I know and love," I say with a smile even though tears are prickling my eyes.

She takes a sip of her shot. "It's hard to watch. I know. I'm sorry."

"I think maybe it's me who should be sorry. Were you really going to tell them that you were in love with me?"

She closes her eyes and nods. "I was. What we had—it was special, Chase. And I know that I was nervous about it, about telling everyone. But when push came to shove, I wasn't going to let some stupid, vapid girls stand in the way of what I wanted."

I lean over and press my lips against hers. It's just a soft kiss. But one I have to give her. When I lean back, her eyes look like mine, shimmering with tears.

"Maybe we don't need to watch the rest," I tell her. "I get it."

"No, I think we do," she says. "Remember how I said we weren't ready? That we included you. And I don't want us to make the same mistakes again. I want to get it all out. Then put it behind us. Learn from our mistakes."

"Okay," I say as she starts the video again.

"What?" Dani says, crossing her arms tightly in front of her chest in determination.

Hunter shakes the football in his hand toward the end zone and says, *"Go long. I know you can catch."*

Dani squints her eyes at him, then says, *"No,"* and turns away.

Mostly, probably, because she hates being told what to do.

"Dani," Brandy says, rushing toward her with a horrified expression and pushing her toward Hunter.

"What?" Dani asks her.

"Just do it. It's Hunter. He likes you. He told me."

"More like he's still in love with Taylor, and they are back together," Dani whispers back, looking frustrated.

"You're so out of the loop. They are not. At all. And trust me, you're going to love this. Just go out for the damn pass."

Dani looks behind her and sees that the cheer squad has now

formed a semicircle behind her, almost pushing her toward him.

"Come on, Diamond," Hunter heckles. *"I thought you said you could play just as well as your brother?"*

A group of football players come into view, and you can hear a few snickers over his taunting of her.

Dani narrows her eyes at Hunter in challenge.

And I know exactly what she's thinking. The girl doesn't back down from a challenge, and she certainly knows how to catch a football.

She takes off, jogging from the twenty-yard line, where I am stretching, to the end zone.

Hunter tosses her the ball. And it's not a very good throw.

His spiral is wobbly, and the pass is too high, but she leaps up and grabs it anyway.

The cheerleaders break out in, well, cheers.

And then the camera flashes to the scoreboard, where a message is running across it.

YOU JUST SCORED A DATE TO HOMECOMING.

Hunter runs up to Dani. *"Pretty creative way to ask, right?"*

The cheer squad is clapping, yelling out their names, *"Hunter and Dani. Hunter and Dani. Go!!! Hunter and Dani!"*

Dani is wide-eyed. Not saying anything.

I watch as her eyes seem to frantically search the crowd off camera.

I don't ask her to pause it, but she does.

"Based on the look on my face, what do you think I was thinking and doing?"

"Well, you don't look happy."

"I wasn't. I was surrounded by people, and I was trying to find you in the crowd. I wanted you to know that I hadn't expected this to happen. I never would have gone out for the pass if I had known. Brandy and Megan rushed up to me and told me they'd helped him plan it. They thought I was so lucky. Hunter was getting high fives, but all I could think about was you. How it must look. How I needed to get out of there. Also, I should point out, I never said yes."

"No, you didn't." I take a deep breath and take another sip.

"Why did you just drink?"

"Because I think I know what happens next."

She presses play, and I was right. When she moves toward an open space in the crowd, Hunter picks her up, swings her around, and kisses her.

"That," she says, "was a horrible kiss, by the way. He shoved his fat tongue in my mouth. I felt like I was going to cry. I wanted nothing more than to get away from him."

"That's when I got involved."

"Yeah."

"This part I've seen. It's been a while though."

"We're going to have a great year, Dani," Hunter says, slinging his arm around her again.

"Let go of me!" she says to him, struggling to get out of his grip.

"Oh no, you don't, Diamond. We're going to celebrate." He whispers suggestively but loud enough for everyone to hear, *"All night long."*

"Get your hands off her," I hear myself say as I rush up to the asshole.

"Whoa, whoa, whoa," Hunter says, holding up his hands. *"Relax. Dani and I are just having some fun."*

"It doesn't look like Dani is having fun. She is trying to get away from you. She even told you point-blank to let go of her," I say in her

defense.

The cheerleaders back up at my outburst, expecting a fight. And they are right to do so because I am pissed.

"What are you, like, twelve? Obviously, you don't know girls. Just because she said it doesn't mean she meant it. It's called playing coy. Dani and I have had lots of fun together already. Right, Dani? And we're going to have lots more. I always get my way," Hunter says, shooting Dani a wink and then giving me a look that causes me to visibly flinch.

Dani pauses the video again.

"I was pretty pissed at this point," she says. "Because I was like, Did he really just say that he could do anything he wanted to me?"

"I was ready to kill him, honestly," I say. I'm breathing heavily, like it's happening now, not more than two years ago.

"And do you want to know what my next thought was?"

"Uh, maybe?"

"That if you and Hunter got into a fight, you could get kicked off the team. I didn't want that to happen. That's why I was so upset. He wasn't worth you risking your dream."

Tears form in my eyes again. "That's what you don't get, Dani. It's that you were worth it. I never thought once about the repercussions. I just knew that I needed to protect you."

"Which was the problem. But now, since we know that you didn't end up getting in trouble, we can watch it and enjoy this. In fact, I might have rewound it and watched it a few times," she says with a laugh.

And I can't help but laugh with her. "Let's see it."

I watch as I throw a right hook, following through with my hips, like I do with a pass. A motion that adds the momentum of my body to propel the pass further or, in this case, puts the weight of that motion behind my fist, which lands squarely on Hunter's jaw.

"If you touch her again," I say to Hunter, venom in my voice.

"Of course, Hunter wasn't smart enough to just go down," Dani says with a laugh as on-screen Hunter makes an obscene gesture, causing me to jump on top of him, pin him to the ground, and punch him in the face again.

"Dani! Do something!" Megan yells out.

"Chase, stop it!" Dani yells, rushing toward us.

But within a second, Damon pushes through the crowd, shoves Dani out of the way, and pulls me off Hunter.

"What the fuck?" Hunter yells, spitting out a mouth full of blood.

"Don't you ever talk about Dani like that again," I growl at him.

"Chase!" Dani hisses at me.

And if things weren't already bad enough, this is where things go south fast.

"This moment, coming up." I say, feeling my emotions rise to the surface again as I hit pause. "I think I've seen enough. I'm sorry. I should have trusted you. It wasn't your fault. I've blamed you this whole time. And you've taken it. Why?"

She lowers her head, looking down at her hands, which are twisted up in a blanket. "Because you didn't have faith in me. In us. It was a big blow, Chase. To me. To my heart. And I didn't want you to get kicked off the team. While I appreciated your help, it kind of wasn't your battle. It was mine. You never gave me a chance to handle it."

I throw back the rest of my shot. Rub my hands across my face. Press play.

"Dani, let's go," I say to her even though I'm not looking at her. My eyes are still locked with Hunter's.

"You need to put your little sophomore on a leash," Hunter says to Dani, standing up and wiping the edge of his mouth on his shirt.

"Shut the fuck up, Lansford." It's Damon who speaks this time.

"Oh, am I going to have a problem with you, too, Diamond?" Hunter retorts.

"You're not worth it," Damon says, shaking his head. He grabs ahold of my shirt tightly to keep me from lunging at Hunter again.

"Dani, we're leaving. Now," I say, looking Dani in the eye.

When she doesn't move, I wrap my hand around her arm.

"Oh, so that's what's going on here?" Hunter calls out with a sharp laugh. *"Dani, did you go slumming on the family vacay with your little brother's best friend? And now, he's being all possessive? Pathetic."*

"I might need more tequila," I say desperately as Dani gets ready to say the words that have haunted me since.

"Just go home, Chase. You've done enough already."

I hit pause. Get up. Take a swig straight out of the bottle and then wipe my eyes with the bottom of my shirt. Dani's going to think I'm a complete baby, but I can't stop the tears. This is the dream I have. And it always ends here because that's when I stormed off.

But I've seen this part of the video. What comes next.

She ruthlessly turns it back on.

"Chase," Dani calls out, tears in her eyes.

"More like he hasn't done enough," Hunter taunts. *"Don't cry, Dani. I can guarantee you won't be able to get enough of me."*

And this time, it isn't me who hits him. It's Damon.

A second later, Hunter is back on the ground.

Although this isn't where my dream always ends; it's where the video Damon presented to the Coach did.

"Is there more?" I ask Dani.

"Yeah, there is. Come sit back down, Chase. Leave the bottle."

Damon is forcefully dragging Dani off the field.

"I freaking told you," he growls at her.

"Damon—"

"I could have just gotten kicked off the team. Chase, too."

"I didn't ask you to punch him!"

"I couldn't not. He was talking shit about my sister. Trust me, if Dad had heard what was coming out of that asshole's mouth, he would have done it himself."

"Let go of me," Dani says, stopping and digging in her heels. *"I don't need your or Chase's help."*

"I told you not to mess with Chase," Damon says seriously.

"Just leave me alone, okay?"

I watch as tears flow down her beautiful face.

The camera follows her as she works her way through the crowd, where amidst all the chaos, she picks up her backpack, grabs her keys, runs to her car, and peels out of the parking lot, her tires squealing.

A voice says, *"Well, that was pretty darn exciting."*

And the video ends.

"All I could think about was that I had to find you. That I had to make it right," Dani says to me. "And I did find you. You were walking down the sidewalk, still in the red jersey and half pads. I asked if you needed a lift."

"And I said no. That I'd rather walk five miles than sit next to you. But you," I say, shaking my head, "are stubborn. You drove ahead, parked, and then tried to stop me on the sidewalk."

"I told you that you didn't understand."

"And I think I said something about understanding perfectly. I thought you had planned it. Thought you had been talking to Hunter the whole trip. When we had been, so close. I felt incredibly betrayed. And not just by the girl I loved, but also by my best friend."

Knew it was right.

Devaney

CHASE IS IN tears. He's so upset. And I hate that I'm putting him through this. But I know I have to. I know we have to get past it.

"You asked why I went out for the pass, like that was proof, but as you can see in the video, I had no idea really."

"And it went downhill from there. I think I told you to forget about the cupcake, about us. Because you wouldn't walk away with me. You wouldn't stand up for us." He puts his head into his hands and cries harder.

When he finally stops, he says, "Do you remember when your mom told you we couldn't play together anymore after I kissed you?"

"Yeah, we didn't listen to her."

"My mom told me about a similar thing that happened between her and my dad when they were kids. They were going to be in trouble, so they were hiding in a tree, holding hands. But her dad found her and pulled her out of the tree. And my mom said they both stayed that way, their arms stretched out for each other because they didn't want to let go."

"She told me and Jennifer that story at the lake. She said it was then that she realized that her and your dad never listened to anyone. They hadn't listened when people told them that girls and boys shouldn't be friends or when people gave them a hard time about their friendship. They hadn't listened when the people they dated threatened to leave them if they didn't stop spending so much time together. She said their relationship had survived over twenty years because they didn't listen to anyone."

"Maybe that's the difference between them and us," Chase says. "My dad knew they'd never let go. I was afraid to let go, Dani. Because I didn't think you'd come back to me if I did."

I think about what else his mom said. The advice she gave me. That if I ended up with Chase, it would be because I came to a time in my life when I was finally ready. When I knew it was right. The problem is, I think she got it wrong. It would be when *we both* knew it was right.

"I thought it was the start of our forever," he continues. "And although I appreciate what you did, showing this to me, I've blamed you all this time, and I shouldn't have. I'm to blame, too."

"Thank you," I say to him softly. "I know it was painful, but I didn't want you to not choose the college of your dreams because of this. Because of me."

"I guess Damon told you?" he asks.

"Yeah, he did."

"Um, okay. So, uh, thanks for this. I think I'm going to head home. It's getting late, and—"

"You have the game tomorrow and all."

"Yeah."

He gets up and starts to walk away, but then he turns around and says to me what he said that day, "It was supposed to be the start of our forever."

And instead of saying the stupid thing I did back then—*That was summer, Chase. Everything was perfect there. This is real life*—I say, "Who knows, Chase? Maybe it will turn out to be something better than you even imagined."

A bad feeling.

Chase

I GO HOME.

Lie on my bed.

Stare at the ceiling.

It's only nine o'clock, but I feel thoroughly exhausted.

Worn out emotionally.

And possibly a little tipsy.

But I can't sleep.

So I focus on hydrating myself for tomorrow's game and try to watch the game film I had started before Dani interrupted me.

AT ABOUT TWELVE thirty, I pad quietly down the stairs in search of a snack, only to find my dad sitting at the kitchen counter.

"Do you know where your sister is?" he asks me, his face full of worry. "She's not answering her phone. And it's way past curfew."

"Where's she supposed to be?"

"Out with Pace. I thought they were going to a movie. Called his dad. Pace isn't home either."

I run upstairs, grab my phone, and call Damon. I don't know if it's from watching the video tonight, but I have a bad feeling about all this.

Damon answers, sounding like he's been asleep.

"Do you know where Pace and Haley were going tonight?"

"Uh, no. Why?"

"She's not home. Neither of them is answering their phone. It's late."

"Oh shit. You sure they aren't at his house? Um, like maybe in his room?"

"His dad said he wasn't home. I'm assuming he checked."

"Yeah, I'm coming over."

I run downstairs. "Damon doesn't know. Did Pace's dad, like, double-check his room?"

"Yes. Plus, his car isn't home."

Just as Damon rushes in the front door, Dad's phone rings.

And based on the way the color immediately drains from his face, I know it's not good news.

"Go wake up your mom," he says as he scribbles down notes.

I run to my mom's room in a flat-out panic, afraid my sister is dead.

"Mom, wake up," I say, shaking her shoulder. "It's Haley."

Mom's eyes fly open. "I just had a dream about her. Oh my God." She jumps out of bed, runs into her closet, and comes back out in jeans with her pajama top on.

"Damon," she says, "will you stay here with the kids?"

"Uh, sure," he says to her, his eyes big.

"How do you know—" I ask, my hands shaking.

"I don't know. I just do," Mom says.

"Pace and Haley were involved in a car accident," Dad says when he sees her. "She's having emergency surgery. I don't know much else. We need to get to the hospital."

"Let's go," Mom says. "Chase, you come with us. Grab a phone charger."

We're just pulling out of the garage when Dani knocks on the driver's window and scares the shit out of all of us. Dad rolls his window down.

"I'm coming, too," she says. "So is Damon. He's on his way out. Jennifer is going to stay at your house."

Dad hits the unlock button, and Damon jumps in the back with me, followed by Dani. We're still getting buckled up when Dad barrels out of the driveway.

He drives fast but not too fast. None of us really says anything, but Damon is on his phone. I can see that he's already texted Pace's parents and that they were just called by the hospital as well.

My mom is braiding and unbraiding her hair and seems to be repeating some kind of mantra. I lean forward, closer, and hear, "Please let them be okay. Please let them be okay. Please let them be okay."

Dani reaches across her brother's lap and grabs my hand, squeezing it tightly.

Damon puts his hand on top of both of ours, tears filling his eyes, and says, "My Hay Girl needs to be okay."

His phone dings with a text. He reads it, turns the phone upside down so he doesn't have to read it again, and looks up to the ceiling of the car.

He takes a deep breath, trying to hold back his emotions. "Pace is in bad shape. His mom isn't sure."

"Are they at the hospital already?" my mom asks him.

"On their way. Pace's dad is on staff there. I think someone called him and possibly gave him more info."

"Oh my gosh, no," my mom says from the front seat.

And I see why.

There are red and blue flashing lights everywhere ahead of us.

Dad grabs her hand, holding it tightly.

"Close your eyes, kids," Dad says. "I have a feeling this might be the scene of the accident."

Damon and Dani do as told, tightly shutting theirs.

I can't.

I have to see it. I reach up and touch my mom's shoulder.

She turns to me and whispers, "It looks like a similar crash to what you and I were in. Wide intersection. Based on the damage to the cars, one car was going straight while the other car turned."

"Which car were we in?" I ask her.

"The one that turned."

"Is that what happened to them, you think? Pace's driver's door is smashed completely in."

"Yeah," Mom says breathlessly.

"And we were okay, so that's good, right?"

"I sure hope so."

"And what about the person who hit us? I don't think you ever told me. Were they hurt at all?"

"Uh, well," Mom starts to say, but then she starts sobbing.

I squeeze her shoulder again in comfort, which only seems to make it worse.

"The person who hit your mom died at the scene, Chase," Dad says. "But we know that didn't happen to Pace or Haley, or they wouldn't be in surgery."

WE GET TO the hospital and rush into the emergency room, where we are basically told to sit and wait. Mom has to sign a bunch of papers. Dad paces but never really takes his eyes off Mom. Pace's parents arrive shortly after we do.

And finally, a nurse comes out.

"Phillip, Jadyn," Pace's dad says, "are you okay with her discussing both the kids' injuries in front of us all?"

"Yes," my mom says.

"As are we," Pace's mom says.

I can tell she's been crying. And I can't blame her.

Damon, Dani, and I haven't really said much, but the three of us have been sitting in the waiting room in the same position we were in the car. Damon in the middle. Dani on his left. Me on his right. And one of each of our hands is stacked on top of each other, resting on Damon's knee.

"I can only speak to your children's condition when they came in through our emergency department." She checks a chart. "Haley Mackenzie was with us for just six minutes. She had an open fracture of the left leg, complicated by an arterial lesion. She was conscious and stable when taken to surgery. EMTs indicated that she was riding in the passenger seat, wearing her seat belt.

"The car was struck on the driver's side. Pace Williams was with us for twelve minutes. He suffered multiple injuries to his left side—dislocated shoulder, cracked ribs, fractures of the wrist and fingers, open fracture of the arm. Head trauma and internal injuries were also likely. He was unconscious, but his vitals were pretty good. Both will be taken to the ICU post-op, so why don't you follow me? I'll get you to the waiting room there, where their team can keep you updated."

"I don't know if I can go up there, Phillip," I hear my mom whisper to my dad.

"Sure you can," he says. "I'll hold your hand the whole time. Just like I did back then."

And I realize they must be talking about when her parents died. I know they were in a really bad accident. But I don't know much more than that.

"MOM SEEMS REALLY freaked out," I tell my dad later when we go get coffees for everyone.

We've been waiting to hear more news for a couple of hours. Nurses come out every so often to let us know that the surgeries are going well and that Haley and Pace are stable, but that's about it.

"Being in the ICU brings back a lot of painful memories for her, Chase. I was there with her though, and I'm still here."

"I know they died. I guess I just don't know the story."

"When we arrived at the hospital, my parents were already here. They had been following them home. Saw the crash happen. When we got to the ICU, she was told that her mother had already passed. Her father was in the ICU. She got to see him, speak to him a little, but he passed a few hours later. It was rough."

"I can't imagine," I say, feeling so bad for her. "It sounds like Haley is going to be okay though, right?"

"She's going to be fine. A little dinged up."

"Don't sugarcoat it for me, Dad. I can handle it."

He looks me in the eye. "I forget you're a grown man now. Sorry. I'm very worried by the fact that she had an arterial injury. That means, she could have lost a lot of blood. I'm worried about what kind of shape she will be in. But mostly, I just want her to be alive and healthy when this is over. And I'm really worried about Pace."

"Me, too."

We get back up to the ICU and hand out coffees.

A doctor comes out, and Damon is the first one on his feet. "How are they?"

"Are you the family of Haley Mackenzie?"

"We are," Damon says then points toward my mom and dad. "Parents."

The doctor shakes hands with my parents and then tells them Haley is out of surgery and stable, but that she will be in the ICU overnight. He produces an X-ray, holding it up to a light bar.

Damon is like, "Whoa, she's going to set off the metal detectors, isn't she?"

The doctor then explains the surgery she had, showing where the rods and pins are holding her leg together.

"The break, although open, wasn't that bad. We only had to put a rod in the tibia, and once we did, the fibula lined up on its own. The surgery took a little longer than normal, as we wanted to make sure we handled the vascular injury with care. The blood flow after looked to be pretty good, but we'll be keeping an eye on it."

As soon as he leaves, Mom puts her head on my dad's shoulder and cries with relief.

Damon, Dani, and I are back in our spots, our hands stacked on each other's, as they have been for most of this time. Mom looks up and sees us, and then she puts her hand over her mouth and starts crying again.

I go over to her immediately and give her a hug. "It's okay, Mom. She's okay."

"I know," she says. "It's you kids. Your hands."

"What do you mean? Like, how we were holding them? We've been doing that since we got in the car at the house."

"You have?"

"Yeah. Why?"

"You know how when you play sports, you do that and then break to start the game?"

I nod. Not really following.

"I had some, um, unusual experiences when we had our accident."

"I read in the diary pages how Dad said he thought he'd lost you. Did you die?"

"I lost a lot of blood. They did surgery to get you out. And then my heart stopped beating, I guess. They say people this happens to have, I don't know, dreams, out-of-body experiences, that kind of thing."

"And you had that happen?"

"Yes. And while it's common to hear stories of people floating over their own bodies, it's not as common to hear they saw things outside of that space. In my head, or wherever, I was watching scenes on a television. They ranged from memories to possible futures. But at the end, I saw Danny rushing down the hall to where your dad was sitting in a folding chair, sobbing outside of the operating room. Danny put his hand on top of your dad's. I was drawn to it. I put my hand on top of that pile, but then I saw myself on the television, standing there with them, but I was faint. And I thought it was going to be the last time I would ever touch either one of them. You'd think that would make me feel sad, but it gave me comfort. As did when you touched my shoulder in the car." She wraps me in a hug. "It's hard, not being able to go in there and hold your sister's hand. But seeing the three of you do that and knowing that Haley's hand belongs in the picture gives me a lot of comfort. I know she will be okay. And I think so will the friendship between you four."

"I don't know what I'd do without them," I say, tearing up.

ANOTHER TWO HOURS later, we learn that Pace is finally out of surgery. Most of his bodily injuries, although significant, involved bone and tissue damage. We're happy to hear that he suffered no internal injuries. The question mark in the equation though revolves around the head injury he suffered. Definitely a concussion and some swelling, so they will be monitoring that closely for the next forty-eight hours.

We're all relieved he's out of surgery but really worried about the swelling.

And eventually, we're allowed to go in to see Haley, who is somewhat alert. Mom and Dad go first.

I grab Dani's hand. "Will you go in there with me?"

She squeezes it. "Of course I will."

The second we walk into the room, Haley says, "You're holding hands. Did watching the video of that day help? Are you finally back together? Like, for good this time?"

"Uh, Haley, you were just in a bad car accident—you know that, right?" Dani says.

"Yeah, I know. And I also know that you just walked into my room, holding hands. I want to know why."

"I'm trying to support your brother," Dani says. "He's been—we've all been—worried about you."

Haley rolls her eyes, says, "You didn't answer my question," and then dozes off.

"I am glad you were here with me," I tell Dani.

"Nowhere more important than this," she says.

I suddenly feel exhausted again. Only this time, I'm pretty sure I wouldn't have any problem falling asleep.

Damon peeks his head in the room. "It's my turn."

Dani gives me a smile and lets go of my hand. "You'd better stay with him, so he doesn't get into any trouble."

Haley wakes up again when Damon goes, "Hay Girl, damn. I just saw the photos of your leg. You're like half-bionic now."

Haley starts crying. "Is Pace dead?"

"What?" Damon says. "No, he's not. He's fine. No one probably told you anything because you were in surgery. And he was in surgery for quite a while too. He has a lot of broken bones and is pretty banged up, but they think he'll be okay."

"It was scary, Damon. I was shaking him, but he wouldn't wake up. I thought he was dead. Right there in his car."

Damon slides his hand across the top of her forehead and pushes her hair out of her face. "Shh," he says. "Don't cry, Hay. It's going to be fine. I promise."

"And what about Chase and Dani? Are things ever going to be normal again?"

Damon glances over at me and lets out a tired-sounding sigh. "I sure hope so."

"WHAT WAS THAT all about?" I ask Damon as we leave her room.

"That's why kids shouldn't do drugs," he replies with a laugh. "They must have her on some pretty good stuff."

"She just had major surgery. It would make sense. And you're avoiding the question."

"I told Haley about what you told me about school," Damon says.

"*And* you told your sister."

"I did. It affects me, so therefore, I can tell whoever I want."

I nod in agreement. "I guess that's true. I'll figure it out after the game."

We look at each other, eyes wide.

"The game," he repeats.

"We need to get home, get some sleep. We're supposed to be on the bus to go to the stadium at three."

"It's six in the morning. Wow. Time flies when you're having fun," Damon deadpans.

"We need sleep. I don't think the dozing off we did in those hard chairs counts."

"No, it doesn't. Let me call Dad. Have him call Coach."

"Coach already knows, boys," Coach says as we step back into the waiting room.

Dani comes to stand next to me. "I forgot all about your game," she says.

"So did we," I admit. "I guess in the big picture, a state championship isn't all that important."

"Now, now," Pace's dad says, "Pace wouldn't want to hear that from you. He wants another ring. So, go out there and win him one tonight."

"Yes, sir," Damon says.

Questioning my decision.

Devaney

ON THE WAY home, I sit next to Chase. Although we've been holding hands all night—well, the three of us have—things feel different between us. And I can tell Chase is still struggling. Not just because of his sister's accident, but also from what went on with us before.

And now, I'm questioning my decision to make him relive that day.

I thought it would help us heal, but I'm not sure it did.

Because instead of him blaming me, he has to now take on some of the burden for what happened.

And I'm not sure he wants to.

Or if he thinks I'm worth it anymore.

But holding his hand. Holding my brother's hand. And worrying about Haley together—I know that when she comes home, I'm going to be here. And I don't care if Chase likes it or not. I'm going to fight for it. Fight for them. Fight for us.

"Why don't we all go sleep in our movie room?" I suggest. "It's quiet and dark down there."

"Uh," Chase says, "I need to go to my house. Tell Madden and Ryder what happened. I'll see you later, okay?"

"I'll be at your game, so you definitely will."

SATURDAY, DECEMBER 7TH

a little off.

Devaney

THE GAME IS not going well.

It's been a tough twenty-four hours, and it's obvious that the team is still reeling over the news about the accident.

Not to mention, our star running back isn't in the game.

Chase looks a little off. Damon has missed numerous passes, and honestly, it's sort of a miracle we're still in the game.

Normally, the whole family would be here to cheer them on, but most everyone is either helping out at home or at the hospital, so it's just me, my dad, and Chase's dad.

Haley and her mom video-chatted with Chase before the game, which was nice, but they also shared that Pace had a setback—some increased swelling on his brain—which didn't sound good.

At the end of the third quarter, the scoreboard shows us trailing by three, a score of 24-27.

And although we clearly know that this game doesn't mean that much in the grand scheme of life, it is a pretty big deal. If they win this game, it will mean that this team has lost only two games in four years and will have won four consecutive state championships.

The dance team is out on the field, doing their usual routine, when our sideline erupts in cheers. Like, the guys are whooping it up, hollering, and high-fiving like they'd already won.

Our phones all ding at the same time with a text from Haley.

It's a photo of Pace, awake and sitting up in his bed. He's got a team jersey wrapped around him, and he's got his hand, the one not in a cast, held up in the air to form a claw. For his team, the Jaguars.

But it's the words below the photo that matter the most.

Haley: *We're listening to the game. Pace is awake. Swelling has dissipated. Brain is normal—well, as normal as it was before the crash.*

And he says you'd all better stop messing around, score a few touchdowns, and win this thing!

Go Jags!

A moment to appreciate.

Chase

HEARING THE NEWS that Pace is going to be okay pumps the team up and allows me to breathe a little easier.

"What do you say, Coach? A little razzle-dazzle in his honor to take the lead?" I ask.

"Hell yeah!" Damon says as Coach nods his head in agreement.

"Who wants under center?" I say to the team.

"Me," Reed, who plays cornerback on defense, surprises me by saying. "I'll get you the ball, Chase. Then you and Damon can do your thing."

I look at Coach, who nods at me.

Although pretty much every team in the state has seen *the play*, this setup is different. Instead of Pace or our backup running back lining up in the wildcat, we have a cornerback, a guy who isn't normally on the field with the offense. You can tell the other team is scrambling, trying to figure out what we're going to do.

Playing cornerback is one of the hardest positions in football. Not only do they have to defend against the fastest guys on the other team—the wide receivers—but they are also called on to blitz and defend running plays. If I saw a guy like him lined up, I'd think we were going to call something like double reverse.

The defense brings both of their cornerbacks in to cover trick run plays, but our line holds them just long enough for Reed to toss me the ball. And by the time they realize what we are about to do, I've already thrown a pass so on target that it literally falls into Damon's hand, mid-stride, as he races into the end zone.

I take a moment to appreciate what was literally one of the most perfect passes I had ever thrown.

And while the team is celebrating and the crowd goes wild, somehow, I'm able to find Dani in the stands, our gazes connecting.

My real-life perfect pass.

TUESDAY, DECEMBER 17TH

Adds to the drama.

Chase

"I STILL DON'T know what to do," I tell Damon the day before we're set to sign.

He's over at the house, chilling with Haley, who has been back home for a few days.

"That's okay," he says with a grin. "It just adds to the drama. I like it."

"You decide," I tell him.

"Sorry, buddy. We already chose together a long time ago. I get things have changed, and I'm gonna roll with that and with you, so I have a plan."

"What kind of plan?"

"Okay, so spread across our table will be all five contracts. On top of each contract will be a baseball cap for that school. You don't even have to really say anything, although you can. If you do, mention what a tough decision it was, throw some goodwill to the other schools, but ultimately, you're going to need to look at me and touch a hat. And when I say look at me, that's exactly what I mean. I want you to look me in the eye and let me know that it's your final decision. It's where our next adventure lies. And then we'll both put those hats on, indicating our choice. And sign those bad boys."

"And you'll really be okay with whichever school I choose?"

"Yeah. Why do you think I made us go on those visits? So we'd know for sure."

"And if I can't decide, do you have any advice?"

"Go where the boobs are."

To this, I can't help but laugh.

WEDNESDAY, DECEMBER 18TH

Separate ways.

Chase

I'M SHOCKED AT how calm and cool Damon is about today. In just a few minutes, we'll be live on television, announcing which college we'll go to.

We're all set up in the school gym, and there are numerous local news stations as well as reporters from each conference we're considering—not to mention, a few sports channels.

I've been so torn. I wish more than anything that I could just go where I dreamed of going as a kid, but it's not that simple.

Because Devaney is there.

I know watching the video was supposed to be eye-opening, and it was—but probably not in the way she'd thought it might be.

All she really proved is that I don't deserve a girl like her.

I'm pretty sure I'm choosing the taco school.

It doesn't feel right, but it doesn't feel wrong either. And it had the overall best score in Damon's ranking of all the schools we'd visited.

"WE'RE ABOUT FIVE minutes out," our high school's athletic director says. "You'll be interviewed by a local reporter, and then you will make your decision. Damon tells me you're both going to simultaneously put on your chosen school's hats and then sign the agreement."

"That's correct," I tell him.

The gym is pretty crowded, but I easily spot my parents and younger siblings in the front row, minus Haley. Her leg is fully wrapped, as opposed to being in a cast, because they have to be able to monitor her wounds. She's not allowed to put any weight on it, so she's either on crutches or in a wheelchair.

"Two minutes until we're live," is announced.

Haley is wheeled up to the front of our table by one of the girls on her cheer squad, and she's followed by a four others. Each girl has two small white boxes in her hands, the name of each of our five schools written on top of it.

The boxes are laid on the table next to the appropriate hat.

Haley smiles at me and says, "Choose well you must." She's rolled over to where the rest of my family is.

I notice that Danny, Jennifer, and the girls have joined my parents along with Damon's mom and her husband. And Damon's family is all wearing Nebraska jerseys.

Nothing like a little pressure.

I take a deep breath, trying to remain calm.

If this decision was just about football, it would be easy, but there's so much more involved.

And I hate that I'm going to disappoint everyone.

"And we're live."

"We're here live," a familiar voice says as the crowd parts, and Dani walks toward our table, "with two five-star recruits, quarterback Chase Mackenzie and wide receiver Damon Diamond—son of retired professional quarterback Danny Diamond."

Dani looks like a natural with a microphone in one hand as she rattles off our stats without even a glance at the paper in her other hand.

"We know the recruitment process has been a challenge for the two of you. Most of us here know that you have been best friends and teammates your whole life. And a lot of people have criticized your decision to play college ball together. They seemed to think the chances of you both getting scholarships or playing at the same time were slim, but I think you've proven them wrong. You've also gotten a lot of advice, suggesting that you should individually choose the college best for you. And we know that time is coming. You went on official recruitment visits this fall, and your top five colleges are represented here, on the table in front of you. And the world is watching, Chase and Damon, wondering if you will put on the same hats, or if the so-called Shock-and-Awe package and two best friends will go their separate ways."

Dani stops and looks at me, her eyes filled with emotion. "How will they choose between what others tell them is best for them and what's in their hearts? That has been the real question in this whole process, but what people don't know is that it's not about just you two. It's about me."

"And me!" Haley calls out.

"So, in order to help you make the best decision, we've made something for you. Because it doesn't matter how old we get. A promise is a promise."

"I think we're supposed to open the boxes," Damon whispers to me.

I lift the lid on the first one and discover a cupcake that looks much like the one Dani made for me in the Ozarks, the picture of which hung in my locker all year and happens to be in my pocket at this very moment. But this cupcake does vary from that one. The first difference is that it is decorated in one of the team's school colors. And the second difference is that there's a volleyball on there for Haley, and the third difference is that instead of just my number on the jersey, there's a triple one—for One Eleven, my and Damon's numbers combined and the name of our company.

Damon has already opened all of his boxes, and I see that there is a matching cupcake for each school, varying only in color. I notice that when he touches the volleyball, his eyes get misty.

"All of us?" he asks Haley.

She nods.

Are they saying that no matter which school we choose, we'll all go there together?

"Anywhere?" I ask in disbelief.

I look up at Dani, and even though she's holding a microphone in her hand, she mimes a boxer's one-two punch combination.

And I know what that means.

That she's here, fighting for me. For us.

And she wants the world to know it regardless of what they might think.

"What's it gonna be, bro?" Damon whispers.

But I don't have a chance to reply because Dani saunters toward me, a sexy sway in her hips and a huge grin on her face.

"All right, everyone, here we go. Your favorite five-star recruits are going to …"

Two pieces of paper.

Devaney

DAMON AND CHASE turn, smile at each other, and nod in agreement. They reach in front of them, pick up the white hats with the red Ns on them, and happily put them on their heads.

The crowd goes nuts.

Chase's parents unbutton their matching chambray shirts to reveal Nebraska shirts.

I walk over to my dad, who has tears in his eyes.

"Danny Diamond, three-time champion quarterback and future Hall of Famer, how does it make you feel to know your son and your godson, who grew up playing ball together in your backyard, are going to your alma mater?"

My dad looks at the boys' smiles but grins at me. He and Phillip hug. The bro hug that is trying to hide their tears.

"Definitely thrilled," my dad finally says.

I go back to the front of the table. "Damon Diamond, do you have any words you'd like to say?"

"Yeah," he says. "I have a message for my friends—you know who you are—let's get it done."

"And what about you, Chase Mackenzie?"

In one swift and athletic move, Chase vaults himself over the table so that he's now standing directly in front of me. And before I can even take a breath, he pulls me into his arms and kisses me.

When we pull back from the kiss, I turn off the mic and set it on the table.

Chase smiles, reaches into his pocket, pulls out two pieces of paper, and hands them to me. "You want to know why I kept winning? What my goal was? It's all right here."

I unfold the paper and find both the *dream* note he put on his window and the cupcake photo I put on mine.

"Where did you get these? I thought they got thrown away when—"

"I made sure they didn't. And they have been hanging in my locker all year."

"And here I assumed, you'd wadded them up, stomped on them, and then burned them."

"Trust me, I considered that."

"I'm glad you didn't."

"So am I."

"You know, you once told me that when what other people think of me is less important than what I think of myself, *that's* when you'd believe me. I'm here for me right now, Chase. Because I love you. And I'm pretty sure the whole world knows it now."

In the house.

Chase

EVERYONE IS OVER at our house, eating celebratory pizza here instead of trying to get Haley into a restaurant.

Her bedroom is upstairs, so she's been moved into the guest suite above the garage since there's an elevator that can take her up there. And I'm pretty sure she plans to never move out.

A national sports channel is playing in the background as the reporters try to rank each college's recruitment class. And I finally understand what Damon meant when he said he had a message for his friends. He's been doing a little recruiting of his own, and because of it, numerous big names shocked everyone by choosing to come play with us.

There's even a clip of Dani interviewing her dad playing on repeat every few hours.

The doorbell rings, so I go answer it.

And, boy, does it make me happy.

"Attention, everyone!" I yell out. "P-A-C-E is in the house!"

Our teammates all cheer for him, but he only has eyes for Haley, who he gingerly walks straight over to and kisses.

"What a day," she says, grinning.

EPILOGUE

Catch snowflakes.

Chase

I LEAD DANI out onto the deck, away from the hustle and bustle of the Christmas Eve party taking place at her house.

"Look, Chase, it's starting to snow!"

I look up at the sky, feeling thankful. And then I look at the girl in front of me, feeling incredibly lucky. She looks like an angel, snow glittering in her hair. But she's got her tongue sticking out, trying to catch snowflakes on it, like we used to do when we were kids.

I place my hands on her hips, pull her toward me, then wrap my lips around her tongue, and kiss her. "I have something I want you to open now."

"Now? Out here? In the snow?"

"Yeah." I pull a small box out of my pocket and hand it to her.

She turns the box over in her hand a couple times, giving it a little shake to try to figure out what's inside before she opens it.

"It's not your gift, more of a surprise."

"Hmm, now, you have me curious," she says, ripping the paper off the box and then opening the lid. She holds up the contents. "A key? What is this? The key to your heart?" she teases.

"Actually, it's the key to my dorm."

"Your dorm?"

"At school. I didn't tell you before because everything felt really complicated, but I had enough credits to graduate midterm. I'm starting college in January, so I can get more time with the team and participate in spring practice."

"Are you really?!" she says, throwing her arms around my neck. "That's amazing! We'll be able to spend so much time together!"

"I know," I say, "but don't forget, I'm an underclassman."

"Oh, please, Chase," she scoffs with a smile. "You're only five months younger than me; none of that matters in college."

"And if anyone says something about it?"

"I'll flip them off and walk away."

I smile big and then start laughing. "I could totally see you doing that."

"I finally can, too. Does that mean you'll be my boyfriend, Chase? Like, for real this time?" she asks me.

"Only if by *for real*, you mean, forever," I reply before I kiss her again.

ABOUT THE AUTHOR

Jillian Dodd® is a USA Today and Amazon Top 10 best-selling author. She writes fun binge-able romance series with characters her readers fall in love with—from the boy next door in the That Boy series to the daughter of a famous actress in The Keatyn Chronicles® to a spy who might save the world in the Spy Girl® series. Her newest series include London Prep, a prep school series about a drama filled three-week exchange, and the Sex in the City-ish chick lit series, Kitty Valentine.

Jillian is married to her college sweetheart, adores writing big fat happily ever afters, wears a lot of pink, buys way too many shoes, loves to travel, and is distracted by anything covered in glitter.

Made in the USA
Middletown, DE
26 June 2022

67829249R00182